gemini

gemini

a novel

Sonya Mukherjee

SIMON & SCHUSTER BFYR

NEW YORK   LONDON   TORONTO   SYDNEY   NEW DELHI

An imprint of Simon & Schuster Children's Publishing Division
1230 Avenue of the Americas, New York, New York 10020

For information about special discounts for bulk purchases,
please contact Simon & Schuster Special Sales at 1-866-506-1949 or
business@simonandschuster.com.
The Simon & Schuster Speakers Bureau can bring authors to your live event.
For more information or to book an event, contact the Simon & Schuster Speakers Bureau at
1-866-248-3049 or visit our website at www.simonspeakers.com.
Jacket design by Krista Vossen
Interior design by Hilary Zarycky
The text for this book was set in Bell MT Std.
Manufactured in the United States of America
First Edition
2 4 6 8 10 9 7 5 3 1
Library of Congress Cataloging-in-Publication Data
Names: Mukherjee, Sonya, author.
Title: Gemini / Sonya Mukherjee.
Description: First edition. | New York : Simon & Schuster Books for Young Readers, [2016] |
Summary: In a small town, as high school graduation approaches, two conjoined sisters must
weigh the importance of their dreams as individuals against the risk inherent
in the surgery that has the potential to separate them forever.
Identifiers: LCCN 2015019774|
ISBN 9781481456777 (hardcover) | ISBN 9781481456791 (eBook)
Subjects: | CYAC: Conjoined twins—Fiction. | Twins—Fiction. | Sisters—Fiction. | High
schools—Fiction. | Schools—Fiction.
Classification: LCC PZ7.1.M82 Ge 2016 | DDC [Fic]—dc23
LC record available at http://lccn.loc.gov/2015019774

For Drew and Maya,
with love for who you choose to be, who you aspire to become,
and who you'll always be, no matter what

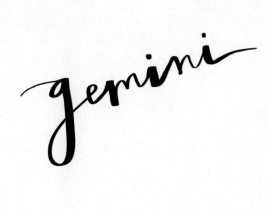

1

Clara

About four years ago, when I was thirteen and still prone to crying spells, my mother liked to show off her so-called wisdom by telling me that every teenage girl sometimes feels like a freak of nature. She claimed that every adolescent worries that everyone's staring at her, and every girl at some point has believed that no one likes her and that she'll never belong.

And sometimes I would just listen and try to believe her, but then this one time (I guess it was the last time she gave the speech) I said, "And does every teenage girl sometimes feel like she has a super-ugly ninety-pound tumor sticking out of her butt?"

And then the tumor started crying, and I felt pretty bad, but not bad enough to apologize.

That was a long time ago, and I have matured somewhat. I'm nicer to my sister now. Nicer to everyone, I guess, or at least I'm trying. I mean, I'm still pretty angry, but what are you going to do? It's nobody's fault, the way things are.

But back then I kind of thought, *If I'm so miserable, shouldn't she be miserable too? I mean, we're supposed to share everything, right?*

We were already sharing the lower end of our spinal column, and sensations in the lower halves of our bodies. We had two totally separate upper halves—two heads, two faces, two sets of arms, the whole works. And for that matter, we also had two full pairs of legs and feet. But we were joined together at the midpoint, in basically a back-to-back position—or butt-to-butt, if you want to get all technical about it. While our stomachs were separate, our guts were, according to the world's leading medical experts, as tangled together as a vat of discarded Christmas tree lights, and partially fused.

We were two complete, full-size people, with two normal, fully functioning brains; and yet, if she ate too much pizza, we both felt a little unwell. If the doctor touched my foot, Hailey could feel it. And if I called myself a hopeless, unlovable freak, well, I supposed Hailey could feel that, too. But only if I said it out loud.

And so it was that when we learned a new boy would be entering our senior class, and every girl in our tiny rural school started speculating and gossiping about him— finally, a fresh boyfriend prospect, for the first time in more than a year!—I refrained from pointing out to Hailey that this was hardly any concern of ours.

Not that it was easy to hold my tongue. Sunday afternoon, the day before he was supposed to show up, we were sitting back-to-back on our bed, cross-legged, our laptops open in front of us. I was trying to concentrate on calculus, but she kept bursting out with these random nonsense questions, like, "So, what color do you think his eyes will be?" or "Do you think he'll speak any second languages?"

And I just kept laughing at her, but it made me want to scream, because it was like Hailey had no idea who she was. When I looked in the mirror, I saw what anyone else would see: a bizarre eight-limbed creature that probably shouldn't have survived the womb. But Hailey acted as if, through a strange mental glitch, she could look in the mirror and see some lovely, fascinating nymphet. And this hallucination was so real to her, she thought everyone else could see it too. Even boys.

I'm not saying I hadn't thought about them. It was hard not to, when at any given moment half our school was either making out in the hallways or discussing the latest school dance. Out here in entertainment-forsaken Bear Pass, school dances were the second-most-popular social events, surpassed only by hanging out at the Taco Bell parking lot with pilfered beers and cigarettes.

So yeah, sometimes I would fantasize about a European exchange student showing up, brilliant and witty, cheerfully amused by our small-town high jinks, with a mind as open as the night sky. I guessed Hailey had her own version of the fantasy (less cheerfully amused, more brooding and dangerous), but even if both versions showed up, so what?

Seriously, who do you think would be the best boyfriend for a girl sharing part of her spinal column with her sister? Be honest.

Exactly.

2

Hailey

Normal, normal, normal. It's this idiotic mantra around our house. We claim we're normal. We build our lives around that lie. It's why we can't go anywhere, or do much of anything. If we did, we'd come up against the truth.

A hundred years ago, if you were a conjoined twin, nobody was like, *Oh, sweetie, you're just like everybody else, you're totally normal, and your life is going to be totally normal, rah, rah, rah!*

Hell no. They were like, *You know what, we're going to put you onstage, maybe teach you a little singing and dancing if you're lucky, and then make people pay to see this bizarre and amazing spectacle! And we're going to keep all the money for ourselves! Mwaaah-ha-ha-ha-ha!*

It was evil, but at least it was honest, and I'm pretty sure it must have been fun sometimes. Traveling the world, playing the saxophone, meeting giants and bearded ladies.

But that's not us. We have to live in this itty-bitty place where everyone knows us, so nobody will stare or freak out at the sight of us. Because, you know, if we freaked somebody out, that would apparently cause us to drop dead or something.

When we heard about the new guy coming to Bear Pass, I could tell Clara's first instinct was to worry about it. Like, what happens when he sees us? Will he scream? Will he faint? Will everyone else suddenly realize that we've been monsters all along?

But me, I just hoped he would turn out to be someone interesting. Because I really needed a few more interesting people in my life.

"You know he's going to ask us all those questions," Clara said at one point, leaning over her shoulder to talk while we worked on our homework. "All the same ones that everybody else always asks. Don't you hate that?"

"Better that he asks," I said. "Remember when Vanessa moved here, freshman year? She was too afraid to ask anything, but you could just feel her wondering all the time. It was way worse."

"Was it, though?"

"You know what we should do?" I said. "We should type up a list of our Frequently Asked Questions. We can hand it to him the first time we see him. Get it all out of the way and move on."

"If you do that," Clara said, "I will stab you with a fork."

"Yeah, we wouldn't want the new guy to think the conjoined twins are weird or anything."

But I typed them up anyway, just for fun.

Clara and Hailey's Frequently Asked Questions

Question: How did it happen?

My answer: We were in a helicopter accident in Panama, and at the moment of impact, the heat and force fused our backs together.

Clara's answer: Actually, identical twins happen when one sperm fertilizes one egg, but then the cells divide and separate and become two people. In our case, we didn't quite separate all the way.

Question: Does it bother you when people stare?

My answer: Yeah, Emma Watson and I text each other about it constantly. We're both thinking about trying to become less beautiful so people will leave us alone.

Clara's answer: Yeah.

Question: Don't you hate never being able to get away from each other or have any privacy?

My answer: Don't you hate never being able to flap your wings and fly? Or breathe underwater? Don't you hate sometimes having to be alone?

Clara's answer: It's true, we all get used to the bodies we have, right? You probably can't jump as high as an NBA player, but how often does it ever bother you? Being attached is just normal for us. We only wish it didn't seem so weird to everyone else.

My follow-up answer: But seriously, how can you deal with sometimes having to be alone? I can't even imagine what that must feel like. It must be unbearable sometimes. It must make you wish you could surgically attach yourself to another person so you wouldn't ever have to be alone. Doesn't it?

Doesn't it?

3

Clara

When we got to school on Monday, Juanita was in the parking lot, scrolling through messages on her phone as she waited for us. As soon as we started our slow, awkward shuffle down the ramp of the family minivan, she put the phone away and started talking.

"Clara, what did you get on that last physics problem? I'm not sure if I did it right."

Hailey was going first down the ramp, with me backing out after her, so I couldn't see Juanita's face, but I could hear her anxiety. I wasn't sure why, but Juanita always seemed to be haunted by the thought of getting even one problem wrong.

"Why didn't you call me?" I asked as I backed down the ramp.

"More importantly," Hailey said, "have you seen the new guy?"

"Yeah, I saw him at Mollie's Market. Will you look at my equations during morning break?"

"What's he look like?" Hailey demanded.

"Not your type," Juanita assured her. We reached the sidewalk and stood beside her, angled so we could both see her. Although our anatomy puts us back-to-back, Hailey and I have stretched ourselves toward each other over the years, so we can both face in pretty nearly the same direction at the same time.

Juanita's thick black hair fell across her shoulders and halfway to her elbows in smooth, glossy perfection. She was president of our class and of half a dozen student clubs, and she was in every honors class that the school offered, but no matter how late at night she finished her homework, she always got up early enough to have amazing hair.

"More details," Hailey demanded.

"He's tall," Juanita said, "and kind of cute, I guess, but he's got one of those really sweet-looking, smiley kinds of faces. Blue eyes, I think. Too sunny for you. No clouds, no dark and stormy secrets. Sort of light brown, almost blond hair." She narrowed her eyes at me. "Pretty much the same as Clara's hair color, actually."

"Ah!" said Hailey. "What do they call that color again? Dishwater? Fish washer? Wishy-washy?"

I shook my head, smiling despite myself. "You know, your hair is the same color as mine, Hailey."

"No, it's not," she said, "because I have enough sense to dye mine. My hair color is a sign of my taste and good judgment. Yours is just lazy."

What you have to understand about my sister is that Hailey is a pink-haired, tattooed conjoined twin. Yup, let me say it again—a pink-haired, tattooed conjoined twin. Her hair, in case I didn't mention this before, is *pink*. Like she's afraid that otherwise no one is going to notice her. Like she might not have any chance of standing out in a crowd if she didn't have *pink hair*. (The tattoo is just a butterfly on her shoulder. I wouldn't let her get one on her ankle, because I can feel what happens to her ankle, and I've heard tattoos are really painful, so I vetoed that. But the shoulder, while I may not approve, is her own body, to abuse as she wishes. Even if spending two hours at a tattoo parlor adjoining a grimy local bar, where Dad secretly snuck us while Mom was away one weekend, is not exactly my idea of a good time.)

"My hair is natural," I said, "and at least it doesn't make me look insane."

My dad, from the driver's seat of the minivan, gave a honk and a wave. I knew he had been listening to our debate, but he'd learned years ago that it's better not to get involved. So he just called out, "Bye, girls. Have a good day!"

We all waved back.

"Anyway," Hailey said to Juanita as we started walking toward the classrooms, "do you think wishy-washy hair is something you can work with?"

Juanita looked from side to side, as if she thought Hailey were talking to someone else. "What, me? Am I a hairstylist now? What do you want *me* to do about Clara's hair?"

"No, I'm talking about the new guy. So his hair is a bad color. But is he cute? Do you think you might like him anyway?"

"Oh." Juanita laughed. "No, I'm not in the market."

"Come on," Hailey said, "I've done the math. Not counting the new guy, there are forty-three guys in our senior class. You won't date anyone who's not in the honors track, so that brings it to thirteen. One is your cousin, three of them you've dated, four are jerks, two are idiots, Timmy still thinks fart jokes are funny, and you've lived next door to Keith forever, so he's practically a relative. That leaves Chris or the new guy, depending on his stats. But you know most of the other girls have done similar math, so when he shows up at school today, he's going to be like a marked-down game station on Black Friday. If you want in there, you can't sit around pondering the pros and cons."

Oh, thank God, I thought. *She wants him for Juanita, not for herself.*

"Wow," Juanita said, "is that the advanced math you were working on while Clara did your calculus for you? I mean, I appreciate it and all, but after that last fiasco, I'm done with boys for good."

"Really?" Hailey perked up. "Why didn't you say so? I've been wanting to have a lesbian friend."

Juanita grinned. "Actually, I just meant that I'm done

with *boys*, because at this point I'm holding out for a *man*. I'm done with all the high school crap. Like, when we're alone, he can look me in the eyes and talk to me about real stuff, but then we go to a party and he's chugging beer and laughing at his friends' juvenile jokes about my boobs? God, you guys, I am so done with that."

I knew that Juanita had been briefly hopeful that her last boyfriend, Leif, had matured into a sensitive soul, rather than being the immature goofball we knew at school; and she'd been crushed when she'd realized the truth. Still, sometimes I had to work pretty hard at feeling bad for her. At least she had dated *someone*.

Hailey and I shuffled forward in our usual way, which is not the most graceful thing you've ever seen, but also not as bad as you might think. We have, after all, had years of practice, and we're able to walk pretty much side by side, though we're angled slightly away from each other. Luckily, everybody at school knows us, so we don't have to worry about them rubbernecking. As we approached the school's central row of classrooms, other students streamed around us like they would around anybody else.

"Anyway," Juanita said after a moment, "maybe college will be better. In a lot of ways, actually." She looked around at the school hallway, all the kids we'd known forever in their jeans and sweatshirts, laughing, pushing one another, a few of them mashed up against each other and making googly eyes. "Sometimes I can't think about anything but busting the gates and getting out of this place, once and for all."

My throat tightened.

Juanita stopped suddenly, looking at me. "Crap, no, I didn't mean it like that. I'll visit you guys all the time. And you should come visit me too, wherever I end up. Seriously, you can do that. Maybe even . . ." Her eyes swept searchingly across my face. My whole body felt tight and closed. "Never mind," she said. "Don't listen to me. There's nothing wrong with Bear Pass. I'm just in a mood."

She glanced at her phone. "Listen, I've got to try to catch Marina really quick before class. I'll catch up with you guys, okay?"

She ran off, while Hailey and I continued toward our first-period class and I tried not to think about the prospect of Juanita *getting out of this place, once and for all.*

We'd always known she would leave. It was just that graduation and college used to seem so far away, and now they were looming ever closer.

Up ahead a *Giganotosaurus*-size poster covered the side wall of the secondary bank of classrooms, where we were headed. It was decorated in big bubbly letters and in all the colors of the rainbow. I was angled to see it a little better than Hailey could, and I tried to keep us that way.

Ladies! the poster shrieked. *Got your eye on a hot guy? Don't know how to catch his eye? Now's your chance! Get pumped for the Sadie Hawkins dance! Boys, sit back and relax. It's your turn to wait to be asked!*

In the roundness of the letters, and in the size of the exclamation points, you could just hear some cheerleader bubbling over with forced glee, as if her life depended on it. Around the corner, I could see the edge of another poster, almost as big as the first. I wondered if the cheerleaders had stayed up all night making these things.

I hoped that Hailey would somehow not see it, but no such luck. "What do you think?" she asked, nodding toward the poster.

To the best of my knowledge, it was the first time our school had ever had a Sadie Hawkins dance. I wondered if I had some secret enemy who had come up with this idea just to spite me. If so, they were pretty smart, because this was perfectly designed to tempt my sister into humiliating us both. She had been known to flirt with guys, but she had never gone so far as to ask anyone out. But she'd never had an opening quite like this. And she didn't seem to grasp the fact that even if certain boys were maybe nice to us and friendly and even seemed to treat us almost like regular *people*, it did not mean that they would ever in a million years view us as actual *girls*.

So my instinct was obviously to knock Hailey

unconscious and keep her gagged and bound in a secret hiding place until after the dance, but with great restraint I responded, "I'm just trying to figure out whether the rhymes and near-rhymes were intentional, and if so, whether they shouldn't have tried for better meter."

We arrived at our first-period class, AP English, and took our customary spot in the front left-hand corner of the room. Actually, it's not just our customary spot but the only one where we fit. Each of our classrooms has one extra-wide, deep bench, custom-made for us by the guys in woodshop, behind two desks that are almost side by side, but angled away from each other. The trick is to pull the desks out, slide-shuffle ourselves onto the bench, and then pull the desks back toward us.

Right next to us, Kim and Amber giggled and whispered, and occasionally one of them would cry out "No!" or "Yes!"

Hailey had the good fortune to be sitting next to the wall (she's always to my left, and by "always" I mean abso-freaking-lutely *always*), so I was closer and more vulnerable to getting sucked into the mindless void of their conversations, which generally flitted around among such topics as nail polish, cute animal videos, reality TV, and who had thrown up in the Taco Bell parking lot over the weekend.

I tried to focus on getting my notebook and *Invisible Man* out of my messenger bag. As usual, Hailey and I had each worn a bag slung over our inside shoulders, so the bags hung on our outside hips. After sitting down, we pulled our bags in front of us to take out our stuff, but then we had to take turns leaning down to set the bags on the floor. We had to pay attention to each other's timing to avoid getting jerked around.

Kim turned to me. "Clara, have you and Hailey seen the new guy yet?"

"Nope. Heard about him, though."

"Anything juicy?"

I thought about it. "Well, I mean, you know about the thing with his face, right?"

"What thing?" Kim pursed her cherry-red lips and raised her overplucked eyebrows all the way up to her bangs, leaning forward in a way that gave her serious cleavage. I guess just talking about this unseen, unknown guy was enough to put her into seduction mode. I've known Kim since kindergarten, and even then she was kind of a tramp.

Wait, let me unbitchify that statement. What I mean to say is, sure, Kim and I are friendly, and we've known each other a long time, but we've never been particularly close.

Yeah, that's much better.

Since I hadn't answered her question, she leaned forward even farther and stage-whispered it. *"What thing?"*

"Well, the fungus?" I said, like I didn't really want to

mention it. "Not that I really know anything about it. I mean, it sounds like it doesn't cover his *whole* face."

Kim and Amber looked at each other with alarmed expressions, and then they both started giggling in a nervous way, probably wondering whether this was one of those occasional-but-not-too-frequent times when Clara Cannot Be Trusted; and that was when he walked in.

Juanita's description had been completely wrong. He was tall, like she'd said—almost awkwardly so—but he wasn't "kind of cute." He was Cute with a capital *C*. Cute in a sweet-looking, gangly, 97-percent-grown-but-still-3-percent-boy kind of way, with deep blue eyes like the sky before sunset, when it's just about to throw itself open and let in the stars.

Also, there was absolutely no visible fungus on his face whatsoever. Go figure.

I checked Kim's reaction first, and she was all attention. Amber's lips were parted, and her eyes were wide. Then I twisted to look at Hailey, though I could really see her only in profile. She shrugged and actually said out loud, although without looking in his direction as she said it: "Meh."

Kim and Amber couldn't control their laughter at that, but because they were still looking at this tall, cute guy who had just walked in, you could tell he thought they were laughing at him.

Also, he didn't know where to sit.

Luckily, the teacher, Miss Young, walked in right behind him. She held out her hand to him and cried, "You must be Max!"

Was she actually batting her eyelashes at him, or was I projecting?

"I am," he agreed, shaking her hand.

She introduced herself and told him where to sit, at the back of the class.

As Max walked in our direction toward his seat, he caught my eye, and I felt myself turning red. Two reasons: First, he'd caught me staring at him, and while half the class was probably staring too, I of all people should have known better. And second, in our small town I usually saw only people who were used to me and Hailey. In the presence of a new person, I couldn't deny being a spectacle. Or half a spectacle. But a gigantic one. Like a car crash on a freeway where a car is turned upside down and another one is wedged under a semi, and you can still see the smoke. I was half of that.

But for some reason I didn't look away from Max as quickly as I meant to, and maybe that was good, because he smiled at me. And his smile was like, I don't know, whatever thing would magically wipe away that huge car crash and turn it into some kind of stellar rock concert, and before I could even think about it, I smiled back.

4

Hailey

"But it turns out he's really weird," Bridget announced at lunchtime.

We were eating on a couple of picnic blankets spread out on the grass, as usual—me and Clara, Juanita, and Bridget. It's not exactly easy to plop ourselves down onto a blanket, but it beats the awkwardness of trying to sit at a picnic table with an attached bench, like the rest of our class.

I could feel Clara tensing up behind me right away, but I jumped in with what we surely all wanted to know. "Weird like fascinating? With an encyclopedic knowledge of obscure Norwegian comedians? Or weird like scary, with a private taxidermy station in his basement?"

Bridget gave me a blank look. "Are those the only choices?"

Bridget is a very sweet girl, but keeping up with a conversation is not her strong suit. It's funny, because she looks like one of those precocious little kids you'd see in a movie. She's tiny and dark-haired, with thick bangs and black-rimmed glasses that hide most of her itty-bitty face. She's smart, too, but in a grades kind of way, not an on-the-ball kind of way.

"Never mind. What's weird about him?" Juanita asked as she bit into a baby carrot.

Bridget poked at her pasta with a plastic fork. "Well, for one thing, there's the fact that he switched schools during October of his senior year of high school. Who would even do something like that?"

"I doubt it was his choice," I pointed out. "Something must have come up with his parents."

"I guess so," Bridget conceded, "but how do you explain the fact that he's, like, seven and a half feet tall but he claims he doesn't play basketball?"

Juanita patted Bridget on the arm. "Sweetie, he's not seven and a half feet tall. I'm pretty sure he's not even *six* and a half feet tall."

Bridget shrugged. "And then also, he moved here from LA, right? But in history class Amber asked him if he had ever seen any stars when he lived there. She was thinking maybe he'd seen one of the Hemsworth brothers when he was standing in line at Starbucks or something, right? But he was like, 'No, are you kidding me? There's way too much light pollution in LA to see many stars at all.' I mean, what does that even *mean*?"

My head whipped toward Clara, but I couldn't see her

expression. Because of the way we're conjoined, we can never look at each other's faces straight-on, unless it's in a mirror or a photograph. If we both turn our heads as far as we can, we can come pretty close to a full view. But mostly we just catch glimpses of each other—at best a profile.

So when Max had walked into our English class earlier, I hadn't actually seen Clara's pupils widen. But I'd caught sight of her smile. I could tell she thought he was cute. And now we were to learn that he was a stargazer, too? She was bound to be intrigued by *that* bit of news.

"Come on, Bridget," Juanita said. "You know what light pollution is. That's when the city lights keep the night sky from getting totally dark. Right, Clara?"

Clara set down her turkey sandwich and clicked into Junior Professor Mode. "Yes, that's the most common definition. Remember the observatory at Sutter College?"

"Oh yeah," Bridget said. "We went there, what, like six months ago? You could see a ton of stars."

"That's because it's so far away from any big cities," Clara explained. "You'd never be able to see so many stars in LA."

Bridget took a big swig from her water bottle and nodded thoughtfully. Her little face was all tight with concentration behind her giant glasses. "Yeah, I figured it was something like that, because then he also said that he was totally relieved to get up here in the mountains, where he could get a decent look at the Andromeda galaxy. But I still don't understand why he would even think that was what Amber was asking him."

Clara shrugged. "Hey, if you think movie stars are more exciting than a spiral galaxy that's on a collision course with the Milky Way, you're entitled to your own opinion."

I studied Juanita for a minute, wondering if she was really serious about not being interested in Max.

Juanita caught my eye, and a hint of a smile twitched at her lips. "You know what I was thinking?" she said. "I bet Max would love that observatory we visited. I wonder if he even knows about it yet."

Was she talking about inviting Max up there for Clara's sake? Or for her own? Did she understand that Clara was interested in him? And even if she did understand, would it occur to her to treat it seriously—to back off if she did like him, like she would for another friend? I had no history to go on here.

"Someone should tell him about it," I said slowly, looking for clues in Juanita's expression.

Bridget lifted her tiny eyebrows behind her giant glasses and leaned forward eagerly, as if in great suspense—which she probably actually was. "But who?"

Juanita smiled. "Here's what I'm thinking. We tell him we're going up there to see it, and we invite him to go with us. You know, just a casual group thing, no big deal."

"Really?" Clara asked without looking up, and with maybe just the slightest quaver in her voice. "I thought you said you were done with boys."

Juanita's laugh verged on a slight cackle. "Oh yeah, I'm done with them, but you're not."

I almost cackled myself. Of course, I should have known that Juanita would be on top of this, and totally on my side. She didn't want to invite Max to the observatory because she was interested in him herself; she wanted to invite him so Clara could get a chance to know him. In a dark, quiet, beautiful place, where my sister would be totally in her element. And where, because of the darkness, our conjoinment would become all but invisible.

Clara stiffened for a moment, but it passed. "Nice try," she said, her voice so close to normal that I was pretty sure I was the only one who could hear its thin, sharp edge. "But the observatory is sacred. I won't go there with just anyone."

"Who says he's just anyone?" Juanita asked. "Don't you want to find out?"

Clara shook her head. "Not particularly, no."

And this was such a freaking pathetic lie that I couldn't take it anymore. "Well, I do," I said, "so we're going. That's that."

"Really?" Juanita looked puzzled. She looked at me, at Clara, and back at me again. "Um, okay, then when should we go?"

"Friday night," I said.

"Hailey!" Clara hissed. "Cut it out! I don't want to go."

"But I do," I said, "and Juanita does, and Bridget does. Right, Bridge?"

"Sure," Bridget said, "it'll be totally fun. I like the observatory. Plus, it's the perfect place for Clara to ask Max to the Sadie Hawkins dance."

I cocked my head to one side. Had Bridget just pulled a random idea out of left field, or was she actually a step ahead of us all?

"Ha!" Clara said. "Now, that's a good one. I'm sure one of the cheerleaders has snatched him up for *that* already."

She jerked her head in the direction of the senior A-list picnic table, where at that very moment Max was surrounded by a veritable swarm of cheerleaders and jocks.

Bridget frowned behind her heavy glasses. "Maybe they haven't gotten around to asking him yet. Or maybe cheerleaders aren't his type."

Clara shook her head sadly at Bridget's hopeless naïveté. "Bridge," she said, reaching over to pat Bridget on the knee, "you know I don't like to dance."

By which she meant that she—*we*—had never danced. Not once. Not even in the privacy of our bedroom.

"Maybe you could go and not dance," Bridget suggested. "Maybe he would understand."

Clara froze for just a second, then started talking rapidly, with forced cheerfulness. "You know what I was actually thinking? This whole Sadie Hawkins concept is pretty sexist and backward. Girls can ask guys out anytime they want, so why do we need a special occasion for it? Maybe we should all boycott this event on feminist grounds."

Juanita stared at Clara, her eyes alight. "I'm not saying you're wrong, but you seem to feel very strongly about this all of a sudden. What's up?"

"Nothing. Could we just please change the subject? Please?"

Juanita squealed. "Oh, look at you! You're nervous because you *want* to ask him out! Otherwise you would just be ignoring us."

Clara shook her head, and her voice rose to an unnaturally high pitch. "I don't even know him! I haven't even spoken to him!"

"Yeah, I know," Juanita said. "But you think he's cute, don't you? Cute plus telescopes—what more do you need? So it seems that Bridget has once again accidentally hit the nail on the head. You are *definitely* asking Max to the dance."

"Can anyone hear me?" Clara asked. "Am I not speaking out loud? That is not going to happen, I promise you."

"Sure it is," I answered, brushing the crumbs from my fingers. "Because if you don't ask him, then I'm going to ask him for you."

5

Clara

My main priority for the rest of that day was to avoid Max at all costs, which was a little tricky, since I didn't even know which classes he was in. I wasn't sure if Hailey was serious about asking him to the dance on my behalf, but I wouldn't have put it past her. This was the girl who had convinced our fifth-grade teacher to make me go first for every class presentation, in order to help me get over my stomach-churning stage fright. Which didn't even work.

I had spent the last seventeen years trying to camouflage my shocking self with all the bits and pieces of normal life I could grab. My wardrobe was bland but never out of style; my musical tastes were borrowed from my classmates. My opinions, often sharp inside my head, were normally softened before being spoken out loud. When people talked about doing things that, because of my situation, I couldn't possibly do—driving a car, riding a bike, skiing, kissing a guy—I tried not to point it out to them. I tried not to make anyone uncomfortable.

And this, of course, included never attending a school dance, let alone asking a boy to one. I wasn't sure what it would look like if Hailey and I tried to dance, but I was pretty sure it wasn't a sight that anybody needed to see.

Hailey, on the other hand, followed none of my rules. And she adored making people uncomfortable.

So when I saw Max walking in the hallway up ahead of us, grinning and chuckling at something that Lindsey Baker was saying to him, my fear was instantaneous and instinctive. Before I even had time to think about it, I was babbling something to Hailey about needing to go back to our locker, and yanking her bodily away from Max and Lindsey.

Later, when I saw him crossing by a few yards away, I was more prepared, and managed to distract Hailey with some questions about a recent scandal in the art world.

The closest call came when he turned up in our fourth-period physics class. He arrived just as the teacher started to lecture, so Hailey couldn't accost him, but all through class I didn't hear a word that anyone said. Luckily, as soon as class ended, some guys got him involved in a discussion about sports. Hailey didn't try to break in.

Finally we arrived at our last and most pointless class of the day—art.

Yeah, yeah, yeah, art is probably the most unique contribution of the human species, now that we know that chimpanzees can create tools and dolphins have a type of language. Art may, in fact, be the one thing that elevates us above our animal natures.

I heartily despise it.

"You know why you hate art?" Hailey asked me as we walked into the art room.

"Cut that out," I said. "I hate it when I'm thinking about something and then you just start talking about it, like you can read my mind. Try to remember that we're not tele-pathic, okay?"

"I'll tell you why," she said as she led me over to the cabinet where she always stashed her favorite paints and brushes. "It's because you suck at it."

"Well, obviously I suck at it," I said. "That's a given. But also, art itself sucks." Okay, I don't always soften my opinions when it's Hailey that I'm talking to.

She shook her bright pink head. "You just don't get it."

"Or," I suggested, "maybe there is nothing to get."

I helped her carry her paints and brushes over to her easel, where she had already sketched out and begun to paint a portrait in the medieval style.

This was something she'd been doing since the end of junior year. She'd copy the painting techniques from the Middle Ages, back when nobody had figured out things like perspective to give dimension to things, so it all looked flat and depthless. Back then the one thing that everybody wanted to paint was the Madonna and child. So Hailey adapted that format to paint things like a curvaceous pop star holding a tiny photographer on her hip, or in this case, a woman in a burka cuddling a naked baby girl.

If it were anybody else, I would have guessed she was just pretending to have a point, but Hailey is always sincere. Still, when it comes to her art, she keeps her words to herself. Whatever she's trying to say, she says it only with paint.

Hailey took her time setting up her equipment. There were maybe fifteen kids in the art class, and lately Hailey had been grabbing a spot near the window each day. She said it was for the light. She never said it had anything to do with being near Alek Drivakis, who just happened to always work nearby.

Alek had been doing this thing where it would be like a Thomas Kinkade painting, one of those cute English-cottage-and-flowery-garden scenes, except there would be a corpse rotting in the yard, or half the cottage would be burned to the ground. Two months into the school year, he had nearly finished the third painting in the series.

When he arrived that day, Hailey was swirling a brown oil together with a cream on her little palette. It seemed to me that she glanced up at Alek, then too quickly away, as he stowed his black messenger bag and got out his supplies. But I might have been making this up, because I can't ever see Hailey's face that well. It's hard to say how much my reading of her is sisterly instinct and how much is pure invention.

Alek is always dressed head-to-toe in black, and his hair

and eyes are dark, dark brown. He's only a hair taller than we are (and we're average-size for girls), but I have to admit that when you look him right in the eyes, he turns out to be surprisingly good-looking.

It's funny how a face like that can slip through the cracks, going unnoticed by most of the girls, maybe because he's short and doesn't play any sports, or maybe because people still remember when he first came to town, moving in with his grandparents back in seventh grade. He would sit in class drawing pictures of people being killed in a startling variety of different ways, and he kept his head down, his face obscured by his hair falling across it, and never spoke to anyone if he could help it. There were rumors that he had murdered his parents, or alternatively, that he had witnessed them committing murders and that they were now in prison. Those rumors had long since faded, but I supposed they had left their mark.

Today he brought his paints and his brushes, canvas, and palette over to the easel where he liked to work, but before beginning, he came over to look at Hailey's painting. They faced it together, so I couldn't see either of their faces clearly.

He said, "How did you make her eyes look so sad?"

"Well," she said, "see, there's this line here, and I thought the shape of the eyebrow, like that?"

For a moment I could hear my own breathing, and Hailey's, too, hers a little faster than mine.

"Your paintings rock," Alek said at last. "They make my brain feel the burn."

"Thanks," she said quietly, in a way that she was never quiet. And then, after hesitating in a way that she never hesitated: "That means a lot, coming from you."

I knew he wanted to say something else. They both did. And it hit me. She was going to ask him to the dance. Maybe even right that minute.

The invitation was inevitable—I could see that now—but did I want her to just go ahead and get it over with? No, I did not. Even Alek wasn't enough of a weirdo not to be horrified by the thought of dating a conjoined twin. He would turn her down—maybe nicely, maybe not—and from that point on, every moment that we spent around Alek was going to get more and more painful, full of awkward humiliation on all sides.

To stir up some distracting controversy, I said, "I don't know. I mean, I really like the colors you're using, Hailey, and maybe I'm missing something, but doesn't it all look a little flat?"

And then they both jumped in to explain about how Hailey *meant* to do it that way. Mission accomplished.

After about five minutes of their joint lecture, Alek turned to Hailey and said, "Well, good luck with that painting. You better let me see it when it's done," and he went back to his own easel, and that was it. Crisis averted—for now.

But Hailey painted in fits and starts, and I was aware of it because I was distracted too.

Since I do indeed suck at art, I use the class time for independent study. I was doing a semester-long unit on cosmology. This is the sort of thing that normally interests me more than I want to admit, even to myself; I don't think normal people get this kind of thrill from the mysteries of dark matter and dark energy, or from knowing that the distant galaxies are racing away from us at such an accelerating rate that someday they will disappear beyond the cosmic horizon, no longer knowable to us. I don't think normal people look up at the night sky and feel this weird, almost painful yearning to be up there, looking back at Earth and seeing it whole, even while knowing that they never, ever will.

But today was different. I couldn't concentrate on my book because I was too conscious of the tiny, suffocating details that pushed right up against me, from Hailey's little huffs of painterly frustration to the way that Alek kept his head bowed down tight over his work.

I stared at the scratched-up window. I tried to think about the big bang and about how even now, at this very moment, another big bang might be happening somewhere, creating a whole new universe with its own set of rules. But all I could think was, *My sister hasn't even learned the rules of our own universe. And she's about to mess up our world.*

6

Hailey

Every Monday we go to the Sandwich Shack after school, even though the Sandwich Shack sucks. We're talking stale sandwiches, bitter coffee, flat soda. On the plus side, it is right next door to our school.

Monday's the one day when both our parents teach late afternoon classes over at Sutter College—eighteenth-century lit for him, freshman writing for her. If Clara and I wanted to get home right after school, we'd have to squeeze into the back of Bridget's aging VW bug. It can be done, but let me tell you, it ain't pretty. So instead we meet up with Bridget and Juanita for disgusting snacks and drinks.

Clara and I were already sitting down with our crappy coffee and mercifully pre-packaged Rice Krispies Treats when Juanita rushed in and dropped into a chair across from us. She dumped her bags all over the scratched linoleum floor.

"Oh my God," she said, "I am going to strangle someone. Maybe myself." She dropped her head into her hands.

"Hey, Susie Sunshine," I said brightly, "what's going on?"

"Oh, just this whole stupid thing with the college apps. Pletcher made me stay after class again today, so she could give me another freaking lecture about my future. Like it's any of her business anyway. She's just my calculus teacher, not my guru. I need some sugar. Caffeine. Anything."

Clara handed her a Rice Krispies Treat. "Let me guess," she said. "Pletcher still wants you to apply to Stanford."

"Duh," I said. "Because she's a shoo-in."

Juanita yanked open the Rice Krispies Treat. "Thank you. This is awesome. But no, I am not a shoo-in." Her voice was tense and exhausted. She bit into the Rice Krispies Treat and talked around it as she ate. "But it doesn't even matter. The point is, she's hounding me about it, and not just Stanford, either. She has a whole list of places where she wants me to apply, and they're all private, and my parents will have a conniption if I even bring it up again, so whatever I do, somebody's mad at me."

I held in a sigh. Juanita was always far too worried about people being mad at her. But we'd had that discussion many times before, and there was no point having it again.

"But can't you explain to them—" I began.

"Don't you think I've tried?" She took another bite. "They've seen all these news stories about the rising costs of college, and I keep trying to explain about financial aid, but they just don't understand that I'm not going to bankrupt them. And of course most of the places Pletcher is talking about are on the other side of the country, so you've got to think about airfare and not being able to come home very often and all that. Anyway, they won't even pay the application fees, so that's it."

Clara twisted toward Juanita. I shifted away to accommodate her, although it made it hard for me to see Juanita's face.

"Okay," Clara said, "but what's wrong with Cal? I really think you'll get in, and then you won't have to worry about all these other places, right? I mean, I know it's nice to have options, but Berkeley is one of the best universities in the world, and it's public. Can't you just tell Pletcher that's where you really want to go, and then maybe she'll drop it?"

In my peripheral vision I could see Juanita sinking down lower in her seat. I twisted my head toward her and saw the way she curled into herself.

"Something else is wrong," I said.

"Yeah." Juanita's breath caught, almost like she was trying not to cry. "You guys, I don't know why I haven't told you. I guess I've been trying to block it out, like if I don't say it out loud, it won't be real. But my mom has been saying that even the UC system might be too expensive. She's been saying I could live at home and commute to the community college a couple of days a week, and maybe transfer after a couple of years."

Something inside me went cold. "She's not serious,"

I said. "After a couple of *years*? Two more years of living in Bear Pass? The place you can't wait to get away from? There. Is. No. Way."

Clara shifted behind me, with a tense little breath that was not quite a sigh.

I pressed on. "Not after all these years of working your ass off in school. Which you didn't even have to do, because you're so much smarter than everyone else in our class. You could have been valedictorian without even trying."

As I spoke, I twisted myself back around to face her, pushing Clara away in the process. But Juanita wouldn't look up and meet my eyes.

"I don't know," she said quietly. "I think my mom might be a little scared of me leaving. Scared she'll hardly see me anymore. Scared I'll turn into someone different. I'm not sure."

I shook my head. "That's not fair to you."

Juanita bit her lip. "It's not so bad, I guess. I made the best of high school, and I can make the best of this. I can always transfer later." She squeezed her lips together, and I thought of all the kids we'd known, a few years older than us, who had said they would transfer later, and never did.

"But it's ridiculous!" It came out as a shout, but that was fine. I wanted to scream. "You can't stay home and commute for no good reason! The Ivy Leagues have amazing financial aid! They'll give you a free ride!"

Juanita played with her Rice Krispies wrapper, still not looking at me. "You're with Pletcher on this? You want me to go off to, like, Princeton or Brown or something?"

It was weird how cold I felt, like someone had taken away my body's ability to warm itself.

Juanita had been best friends with me and Clara since the sixth grade. Sometimes she seemed like the only person in the world, outside of our parents, who could honest-to-God see us not as the Twins but as just plain Hailey and Clara. The farther away she went, the less we would see her. And who else would ever be able to see us like she did?

But all these years, knowing that Clara and I were destined never to leave Bear Pass, I'd hitched my fantasy life to Juanita's.

My own future, along with Clara's, had been laid out since infancy. Our parents had searched the whole state of California until they'd found the perfect place for us to grow up and live out our lives. A small community where we could get a complete education, and maybe even find suitable work, without ever having to deal with all those scary hordes of staring strangers.

Starting college would be the hardest part—even Sutter would involve a lot of new faces—but with only about five hundred students, Sutter would be small enough for everyone to get used to us pretty quickly. And then we could go back to disappearing in the crowd.

But Juanita wasn't tied down. She had no limits. She was the one who would go to the East Coast. She was the one who would backpack through Europe and Southeast Asia. If we had to stay holed up here, unseen and unseeing, she would be the one to fly.

"I just want you to do everything you ever dreamed about doing." My voice sounded weirdly bitter. "Is that too much to ask?"

Juanita gave a short laugh. "Okay, I need a soda. Can I get you something?" She looked at Clara. "Another Rice Krispies Treat? I kind of inhaled yours."

We shook our heads. When she was gone, I said quietly to Clara, "Don't you ever want to get out of here?"

Clara snorted.

"I'm serious," I said. "We've lived our whole lives in a town of four thousand people. We go to a school where we basically know every single person, and there's never anybody new to talk to—"

"Or anything new to look at," Clara finished for me, with a voice that might as well have been a long, slow, exasperated sigh.

It was possible that I might have mentioned this a time or two before.

"And now," I pressed on, "we're going to go one town over for the next four years, to a college that's barely any bigger than our high school, where they hardly have an art program, and where, frankly, they let in pretty much every-one who applies."

This was the part that I hadn't mentioned for a few months, since our last big fight about it, when I'd backed down once again. Clara always hyperventilated at the thought of leaving Bear Pass, even to go to a restaurant, or to buy new clothes. Which was why we never did those things.

At different times a couple of people had asked us whether we felt stifled and trapped by being attached to each other. This always seemed stupid to me, like asking if I felt imprisoned by gravity. I mean, *No.* Like, *Should I?* And like, *I'm a land mammal. Did you want me to be something else?*

But never leaving Bear Pass—well, that was different. Being attached to Clara made me who I was, and I liked who I was. Being in Bear Pass was just a circumstance. And it was one that I could very much envision changing.

But asking Clara to move away was just too much. Plus, unlike Juanita, we could get a free ride at Sutter College, the private four-year college just an hour away, where our mother was a lecturer and our father was a tenured professor. Expertise in literary theory and British poetry doesn't traditionally come with all that many perks, but free tuition for your kids can be a pretty good one.

"They do have art!" she whispered back, and I tried to let it go, but I couldn't.

A shudder ran through me, and I couldn't stop myself from muttering, "Oh, God help me."

Clara kicked me in the calf, then flinched at the pain. Because of our conjoined lower spinal column, she could feel my leg as much as I could, so it was pretty much like she was kicking herself.

"Nothing wrong with that," she said, smiling at Bridget.

Bridget went up to the counter to order. Juanita was headed back, but there was a moment when they paused to greet each other, and I turned as far toward Clara as I could and said what I had been stopping myself from saying for the past however-many months: "We don't have to be trapped here forever, you know. We could go to any school in the country. We could get in anywhere we want."

After a moment she said quietly, "Because we're conjoined twins?"

I rolled my eyes. What did she want me to say? We basically had straight As and solid SAT scores, and okay, if we hadn't been conjoined twins, maybe that wouldn't have been enough. But we were, and it would.

"It's not too late," I said. "We have time to apply."

"Can you imagine what Mom—"

"Anywhere we want!" I whispered, and then Juanita was back, sipping her coffee, the gloom mostly gone from her face.

"Did I ever mention," Juanita asked with a forced cheeriness, "that this is the worst coffee in the entire world?"

"You know the painting faculty sucks. They're all stuck in the twentieth century."

Okay, maybe I did have a flash of guilt as I said this, remembering how a couple of years ago Dad had gotten this one Sutter art professor to come and work with me every other week for six months. He'd paid her, but I knew that wasn't the main reason she'd done it. And she had helped me a lot back then. But still.

"Well," Clara said, "the film studies—"

"Film studies! Great. Okay, Clara, yeah, I'll do film studies, and then we can move to Hollywood."

"I just meant—"

Just then Bridget breezed in, smiling and waving to us, and we both shut up.

"*You're* still sticking to your plans for next year, right, Bridge?" Clara asked as Bridget scooted into a chair across from us. "Still coming to Sutter with us? You haven't scrapped that so you can go do missionary work in Peru or anything?"

Bridget laughed. "Can you imagine? I'd be lost and confused all day. The locals would waste oodles of time taking care of me. No, it's Sutter for me." She shrugged.

"You sound pretty thrilled about it," I said.

She didn't catch my sarcasm. "Yeah, I'm totally excited. My brother's already there, you guys will be there, and a bunch of other people we know. It'll be great. It'll be just like high school."

She looked back and forth between us. "What are you two arguing about, anyway?"

"I would like to find out if you're right," I told her. "I would like to travel all over the world, sampling all of the planet's worst coffee, in order to determine whether the Sandwich Shack would actually win the prize." I smoothed my hair back behind each of my ears and pulled on the ends so they pointed forward the way I liked them, in sharp pink daggers just below my chin.

Juanita sat down across from me. "And that's what you're fighting about?"

I glanced in Clara's direction, wishing I could see her whole face. I wanted to tell Juanita the truth, that I wanted us to fly away too, that I was as claustrophobic as she was and as desperate to leave this tiny little town behind.

But all I said was, "Yes, because Clara doesn't want to go. She wants to sit right here, giving the Sandwich Shack the benefit of the doubt for the next few decades, and then die in her sleep, having never seen anything at all."

"Yes," Clara said, sighing, "that is my dream."

Juanita nodded thoughtfully for a minute, considering this. "All right," she pronounced at last, "it is a worthy project. I accept your offer to bring me along as the third bad-coffee judge." She looked over to Bridget, who was in the middle of ordering at the counter. "Hey, Bridget," she called out, "do you want to come on our epic mission to find the worst coffee in the world?"

The door swung open behind her, and Max walked in alone. His wishy-washy hair was slightly tousled now, and he had a faded blue backpack slung over his shoulder.

I felt Clara staring at him, and without allowing myself to stop and think, I turned to wave at him.

"Max! Come hear about our mission. I think you'll definitely want to join!"

He stopped just inside the doorway. He looked at me, at Juanita, then back at me, and finally at Clara. I swear I could feel the moment when their eyes met, like a shock that passed through Clara and right into me.

Max opened his mouth, shut it again, and closed his eyes for two full seconds before refocusing them on me.

He said, "I—"

"Come on, come on," I said, starting to speak before I heard him, and realizing a moment too late that I'd cut him off. "The mission starts immediately. We shall bravely traverse the globe to find the world's worst coffee. None shall rest until the matter is settled once and for all. So it's time to choose. Are you with us, or are you against us?"

He stared at me a moment longer, then turned around and walked right back out the door.

For a minute no one said anything.

"Well," Juanita said at last, "I would not call that a great success."

7

Clara

"Juanita, you have to help!" Hailey said. "We need you now. The mission is failing, but we can't let it go up in flames."

"Um," I said, "are we still talking about the mission to find the world's worst coffee?"

Hailey scoffed. "Like you don't know. The real mission, obviously, is to get Max up to the observatory so he can fall in love with you, and then you can ask him to the dance, and then you'll live happily ever after in a fairy-tale castle or— Well, at the very least, let's just start with the observatory, all right?"

"Oh, was *that* the plan?" A little smidgen of tension drained away from me as I realized that Hailey hadn't mentioned anything about asking Max to the dance *for* me. This was still bad, but not as bad as I'd thought.

"Come on," Hailey urged Juanita, "earn your stripes!"

"Are you sure you want me to?" Juanita asked, frowning. "I mean, what's his problem, just turning around and walking out like that?"

"Oh, please," Bridget said. "After that nonsense Hailey was shouting at him? You can't really blame him for running."

"That's true," Hailey said. "I *was* shouting a lot of nonsense. Well, not shouting, but saying loudly."

"Oh, *I'll* get him," Bridget said, and she hurried out the door.

A minute later Bridget was leading Max to the counter. I could see her pointing out various menu items, probably giving advice about which ones to avoid, which was almost all of them.

"Better watch out for that one, Clara," Juanita teased me as we watched Bridget leaning in toward Max, whispering something to him. "I can't remember if she ever officially signed on to our plan of letting you have Max."

"Poor guy," I said, "he probably doesn't even realize you're in charge of his life."

Max completed his purchase and came over with Bridget, looking distinctly pink-faced and uncomfortable.

"Max," Bridget said brightly, "have you met everyone?"

"Um, no." He cleared his throat. "Not exactly."

"Well, don't worry," she said. "No one is really going to force you to travel the world looking for bad coffee. At least not right away."

As she introduced us all, I got the sense that Max was having to push himself to make eye contact with each of us—not just me and Hailey, but Juanita too.

As far as I could tell, he did not pause to inspect the area where Hailey and I were conjoined, or spend any time trying to visually figure out how it worked. I guessed that it must have taken a lot of self-control.

When Bridget finished, there was about half a second when Max looked nervous and unsure what to do, and I almost thought he might bolt again; but then, out of nowhere, he unfurled that broad, twinkly smile and said, "Nice to meet you."

And immediately a boxing match was on inside my brain.

See, some people apparently have a little angel that sits on one shoulder and a little devil that sits on the other, just politely debating back and forth. But in my case it's more often a showdown between Idiot-Girl and the Cynic. So over here in one corner of my mind, we've got Idiot-Girl jumping up and down and shrieking in a high-pitched voice, *Omigod, did you hear what he said? He said 'Nice to meet you'! That is the most charming and witty line I have ever heard in my life!*

And from the other corner the Cynic comes running to punch Idiot-Girl in the nose and shouts, *Calm down and get some sense into your stupid head!*

"Have a minute to join us?" Hailey asked calmly. "We're still planning this bad-coffee-finding mission, and we could use your advice."

"Um," he said. He looked at the package of mini

chocolate doughnuts in his hand, then looked over at the door. "Actually, I was just going—"

"But we just want to know," Hailey interrupted, "what is the worst coffee that you've ever had?"

"Ah." He cleared his throat, hesitated a moment longer, then pulled out a chair and sat down at our table. "Well, I don't really drink coffee."

"Oh. Oh, all right." Hailey leaned in Max's direction, while I did my best to pull her back the other way. "I'll ask you something completely different, then. How are you liking Bear Pass so far?"

He nodded and cleared his throat, two of his fingers tapping against the pack of doughnuts in his hand. "Good, good, it's been great," he said. There was an odd precision to his words, or to the way he articulated them, but it faded as he continued to talk. "You know, everybody's been really friendly." He looked at Hailey thoughtfully. "To be honest, I kind of expected nobody would talk to me the first day, but it's actually been just the opposite."

Bridget's brown eyes were wide behind her giant glasses. "You thought nobody would talk to you? At all? The whole day? Why wouldn't they?"

Max cracked a half smile, which somehow managed to be just as dazzling as the full display he'd given us earlier.

My inner Idiot-Girl swooned a little, and the Cynic actually forgot to slap her.

"I'm from LA, you know?" he said. "I've never lived in such a small town before, and I guess it's different. It seems like a really nice place."

"Yeah, LA, that's right," Bridget said, peering at him. "So why did you leave? I mean, like, in October of your senior year? Doesn't that sort of suck?"

He nodded. "Yeah, but my dad's university decided to eliminate its whole classics department last spring, and it was looking like he wasn't going to find another job. I mean, all the schools had started their fall semesters and everything, and he was, like, looking for freelance translation work and stuff. It was pretty bad. Then some poor dude at Sutter College had to go on long-term medical leave, and here we are." He shrugged. "At least until Sutter decides to eliminate classics too."

Then Max's father would be working with our parents—sort of. Our parents were both in the English Department, but they might cross paths with a classics guy every now and again. More of the faculty lived around Los Pinos, but a couple of others were here.

Hailey leaned in, pulling us toward Max. "Did you love LA?"

He shrugged. "We were in Santa Monica. You ever been there? I don't know, it's like you've got no right to complain. You've got the ocean right there, amazing beaches, great weather. It's not even that far from the hills, but the place itself is just . . ." He opened one hand and spread out his fingers, palm down, and made a small circular motion. "Flat." Shrugging, he opened his doughnuts and popped one into his mouth.

Though I'd been doing my best to silently disappear, I somehow heard myself saying as I looked up at him, "You like the mountains more than the ocean."

He turned his head to look my way, his lips turning upward with a hint of a smile. "I guess I do. Is that weird?"

I shook my head. I couldn't seem to look away from the deep blueness of his eyes, and I wondered if that was what the ocean looked like when it was calm, and reflecting a clear blue sky.

"What about you? Which one do you like better?" he asked, and I thought at first that he must have been speaking to someone else, but he was looking right at me.

I cleared my throat, and my gaze fell away from his. "I've never seen the ocean."

All at once, and for the first time in my life, I found myself wanting to stand at the water's edge, feeling it lap over my toes while my feet sank into the wet sand, looking all the way out to where the sea reached up to meet the sky.

"I would kill to see the ocean," Hailey said.

"You should go sometime. It's not that far. Just a few hours' drive. Give it a chance." Max spoke confidently, but then he suddenly looked embarrassed, and for the first time his gaze went to the place where Hailey and I were joined.

While I tried to think how to gloss over this, Bridget leaned forward eagerly. "What's the air quality like in LA?" she asked, her eyes wide behind her oversize glasses, her voice so sweet and childlike that it made you forgive the oddness of the question.

Max looked at her curiously for a second and then gave a short, bewildered laugh. "It's better here."

Bridget waved her hand toward me. "Clara here—you know Clara, she's the pretty one—she says we have the best conditions for stargazing. Because there's no air pollution."

"Light pollution," I corrected her, even as I winced at her ridiculous characterization of me as "the pretty one." I figured that Max was now wondering whether Bridget was "the blind one." The truth was that even if you were just comparing me and Hailey, it was Hailey who somehow, despite being my identical twin, always managed to be a little more attractive than me.

Bridget whacked her forehead with the heel of her hand, a gesture that was not common for her, and it occurred to me that she had actually made the mistake on purpose. Not the mistake about me being pretty, but the mistake about the pollution. Well, actually, both.

"Light pollution!" she agreed. "See, Clara's the astronomy expert, not me."

Max tilted his head toward me. "You're into stargazing?"

I shrugged. "I guess so."

"How often do you go to the observatory?" Juanita asked me pointedly.

"Um, I don't know, two or three times a month, if Hailey will let me?" Unfortunately, Hailey loved the observatory about as much as I loved art class. And at the observatory it was too dark for her to bring a book. I didn't mention that if it weren't for Hailey's resistance, and if I didn't care what anyone else thought, I would probably go up there several times a week.

"Case closed," Juanita said. "She's practically obsessed."

For the first time Max scooted his chair in closer to the table and leaned into his words. With perfect seriousness and not a shred of self-consciousness, he said, "So am I. What observatory do you go to?"

Idiot-Girl screamed shrilly, echoing through my brain, *Did you hear that? Did you hear? He's practically obsessed with stargazing, just like me!*

But as fast as lightning, the Cynic had her pinned down on the floor, and she growled back at her, *Yeah, but that doesn't mean he wants anything to do with a freak like you, you freak!*

I tried to block them out and do my best imitation of speaking like a normal person. "Over at Sutter College," I said.

Shut up, said the Cynic. *Just shut up! Or find a way to change the subject!*

But Idiot-Girl kept me talking: "It's pretty good, I

think. Well, actually, it's the only observatory I've ever been to. But to me it seems amazing, and I've heard other people say there's good viewing there."

"What type of telescope do they have?"

Idiot-Girl found this question profoundly brilliant. The Cynic gave Idiot-Girl a whack upside the head.

I looked down at my hands, which were wrapped tightly around my now-cold coffee cup.

"A Schmidt-Cassegrain," I said, my voice coming out all quiet and breathy, like some kind of moron. I tried hard for a regular voice as I added, "Sixteen inches."

He was on the edge of his seat. "When are they open?"

I glanced nervously at Juanita. Max was playing right into my friends' plans, and I couldn't think of any way out.

"It just so happens," said Hailey, with a note of triumph, "that all of us are going there this Friday night. Would you care to join us?" A playful, almost flirtatious note crept into her voice as she added, "Maybe let Clara show you where Orion meets up with the Gemini constellation?"

I would need to strangle Hailey in her sleep. Had a conjoined twin ever successfully murdered her sibling? I would have to look into it.

"Oh." Max drew back into his chair, his shoulders straight. His hand must have tightened around his pack of doughnuts, because it made a loud crinkling sound. He looked again at the door.

It was, I saw, exactly how I'd predicted. Hailey's two-headed invitation had completely freaked him out. Of course. Of course it had. How could it not?

"Have somewhere to be?" Juanita asked Max, seeing him look toward the door.

"W-well, I did plan—"

"You planned what exactly?" Juanita said sharply.

I drew back, pressing my shoulder into Hailey's so hard that I could feel her bones. It was rare for Juanita to take this tone with anyone, but I had heard it a few times before, when she'd felt the need to defend me and Hailey against other people's hurtful behavior. That was when her claws came out.

I didn't want a fight. I didn't want anyone to make any points. All I wanted was for Max to leave, and as quickly as possible.

Max looked at her uncertainly, and before he could come up with any response, Juanita took a quick swerve in her tactics. Her smile turned mischievous. "What are you so nervous about anyway?" she asked, teasing him. "Never been alone in the dark with four girls before?"

"Er, no, I just—"

"Oh, for God's sake," I burst out, "stop trying to mess with his head. He doesn't have to go to the stupid observatory."

Juanita raised her eyebrows at me. "Oh, now it's the *stupid* observatory?"

"Leave him alone," I repeated lamely.

My gut twisted. Why didn't he just leave? Why couldn't this just be over now?

"It—it—it's okay," Max said. "I—"

I was such a fool. The truth was that from the moment when Max had smiled at me in class that morning, there had been a part of me that had imagined—what? Surely not *dating* him, but . . . Having him smile at me again? Having him become my friend? My incredibly cute friend who made my breath catch with every one of those thousand-kilowatt smiles?

But even that had been a fantasy. I'd imagined that just because he was so good-looking, he must be extra good inside too. See, that's the thing about our species. We can kind of tell the difference between looks and personality, but only kind of. We're always getting the two things mixed up in our heads, even when we know better. That's part of what makes it so hard for people to accept me and Hailey, and it was that very same flawed thinking that had made me fantasize some kind of connection with Max.

But here he was, completely flustered by Hailey's simple suggestion that he come out with us as a group, and after all, the chances were that he was just another skittish, reputation-protecting jock. He was probably afraid of what people would say if he went up there with us.

"It's too bad," Hailey said. "You didn't seem so scared of us when you first walked in."

For a long, drawn-out moment the whole Sandwich Shack fell absolutely silent. Bridget's eyes were wide, and her mouth had fallen open in shock.

Juanita waved a hand in Max's direction. "Oh, forget it," she said. "Just forget it."

Max said, "I j—"

"I said forget it. We'll see you around."

She waved at the door. I was frozen, waiting for him to leave so that maybe, just maybe, I could finally breathe again.

He looked like he wanted to say something. But whatever it was, he didn't say it, and then the moment passed. He stood up, and as he did, his face seemed to contort into a strange, rigid anger. I pulled back in alarm; it was as if he'd turned into a different person from the wind-tousled, broadly smiling guy who had walked in here just a few minutes earlier.

Max turned to look at each of us, one by one—Juanita, Bridget, then Hailey, and finally me. With his eyes on me, he opened his mouth as if to speak, but no sound came out, and then he shut it again. He seemed to be as mute with fury as I was with fear.

He shoved his chair too hard into the table, with a loud screech and a clatter. He turned away, grabbed his backpack from the floor, and walked out. As the glass door swung shut behind him, I noticed his bag of miniature doughnuts sitting on the floor where he'd dropped them. Half of the doughnuts were smashed flat.

"There's some mail for you on the counter," she said, nodding toward a stack of papers. We divided the pile and flipped through it—clothing catalogs and college brochures, as usual. Today it was Anthropologie, Caltech, and UCLA.

"You don't have to save these for us. You can just recycle them," Clara said, frowning at the image of a beautiful, ethnically ambiguous girl in a dazzling flame-colored dress, peering into a microscope. I couldn't tell if that one was from a college or a clothing company. It didn't matter; none of them were just offering us a dress or a biology class anyway. No, they were all offering the same thing: a life of glamorous individuality and perfection.

On her laptop Mom played a clip from a morning news show. A surgeon and his team of twenty-four doctors and staff were getting ready to separate a pair of ten-month-old girls who were conjoined through the abdomen.

My mom seemed to find these news stories about conjoined twins every couple of months. She would always search for all the information she could find and follow the stories for as long as possible. These twins were Americans, which was awesome for her because they would get way more airplay than, say, Zimbabweans. The operation was happening in San Francisco, just a few hours away from us. Bonus!

Ironically, when Clara and I had been born, my mom

8

Hailey

That night, when I'd had enough of homework, Clara and I
headed for the kitchen. I'd been smelling Thai curry for the
past twenty minutes, and between that and the fact that I
kept thinking maybe I should say something to Clara about
Max, make sure she was okay or whatever, I wasn't getting
much done.

We found our mom standing in front of the stove with
two pots going, her laptop open on the counter nearby.

She looked so different these days. Her hair was all
pearly blond and smooth, and she was even wearing makeup.
After years of full-time motherhood, she'd just been hired
as an adjunct lecturer, to teach the freshman writing classes
that the full-time faculty didn't want. Even though most
of Sutter's faculty were more casual-artsy-Bohemian types,
Mom had decided that she had to look professional. She was
busier now too. In the afternoons and evenings she would
often sit on the sofa or at the dining table, with stacks of
papers to grade.

had treated the media like devils incarnate. Instead of just concentrating on staying healthy through a high-risk pregnancy and delivery, she'd focused a crazy amount of energy on keeping almost all the reporters out of the hospital. We ended up with just a couple of newspaper stories, and maybe a mention on TV. If anti-publicity were a career, my mom would rock the hell out of it.

But she was still a fan of everybody else's news coverage. Like these babies now, who between the two of them shared only two legs, one pelvis, one liver, and one large intestine.

The lead surgeon was trying to act all cool, but you could tell that he secretly felt like a little boy with a new box of Legos. The girls' mother cried with joy. Their grandmother praised the surgeons, the nurses, and God, in no particular order. Everybody was celebrating. But the surgery hadn't happened yet.

Clara and I stood beside our mom and stared at the screen as the lead surgeon explained that nine to twelve months was the ideal age for separation, for reasons involving muscular, skeletal, and psychological development.

My mom, predictably, said, "You have to wonder if anyone's weighing the pros and cons. Have they thought about the fact that these girls will have prosthetic legs? That they'll probably have less mobility than they'd have if they stayed together? Or all the health problems they're going to introduce by splitting up their organs and their bones?"

She grabbed a handful of chopped snow peas and tossed them into one of the pots.

"They're not thinking about quality of life," Mom muttered. "They're not asking themselves any questions. They're just letting the surgeons have a field day."

She always went on like this, and we just listened. Or pretended to. But now, unexpectedly, Clara spoke up.

"I don't know," she said. "A lot of people do just fine with prosthetic legs."

Mom looked up in surprise. Behind her, the clip from the news show ended and fed into a commercial for a supposedly magical fitness product.

"All my life," chirped the woman on the screen, *"I dreamed of having the perfect body. And look at me now!"*

"Better than fine," Clara went on. "People are running in the Olympics on prosthetic legs. They're walking around and living their lives and barely getting a second glance from anyone. And plus, you know, a lot of separated twins do really well. A lot of them are thriving."

I squinted in Clara's general direction. What was she getting at? That our parents should have had us separated as babies? That was a useless argument, and seventeen years later, it was certainly a moot one. No twins our age now, or anywhere near it, had ever been separated and lived to tell the tale.

It hurt my feelings a little—the idea that Clara would want to be away from me. I mean, it had crossed my mind before, but more as a momentary thing, mainly if we were having a vicious argument and I felt like storming out of the room.

But even then, in those moments when I had those thoughts, I didn't really want to leave. Even then, feeling the warmth of her body next to mine, the rhythm of her breathing—it was a comfort. Knowing that we would have to sort out whatever we were arguing about and be okay again. Knowing that in the end, nothing could change our closeness. To actually be away from her was a dark, cold, lonely thought.

Is that cowardice? Maybe. But I like to think it's just appreciating what I have. Because who doesn't want unbreakable love?

Anyway, I told myself now, maybe Clara was just trying out her ability to stand up to our mother. If so, I wasn't about to stop her.

The front door opened; from where we stood, we couldn't see it, but we could hear it, along with the sounds of Dad walking in and dropping his keys and wallet onto the table, and his battered leather messenger bag onto the floor.

Mom slapped her wooden spoon down on the counter-top, turning to give us her full attention. "Didn't you hear about that girl, just a few months ago? They cut her apart from her sister, and a full year later she died of complications. But that part of the story gets buried, doesn't it? That doesn't make any headlines."

"Of course I know about that," Clara retorted, "but that's just one case, and there are so many more where the outcomes are great. How come we never talk about *those?* How come we only talk about the ones who die?"

Dad walked over and hovered just outside the kitchen.

"Late office hours today?" Mom asked.

He shrugged. "One of the students had a lot of questions. Smart kid. It was fun talking to him." He tilted his head toward Mom's laptop. "You guys watching something?"

Mom jabbed her wooden spoon into the curry pot. "Another needless separation. And a news media so enamored of surgery that even the survival of one twin gets celebrated as a victory. Even when that separation means introducing a new set of disabilities. What no one seems to understand is that you can keep twins together and they can live perfectly happy, healthy, normal lives."

Clara inhaled sharply but said nothing.

Dad nodded, looking at us for a moment, then back at Mom. "Of course you're right," he said. "Though it's hard to imagine it until you see it with your own eyes."

"I never found it hard to imagine," Mom retorted.

He walked over to her, rested one hand on her waist, and kissed the top of her head. "I know. But you're a visionary. Most of us need more help to get there."

She looked up at him, with what looked to me like wariness—like she couldn't quite decide whether to take his comment at face value.

Then she turned away, stirring the vegetables with one hand while she turned off both burners with the other, and at the same time called out cheerily, "Could you girls help me set the table?"

We both held still a moment longer, and then, without saying anything, we began moving in unison. We went to get the silverware from the drawer.

One of our house's unusual things is its dining table. Since Clara and I can't face in the same direction at the same time, sitting at regular tables can be a pain. Sometimes literally. Outside the house, we might choose a picnic blanket on the ground, or if there's a backless bench and it isn't too narrow, then one of us can face the table and the other can face the opposite way, holding the food in her lap. Or, like at the Sandwich Shack, we perch on the edges of two chairs, both angled away from the table. But at home we have a U-shaped conference table in the dining nook adjoining the kitchen. Hailey and I sit on the inside of the *U*, and our parents sit facing us.

"Perfectly normal lives," Clara muttered as she placed

the silverware for herself and Mom, and I placed the silverware for myself and Dad. "I'm sure it's perfectly normal to have to share the job of putting out silverware because we can't be in two separate parts of the same room."

I raised my eyebrows. "Really?" I asked, trying not to laugh. "That's your sob story?"

With a smile, she brought it up a notch. "I'm sure it's perfectly normal to always balance off the side of the toilet while your sister is peeing."

I shrugged. "That's a *little* better." I knew I was egging her on.

"I'm sure it's perfectly normal," she said, "to have to spend your entire life in the world's smallest rural community so that no one will stare and point and laugh at you when you go out in public and see actual strangers." Her voice dropped to a half whisper. "And it's perfectly normal to terrify any strangers who do come to town."

We headed back to the kitchen for bowls and cups.

"Are we going to talk about that?" I asked. "Because we don't have to do that, you know. Stay here, I mean. There isn't a force field around Bear Pass. We can cross the town line."

Dad, on his way to the dining table with a bowl of curry, stopped short. "Wait. Are you talking about going somewhere? A day trip, like I keep asking you to do? I've got a whole list of places we could go in Sacramento. Or if you want to do San Francisco, there's even more. When do you want to do this? I've got this whole weekend free. We could see about tickets to some kind of show."

I glanced warily in Clara's direction. Dad was so excited, I didn't know what to say.

Mom emerged from the kitchen with another serving bowl. "This weekend sounds awfully soon," she said, her brow wrinkled with worry. "If you want to do something like this, we need to take some time to plan and prepare."

Dad looked at her quizzically. "Why?"

Mom gave me a slow once-over. "For one thing, maybe you could go natural with the hair first. You don't always have to hit people over the head with things."

"Mom," I said, "you are rearranging the deck chairs on the world's largest and most beautiful ocean liner. And I lined them up that way for a good reason, and it's really, really important to me, so don't mess with the damn deck chairs."

Dad laughed, but Mom frowned and shook her head. "You're not the *Titanic*. You're not doomed."

"Unless being stared at counts as doomed," I replied, "in which case, we are our own iceberg. Or at least we're attached to our own iceberg. The iceberg is our conjoined triplet."

Clara and I silently pushed past them to get the cups and bowls, while Mom and Dad put their serving dishes on the table.

The last time we'd tried a day trip had been four years earlier, in eighth grade, and Clara hadn't made it down two blocks of Old Sacramento before she'd fallen apart. The problem wasn't so much the adults looking at us and then quickly averting their eyes, as if they couldn't bear the sight of us, or urging their kids not to look, or hurrying them away from us with fierce whispers—a sight, apparently, too gruesome for the little ones to bear. And it certainly wasn't the little preschool-aged girl who'd grabbed her mother's hand and screamed, "What is that?"

Those things had upped Clara's stress level, sure. And yeah, okay, mine too. But what really did Clara in was the group of kids our own age who poked one another and giggled and gasped like idiots. They were pretending to be quiet, like they thought we couldn't hear them or understand. Like they were trying to be discreet, or they told themselves they were trying, but it was all mixed up with hidden meanness. That was the thing that made Clara run and hide and never go back.

And yeah, okay, if I'm totally honest? Maybe it was also the thing that made me not fight her on it as hard as I should have.

Because those idiot Decepticons had a power over me that I'd never meant to give them. I knew that each one of them was weak and flawed and full of secrets—because who isn't?—but they could hide it all behind a veneer of lip-glossed, plucked, and flat-ironed sameness. And I couldn't. Like an animal at a zoo, I was on display, and I didn't get a vote about that. Only, unlike a zoo creature, I didn't have any bars or barriers between me and the crowd. They could walk right up to me. They could poke and prod. And I didn't have any teeth or claws to fight back with.

That was before I dyed my hair pink, before I got the tattoo and started wearing a lot of thick eyeliner and black clothes. I know I'm still on display. I know I still have no weapons. But a kind of armor, maybe. A gesture toward controlling the conversation.

As soon as we returned with the cups and bowls, Mom leapt back into the argument. "People don't stare at you as much as you think they do. You exaggerate it in your heads. You think of yourselves as more set apart than you really are. If you would skip the outlandish getups, you'd hardly be noticed."

She said this with what sounded like total sincerity. Sometimes I wondered if she could even hear herself.

"Mom," Clara said in a tight voice as we put down the cups and bowls and sat down, "we're one of the rarest mutations in the human species."

Depending on who you ask, conjoined twins occur in something like one out of every two hundred thousand live births. And quite a lot of those die in the first day. I'm sure there are rarer conditions, but if you could come up with a formula for how rare it is plus how visibly obvious it is, we might win. The most common condition leading to dwarfism, for example, is somewhere around five to thirteen times as common as being born a conjoined twin, let alone surviving as one. Booyah.

"I wouldn't go with that choice of language," Dad put in as he took his seat, "but I do have to agree that your hair is not going to have much effect on how much attention you get, one way or the other. It's more a question of whether you can suck it up a little, right?"

"And appreciate the fact that you're able to have these options at all," Mom added. "Appreciate your health and all the abilities that you have, and the fact that you're both even here, alive. I'm grateful for that every day, you know."

I supposed she wanted us to say that we were also grateful—grateful to her and Dad, for making the decisions they had. We probably should have been. I just wasn't sure if I could say it again right then.

"Sometimes," Clara said, "it seems like you're so set on us being grateful and cheery all the time, you're blinding yourself to reality."

"Oh, honestly." Mom shook her head. "You're two completely healthy girls. You go to school. You're good students, you have friends, you do practically everything your friends do. You don't think that's a good life? You don't want to be happy with that?"

"That's not what I'm saying," Clara said.

But Mom went on. "You know, if you'd had surgery, there's an excellent chance that at least one of you would have ended up paraplegic, with a colostomy. Or dead." She bowed her head. "And I just keep thinking about that baby who died, and these two babies going in for surgery, with the parents knowing full well they might die too. I don't understand these parents who just write off those risks in the name of looking like everyone else."

"And what I don't understand," Clara said, her voice rising sharply, "is these parents who just write off the costs of staying conjoined. You think we can do everything our friends do? When was the last time we went snowboarding with them? When was the last time we joined them for a nice day hike? When was the last time we *danced*?"

The answer, of course, was never. We had never danced. Honestly, I had never given it much thought. But all of a sudden, I thought, *Why?* What was stopping us?

We could walk forward, we could walk backward, we could shuffle sideways, and we could even run a little. Why hadn't we ever danced? Why hadn't *I* ever danced?

"You know," Dad said quietly, "some of those things you could do. Probably not the snowboarding. But we could work on the rest of it. Broaden your horizons. And I still think visiting a city might be a good place to start."

No one answered. Mom looked at Clara, then at me. She didn't look upset, just thoughtful, like she was working something out in her mind.

Then she said, "Hold on." She went to her laptop and quickly plugged a cord into a set of speakers. A moment later a popular dance tune blasted through the kitchen and adjoining dining area.

My mother splayed her hands out around her. "Go on then," she said, grinning. "Let's do it! Let's dance!"

Unbelievable. She'd heard some of Clara's words, but not the right ones.

When Clara stormed toward the speakers, I followed without resistance. She turned them off, and a loud silence filled the house.

"No," Clara said. "I'm not going to dance for you. I'm not going to dance for anybody, and I'm not going to pretend that I'm normal for you."

I drew in a breath.

For seventeen years Clara and our parents had conspired to pretend that we were normal. If Clara was even halfway ready to stop pretending, it would change everything.

"We're not normal," she said now, her voice harsh and thick with unshed tears. "You can say that we're two totally normal girls six thousand times, and you can say it as fast as you can like a tongue twister, and you can say it every night before you go to bed like it's some kind of prayer, but I'm sorry, none of that is ever going to make it true."

I didn't say a word. But as I followed Clara out of the room, absorbing her fury and her frustration and her deep well of sadness, I understood those feelings, but I didn't share them. Instead I felt a crazy tug of hope.

9

Clara

Hailey and I didn't talk much as we got ready for bed that night, taking turns at the sink and exchanging our day clothes, with their customized fittings—Mom had become an expert seamstress because of us—for loose-fitting pajamas, which we were able to wear off the rack.

It was my night to sleep on my left side, which was unfortunate because my left shoulder had been bugging me that day. When we're walking—or doing anything else, for that matter—I'm on the right, so my left shoulder gets hunched toward Hailey, and the right one has to stretch. Plus, there are some discomforts that come with fitting ourselves onto chairs and benches, and of course into bed, where it's hard to shift positions during the night.

Basically, our bodies are healthy, but like anyone else, we can get some aches and pains now and then when we have to repeatedly move, sit, or lie in positions that aren't perfectly comfortable. Weekly physical therapy and massage helps, and Mom knows how to do some helpful massage moves between our official sessions, but we also try to make things as ergonomic as we can. For sleep, we've found that the best pillow situation is sharing an extra long one, which was really designed to be a body pillow for pregnant women to prop up their elbows and knees.

I thought about asking Hailey to switch sides, but the pain wasn't that bad. It's better to stick to the schedule as much as possible, lest we degenerate into chaos and bickering.

Lying in bed and doing my best to ignore the pain in my shoulder, I tried to focus my mind on something innocuous. But wherever my thoughts went, some anxiety would creep up.

More than anything else, I kept thinking of Max's twisted, angry face just before he'd left the Sandwich Shack. And the pack of mini doughnuts lying smashed on the floor, as if he'd been squeezing them to smithereens as we'd been talking. It was the oddness of it all that made it stay with me. What had he been so mad about?

When I was younger, if I couldn't sleep, I would mentally trace the stars of the Gemini constellation. Dad had taught us to find it when we were as young as six or seven, keeping us up late on certain clear winter nights, when Gemini would be easiest to spot. He didn't know that much about the stars, but for some reason he needed us to memorize every part of those glittering, dazzling twins, so close to each other that they formed a single constellation. So we would bundle up in sweaters and jackets and follow him outside with our kid-size astronomy books and the star maps that he'd printed out. We would find Orion or the Big Dipper and use them to trace our way over to the bright stars Castor and Pollux, and from there we'd find the rest of Gemini.

For Dad it was all about the timeless beauty of those twins and their love for each other, which was more important to them than life itself. He couldn't have known how for me it would be just the starting point to falling in love with all the stars.

On other sleepless nights I would picture myself in a space suit, floating somewhere near the moon, all alone—no Hailey in sight—unencumbered by the gravitational mass of my home planet and my home body. I imagined looking back at Earth from there, seeing the whole planet all at once, and finally understanding how all the parts of it fit together—the oceans and the continents and the clouds. Because down here on the surface, where I could see only little patches of ground and sky, I felt like a farsighted person trying to read a book. I couldn't understand anything when it was all up so ridiculously close.

But at some point I started worrying about Gemini, the celestial twins. Were they glad to spend billions of years together in the sky, always on display, or would they rather wander apart and explore?

As for traveling to outer space, the wild impossibility of that began to overwhelm me. I was never going to escape the gravity I'd been born to. And what was wrong with me anyway, for even wanting such a thing? I was strange enough on the outside. Did I have to be so strange on the inside, too?

Just when I thought that Hailey must have been asleep, she uttered one of her rarest sentences. "I know you're right."

"I am?" I briefly savored the moment before I asked, "About what?"

"About us not being normal."

Her tone was urgent, but her volume stayed low. We try not to let our parents hear us talking in bed. Maybe it's just a holdover from when we were little and they used to keep coming in to check on us.

"We're not normal," she repeated, "and we never will be. But there's no point fighting against that, or hiding from it. We just have to accept it."

I groaned. Somehow I'd imagined, for just a second there, that she actually had something worthwhile to say. "God, Hailey, is that, like, some brilliant new insight? I've been accepting it for seventeen years already."

"No you haven't," she insisted, with that same hushed urgency. "You've never accepted it. Not ever. You struggle against it every day of your life."

Helpless, I asked, "What do you want me to do?"

"I want you to stop being afraid of living in the world. Stop being afraid of yourself."

"Oh," I said, my voice as small as a little girl's. "Is that all?"

"If you weren't afraid," she said, "we could go to Sacramento. Or San Francisco. And then we could go to Stanford or Berkeley or Yale. Paris. Tokyo. Sydney. Just let everybody stare if they want to."

"The last time we tried it—"

"We were only thirteen. Yeah, I know, it sucked. But you just have to start embracing it. Let them look at you. Show them what you are. Let them be comfortable or not, it's up to them, but it's not our problem one way or the other. Because there's nothing actually wrong with us. And if we would just be okay with being freaks, then we could actually *do* something."

A deep shiver ran through my upper body; sometimes that happens without me fully understanding why. Though I wasn't crying, a slight dampness seemed to wet my lashes and then pass, like one of those blink-and-you'll-miss-it spring rainstorms.

I closed my eyes. "What is it that you want to do, Hailey?"

"I don't know." She shifted toward me, so her shoulder rested against mine. "Just something besides staying here." Her voice dropped to a softer whisper. "I can't let this be all there is. How long are we going to live? Another sixty, seventy years maybe, if we both stay healthy? Do you want to spend all of those years stuck in one place?"

Sixty or seventy more years. Yes, possibly. Though many conjoined twins die at birth, and some have serious health issues, others have lived full lives. Daisy and Violet Hilton, the famous back-to-back, singing and dancing conjoined sisters of the twentieth century, had lived to be sixty. Millie and Christine McCoy, the back-to-back conjoined stage stars of the nineteenth century, had made it to sixty-one—and they'd been born into slavery, in an era before modern medicine.

My bookshelves held a stack of biographies of conjoined twins who'd come before us—some that Mom had bought us when we were younger, and others that I'd ordered for myself. I'd read most of them more than once, looking for any clue about our lives and what we might expect. Hailey was content to skim or ignore most of these, which I couldn't understand. We'd never met any other conjoined twins in real life. Those books were the closest thing we had.

Like the Hiltons and the McCoys, Hailey and I had always been, essentially, perfectly healthy. Sure, we'd had a few extra doctors' visits when we were small, and a bit of continuing physical therapy and extra monitoring—more when we were younger, less and less as time went on—but for the most part, we seemed to have as good a shot at full lives as any singletons we knew.

"It's not such a bad place," I said. "You act like Bear Pass is some kind of hell on earth, but it's actually really beautiful. Do you ever look around? Really take it in? The huge green trees? The mountain air, the stars?"

"Seriously? You're trying to sell me on the scenery? It might be beautiful, but how would we even know? We've never seen anything else. We've never seen any other mountains, or any other trees. We've never seen the ocean. Or a lake, or any other river besides the one that runs through town. We've never seen the New York skyline, or the Eiffel Tower. Or the Golden Gate Bridge. We've never—"

"The Eiffel Tower? How are we going to get there? How are we going to fit ourselves onto an airplane? I mean, how do the seats even work?"

For a brief moment she was actually quiet, and I thought maybe she was seeing reason. But then she said, "I think we could probably do it. It might not be super-comfortable for such a long trip, since we'd have to be stretched away from each other and angled a little weird from the seats and everything, but if the seats are close enough, I think we could make it work. And anyway, even if we couldn't, there are always cruise ships."

I sighed. "Okay, fine, whatever. But what about the

people here? They've been good to us, Hailey. It's like everybody's family here."

"Yeah, sometimes literally. The amount of inbreeding—"

"No. Stop. That's not true. We've lived here all our lives, and in all that time nobody has ever sent reporters after us. Nobody has ever posted anything about us online. They've respected our privacy, they've protected us, and they've treated us like real people. Have you ever thought about how amazing that is?"

"Clara, okay, but don't you understand? I want to see museums. I want to see original paintings, and the churches of medieval Europe. I want to study with real artists, or I'll never be able to become one myself."

"If you would just think about the film studies department—"

"Goddamn film studies." She sucked in her breath. "Okay, fine. You want me to make films so bad? I'll apply for film studies at Sutter. I'll do that for you. I mean, I want to try new things, right? I might as well start with that, but that's not where it stops. I want to try a lot of things."

She paused, and I could feel what she was going to say before she said it, and I wanted to stop her, but I didn't know how.

"Like dancing," she said.

"What, like tap dancing?" I blurted, before she could go on. "Ballet? Or do you want—"

"You know what I want."

She was right. I did.

"I'm asking Alek to the dance," she said, "and you should still ask Max."

"Oh, you have got to be kidding. Didn't you see how much we freaked him out?"

"It was a little weird," she said, "but Juanita and I shouldn't have been so bitchy to him. Anyway, you can't make assumptions about what it means or what he's capable of. You can't go off crying in a corner every time someone acts strangely around you."

I shook my head in the darkness. "Yeah, right, Hailey. The way he was looking at us, we might as well be werewolves. Ogres. Trolls."

"And you don't want to show him how wrong he is?"

"What for? We barely know him. Why is it my job to prove anything to him?"

She didn't answer. She shifted around. She fluffed her side of the pillow and settled into it, and after a few minutes she got quiet. I stopped waiting for her to say something. I thought maybe she had fallen asleep.

But then she said, "Fine, you don't have to ask Max. But I'm asking Alek. I know you don't want me to. I know you're scared that it'll freak him out and that other people will hear about it and freak out too, and I know he's not exactly the best person for improving our reputation as normals—"

"It's not that," I said, my hackles rising at the implication that I, of all people, would avoid a guy because he was considered a freak. Well, actually, a homicidal freak. I hesitated, then added, "Maybe it's 1 percent about that, but only 1 percent. I never believed any of those rumors or anything."

"Fine," she said, "but the point is, you only get to veto things that affect our shared nervous system in the lower half of our bodies. You don't have jurisdiction over this."

And there was nothing I could say. She was right.

10

Hailey

It was a cold, crappy October day. The grass where we normally ate our lunch was soaked. Juanita and Bridget scooted off to some yearbook meeting, and Clara and I decided to move our picnic blanket into a corner of the gym. It was either that or the damp, packed cafeteria, where the tables all had built-in benches. None of that really works for us.

I hadn't slept much after our conversation the night before. First I'd been kind of pissed at Clara for how she kept harping on the film studies thing. I mean, I paint. With oils. On canvas. What did that even have to do with film?

But then I started actually trying to answer that question. Like, okay, you can't make a film out of oil paints. But what were my paintings about? Was there something in them that I could apply to film?

My basic thing lately was these twisted Madonna-and-child portraits. So what was that about, anyway? Each of them took a really standard, familiar design, and then incorporated one or two things that completely did not belong. Was there something I could do with that?

I'd thought about it for a couple of hours, and finally some ideas had started bubbling up in my head. They were pretty vague. But one thing I did know was that I was going to need help. So, while Clara had snored beside me, I'd sent messages to a few people. I figured I would wait and see what they sent me. And then I would go from there.

I'd been working mainly with oil paints for the last couple of years, and I felt like I had a groove going there. But now I started to remember the freedom, the thrill of uncertainty, that came with trying something new—something where I had basically no idea what I was doing.

When I was little, art had always seemed like an adventure to me, and there was always something new to try. Back in preschool, I went mainly for size. We would collect boxes, all the biggest ones we could get from our neighbors and friends, and I would paint them with big strokes of color, stripes and dots and swirls and patterns. We would stand inside the boxes if they were big enough, and I would fill them up with brightness. Sometimes Clara would even grab a brush, or swirl her fingers through the paint to make her own, separate patterns.

Then we started elementary school, and again and again I heard my mother telling teachers, aides, administrators, and other parents and kids, "They can do everything the other kids can do. They're typically developing children who happen to be attached. They're normal. They're just like everyone else. They're exactly the same."

Normal. Normal. Normal.

Just like everyone else.

Exactly the same.

Even then, I understood why she was saying it. Understood that it was the best thing to say. The simplest thing for other people to understand.

But something in me hated it, and I wanted to rebel.

We were not like everyone else. Who besides us had two minds that understood each other perfectly? That worked in such perfect synchrony that they could operate their four legs and four arms in unison without discussion, giving them twice the strength of a regular child? Not to mention twice the imagination and bargaining power, whenever we wielded them in unison, which we often did. We weren't normal. We were magical.

I couldn't rebel at school. This had been made clear. If we didn't behave there, if we didn't act like everyone else, they might want to send us away to a special school, which wouldn't be as well-suited to our needs. The school we went to, a regular school, was the right one for us, and that was why Mom had been there almost constantly—once or twice a week, sometimes more—meeting with teachers and administrators, sitting in on classes, making sure we were accommodated in just the right ways, and in just the right amounts.

Part of the deal was that we had to be perfect, so they would understand that we were okay.

At first my rebellions were so tiny, they went unnoticed. I drew pictures of me and Clara with wings, flying away over the clouds. Or with animal tails and hoofs, or even scales and talons. I drew a whole classroom of kids in one big conjoined circle. I was trying to say something, I think, but nobody seemed to hear. They thought my pictures were cute.

Then one afternoon, when Mom was busy in the kitchen, I took all her favorite picture books off the shelf. All the ones about kindness and compassion and loving yourself just as you are. While Clara looked on in horror, I tore out a few key pages from each one. I painted them with my tempera paints, a collage of patterns and colors. Then, while they were still wet, I folded them into different shapes and pressed them into one another, adding tape and staples to secure them.

By the time Mom came out of the kitchen, I had a strange, unwieldy tower that was taller than I was, and at least twice as wide. Clara and I were both covered in paint, and so was the hardwood living room floor, and part of the closest wall. There were a few spatters on the nearby sofa. Most of the picture books were ruined.

I held my breath and waited for a punishment that never came.

They bought me more paints and paper. Watercolors, ink pens, and pastels. A huge set of brushes. A new easel. Books and videos about art. They rearranged that corner of the living room and made it my studio.

I'd failed at rebelling. But I felt like maybe they'd heard at least part of what I was trying to say.

I didn't expect to see Alek until art class, but as Clara and I walked toward the gym for lunch, I noticed him trudging down the hill from the art room, a thick portfolio slung over his shoulder. His black T-shirt and black jeans hung loosely on his slight frame.

When I caught his eye, he lifted a hand in greeting and walked over.

Calm down, I told myself. *He's just a guy. This is no big thing.*

"You robbing the art room?" I asked, nodding at the overstuffed black portfolio. "You forgot your mask." I made two *V* signs with my fingers and placed them over my eyes, like one of those black masks that burglars wear in cartoons.

"Oh damn, I thought I was wearing my invisibility cloak. Now I'll never get away with these invaluable treasures. And by 'invaluable,' I mean they have no value whatsoever." He pulled one out as evidence. It was one of his own paintings, a pillaged English cottage with flames and smoke rising into the soft blue sky.

"What's going on?" I asked. "That's an awful lot of stuff you're taking home."

"Yeah, I'm getting ready for this interview. There's this program over the summer, in San Francisco. Did you hear about that? It's like a summer intensive with real working artists. Three whole weeks at Golden Gate Arts. I'm going down to show them my portfolio in a couple of weeks, and I thought I'd bring some stuff home to start going through it."

He tilted his head to one side and looked thoughtfully at his canvas, then stuffed it back into the portfolio. Without quite looking at me, he said, "You should come too."

San Francisco. Real art professors. And Alek.

You know how people put Mentos in Diet Coke and it makes the whole thing explode? And it's pretty spectacular? I felt like my heart was the Diet Coke, and each of those things was a Mentos: San Francisco. Art professors. Alek.

But I just nodded, pretending that he had described something mildly interesting at best. "San Francisco, huh?" I stole a quick sideways glance at Clara. There was no way she would ever consider it. And no way that our mom would ever let us go.

Dad might be on my side. But it wasn't likely to do much good. Not when we were up against the hard wall of Mom and Clara.

"Yeah," Alek said, "you stay in the dorms on campus."

His gaze flitted over to Clara. "Um, would that be a problem? The dorm rooms?"

Some of his hair fell into his eyes. A weird thought popped into my head. I wished I could reach up and brush it away for him. I wanted to see his eyes, which in this hazy October light would be so dark, they would look almost black. And I wanted to touch his hair.

I shrugged. "I don't know. We might be able to manage it." I cocked my head toward Clara. "We could probably live in a dorm room for a few weeks, don't you think?" I knew it was impossible. I didn't know why I was even asking her, when the mere thought was bound to give her a heart attack.

Clara answered tightly, "They probably only have twin beds."

Ironically, we cannot sleep in twin beds.

"Maybe they'd make an exception," Alek said, brushing the hair out of his eyes himself. "They could let you live off campus or bring in a bigger bed. Or maybe they have some special rooms to accommodate people with different needs."

His words jolted me. *Accommodate. Different needs.* Not that there was any better way to say it.

He was probably right. The art school had probably never had to *accommodate* conjoined twins before, but they'd probably had plenty of *different needs* come up in the past. I didn't normally think about being part of some larger group of disabled people, those with wheelchairs or canes, hearing aids or service dogs. But there was no reason why I shouldn't.

"Seriously, Hailey," Alek went on, oblivious, "you should really come. I know you'd get in for sure. My cousin did it two years ago, and she said it totally turned her art around. I mean she was good to begin with, but afterward she was— well, still not as good as you, but close. Of course I'm also applying for the fall, but I'm not sure if I'll be going then."

For some reason he looked toward Clara as he asked, "You guys are going to Sutter next year, right?"

Clara gave a slight nod, but I was the one who spoke. "I'd love to go to art school instead, but the thing is, and I don't know if you ever noticed this about me or not? But I'm actually a conjoined twin."

Alek laughed. His laugh was low-pitched and musical, and I immediately wanted to hear it again. "And here I thought the two of you were just really close."

"Yeah, no," I said, feeling warmer now and more hopeful, "and the thing about it is, my sister hates art. She is such a huge pain in my backside, if you know what I mean?"

He smiled. "Yeah, I can see how that might be inconvenient from time to time. Though to be honest, I always thought it must be kind of cool, too. Like, how many people can say there's another person who understands everything about them?" He looked straight up at his eyebrows and added, "Or am I just making a complete corny ass of myself?"

"No," I said slowly, "you're not completely wrong.

Except for the part about how sometimes I don't understand that crazy chick who's stuck to my butt at *all*."

Other people had said these things to us before. Usually it seemed like they were trying to put a really fakey-assed smiley spin on something that, deep down inside, they believed was unimaginably horrifying.

But Alek wasn't doing that. He wasn't the type. He really did see that there was something valuable about being what we were.

And that was when I realized that the time was now.

I grabbed Clara's hand and squeezed it. There was some sweat and coldness going on back there, and a slight tremor. I couldn't tell if it was coming from her hand or mine. But I did feel her squeezing back, and I decided to take it as an encouragement rather than a warning.

"Sometimes," I said to Alek, "it does get in the way of things."

"Well, of course I noticed that you're not on the soccer team," he said, smiling. He seemed comfortable; he showed no sign at all of getting ready to turn and run away.

I gazed at him, and he gazed back. And then, gripping Clara's hand harder, I said, "And dancing. We never dance. But you know, there's that Sadie Hawkins dance. . . . Would you go with me, Alek?"

It was hard to say how long he stood there, not saying anything. There were sounds of students all around us, walking through the outdoor hallway and in and out of the gym, talking and laughing, but it was all a blur. This must be what it felt like to jump from the high dive, and realize only in the moment of jumping that actually, you never meant to do this, and you don't even know how to swim.

He was about to say no.

Alek cleared his throat, and he opened his mouth to say something, but I was already speaking, blurting out, "As friends!"

I cleared my throat too, an echo of the sound he'd just made, and added, "Obviously."

He searched my face. Again it seemed to last forever. I tried to think of what else I could say to erase the last five minutes from time and space.

Finally Alek said, "I've never been to a school dance before."

"I haven't either," I said, with a tiny, pained giggle that didn't even sound like me at all.

"Sorry," he said, "I was just having trouble picturing it for a minute there."

I started backing up, push-pulling Clara along with me, away from Alek. My grip on her hand loosened; my whole body had begun to deflate.

Maybe Clara had been right all along. Maybe I'd been wrong to even try.

"I mean myself at a school dance," Alek went on, and

there was nothing rushed or embarrassed about the way he said it. Either he was really good at covering himself or he wasn't even covering at all. "All these years, even at middle school, I could never picture myself going to one, with all those . . ." He gazed up at the cloudy sky, looking thoughtful, like he was just trying to figure himself out. "Not that I have anything *against* those people that go to them, but I'm just, you know, not . . . They must play a lot of pop music, right?"

Pop music. God. Of course. He would hate that.

"Never mind," I said, backing away farther. "I'm sorry. It was a stupid idea."

I hoped my black eye makeup and pale foundation were thick enough to disguise the mess of emotions that I couldn't seem to tamp down. An impenetrable mask of *whatever*. That was what I needed.

Over his shoulder I noticed Gavin and Max coming out of the gym and then walking in our direction. They weren't looking at us, just chatting with each other. And then Clara was pulling at me in a confused, erratic way, as if she wanted to flee but didn't know which way to go.

"No, no, wait!" Alek grabbed my free hand, and his was so warm and dry that it actually made me halfway relax.

"You see how stupid I am?" he said. "I'm making you feel bad because I'm not paying enough attention to what I'm saying. I was just thinking about the dance part of it. I never thought about going to one before, but there's a first time for everything, right?"

I stared at him, uncomprehending.

Max and Gavin stopped near the edge of the grass, continuing their conversation but no longer walking. Max looked toward us, then away. Behind me Clara was quietly freaking out.

"Hailey," Alek said, holding on to my hand, "I'm trying to say yes."

11

Clara

"You'll have to tell me how these things work," Alek said as he let go of Hailey's hand. "Do we go out to dinner first? Can I pick you up, or should we meet somewhere?"

"Ah, I actually hadn't thought about any of that," Hailey said.

My mind was reeling—*Had a real live boy just accepted a date with my sister? Did this mean that he must really be a serial killer or parent-murderer, or was it still conceivable that he could be semi-normal? If he was, would that suggest that my entire theory of the universe suffered from some fundamental flaw in its basic underpinnings? Also, were they going to DANCE at the dance? And what was I supposed to do while this was going on?*—but all that dropped away when my gaze wandered over to Max.

Our eyes met for just a moment, and then he quickly looked away. I'd caught him staring.

Gavin walked off toward the gym. Max looked my way again. I held his gaze. *Let them look,* Hailey had said. *So what?*

But then he started walking in my direction, and I kind of started hyperventilating. Alek and Hailey were saying things to each other, but I didn't hear a word of it. Max looked at me as he approached. What could he possibly have to say to me, and what would I conceivably come up with to say back? Part of me hated him, part of me felt total sympathy for his fear of me, and another part—well, another part just wanted to throw up.

Max walked right up to me. "Hey, ah, Clara," he said. "And Hailey. Hi there." He nodded at Hailey and Alek, who nodded back before returning to their own conversation.

"Um, hi," I said, frowning, but not failing to note that Max had gotten our names right. He glanced at Hailey. She was whispering something to Alek, whose head was bent close to hers.

Max cleared his throat. "I'm sorry about yesterday." It was there again, that clipped precision that I'd heard at the Sandwich Shack, like he was pronouncing each word a little more carefully than the average person. It made his words seem unnatural and forced, like a coerced apology from a preschooler or a politician.

I shrugged. "We didn't exactly make it easy on you. I'm not sure what got into Hailey and Juanita."

"It was my fault. They were just having fun. So, ah, I'm sorry about that. And, mmm . . . Maybe another time on the observatory?"

Alek and Hailey said their good-byes, and Alek turned away, heading toward the parking lot with his portfolio.

Alek had really said yes to Hailey. He hadn't mocked her, laughed, shouted at her, or called her names. The world hadn't stopped spinning.

And in my mind I heard myself saying the kinds of things to Max that I would normally say in a situation like this: *Sure, another time.* Or: *Sounds great.* Or: *Yeah, just let us know when you're up for it.*

But it was all a pack of lies. Max wasn't ever going to the observatory with us, and we both knew it, so why did we feel the need to pretend otherwise? And why did my friends feel the need to tell me that asking Max out was a good idea, when they had to know it wasn't? And why did Alek feel the need to tell Hailey that he would go to the dance, as if it were a real date, when of course he couldn't mean it to be? And why did my mother keep insisting that our lives were normal, and why did our teachers pretend that we were going to choose our own careers, as if we had the same opportunities as their other students? And why, why, why was I pretending that I wasn't offended by Max's fear of me? Why was I letting him off so easily?

And I thought all of that, and I told my mouth to say, *Sure, great, some other time,* but my mouth just didn't want to listen.

And so instead I heard myself saying, "Nope. Friday's your last chance."

He cocked his head to one side. "It is? Why's that?"

I shrugged. My heart started beating so loudly and so fast, it was like the whole school marching band was doing a drumroll right inside my ears. But I just plunged ahead. I actually tilted my head and said in this voice that was weirdly maybe a little bit flirty, from what I could tell over the sound of the drumroll:

"I don't know, it just is. I'm a nice girl—well, some of the time, anyway—and I'm pretty smart and sometimes slightly interesting, and I'm actually not that bad-looking if you look at me from the right angle, you know, like the angle where you can't tell that I've got another one of me growing out from the back. So I assume that all kinds of guys would actually be really excited to go to the observatory with me. I mean, I can't think of one single reason why they wouldn't be. Can you?"

I looked right up into his eyes, my head angled to one side, my eyebrows raised. A lock of hair fell into my eyes, and as I tucked it back behind my ear, I felt, somehow, like some other girl. Like a girl who knew what it was to be a girl, talking to a boy.

He didn't look away. In fact, he cracked a smile, and I watched as it slowly widened, as glorious as ever, but somehow this time it didn't make me feel so much like I was under his power; instead I felt sort of victorious. I had *made* him smile.

"Nope," he said, "not one single reason."

Behind me, Hailey gave a barely audible squeal of delight.

I shrugged, using every ounce of strength to feign non-chalance. "Well, so you can see why I don't want to wait around to see if you're going to show up some other time. I'll probably be busy some other time. This Friday night is very likely the last chance you'll have to catch me with that kind of free time on my hands."

My palms at this point were so sweaty, I thought they might start dripping right onto the ground.

Max's smile was still there. "All right. Friday night it is, then." He looked sideways, then down at his absurdly large feet, shoving his hands into his pockets. "Um, do . . . you find you . . . can actually *see* very much of the meteor shower from there?"

"Meteor shower?"

He met my eyes. "You do know that's supposed to be the height of the Orionid meteor shower this year, right?"

Hailey cackled.

Max raised his eyebrows, looking at her.

"Sorry," she said, even as she laughed again. "I was trying so hard to be quiet. But the Orionid meteor shower! Is it really this weekend? I can't believe Clara didn't know that!"

I nodded, as all that hot air seemed to seep out of me. "I can't believe it either." An observatory was perhaps the worst place in the world to watch a meteor shower.

Max said, "A powerful telescope . . ."

He let this trail off, but I finished his thought for him. ". . . shows you only a little bit of the sky."

"And for a meteor shower . . ." He looked questioningly at me, openly waiting for me to complete his thought for him.

"You want to lie on your back in an open space," I said, "and take in as much of the sky as you can, all at once."

He sucked in a deep breath and said nothing.

I stared at him—those gorgeous blue eyes, those long black lashes—until Hailey elbowed me in the ribs.

"Were you planning on watching the meteor shower all along?" I asked. "Is *that* what you're planning to do on Friday night?"

He scrunched up his face in a sort of exaggerated embarrassment, as if to say, *You caught me.*

"I know it's supergeeky and everything," he said, "but I've watched it every year since I was four years old, and I kind of, ah, make a point of never missing it." He looked down. "I should have told you. I mean, I tried, but . . ."

I said, "My friends and my sister thought you were afraid of us. Or afraid of being seen with us." I stopped talking. Why was I telling him this?

He looked at me for a minute without answering, and then he said, "Have you seen my house? It used to be the Olsens', over on Ridge Road?"

I shook my head.

He said, "We have a pool surrounded by a deck. It's made of that fake wood stuff, you know that stuff? They make it so you don't get splinters? We have these deck chairs on it that recline all the way back."

I nodded. "Probably a better viewing place than the observatory. To tell you the truth, I just about always watch the Orionid meteor shower too. I don't know how I managed to forget about it this year."

I'd forgotten, of course, because I'd been so caught up in the plans to get Max up to the observatory. And then I'd been enmeshed in the agony of defeat. I hadn't even checked the dates for this year, but I knew that this particular meteor shower always took place about a week before Halloween, so of course this Friday would be just about right.

"I hope you're not offended if I ask you this," he said, "but are you guys able to sit on a deck chair? Or on two of them?"

"Um . . . yeah, I'm pretty sure we could do that. At our house we just sit on the lawn and lean back against each other."

He nodded. "That would work too. My house is up on a hill, and it's a little bit away from any other houses, and the trees and brush are all cleared away around it." He swallowed. "Would you . . . would you maybe want to come over and watch the meteor shower with me on Friday?"

I stared at him. I supposed after all that chitchat about his house and the chairs, a normal girl might have seen this coming.

"Well," he said, with just a hint of a smile, "you did say Friday night was my last chance, right?"

I kept staring.

"Hailey," Max said, looking over at her, "obviously I'm inviting both of you. And your friends too, if they feel like coming, and if they don't mind missing the observatory. It sounded like that was more your thing anyway, wasn't it?" he asked, turning back to me.

"Um . . ."

Hailey, who had been holding herself so silent and still that it was almost like she wasn't there (yeah, right, as if I'd know what *that* would feel like), now took the opportunity to kick me pretty hard in the side of my calf. And then, because she can feel what happens to my legs, she had the gall to cry out, "Ow!"

Max looked confused.

I laughed. "Um, yeah, okay. I'll ask them."

"Great. I'll make popcorn. Um, do you *like* popcorn?" He sounded worried. "Because I could also make something else."

And that was when I realized that all this time, feeling angry at Max for being afraid of me, I'd missed the fact that *I* was afraid of *him*. And all of a sudden, at least for just that moment, I wasn't anymore.

"Yeah," I said. "I love popcorn."

I smiled at him, and lo and behold, that was all it took to make him smile back.

12

Hailey

"So you guys have to help me," I told Bridget and Juanita at lunch the next day, sitting out on the grass. I could feel the coldness of the ground right through our picnic blanket, and we were all huddled inside thick winter coats. "How can I convince Clara to go to a three-week art program in San Francisco this summer?"

Since talking to Alek, my mind had been fizzing continuously with those same three Mentos-like thoughts: San Francisco. Art professors. Alek.

Juanita laughed. "Could we start with an easier problem? Like how to stop climate change?"

"I'm serious," I said. "It's just three weeks in the dorms. With artists! They're all weird anyway. They *love* weird. We'll be gods to them. How can I make her see it?"

Clara nudged me. "Could you stop talking about me like I'm not here?"

"I never talk about you like you're not here," I retorted. "I wouldn't even know how to do that."

"Well, it might be good practice," Bridget said. "Living in the dorms. Since you'll be in the dorms at Sutter in the fall."

I cocked my head to one side, squinting at her. "No, that was never the plan. We're going to live at home."

"Oh." She frowned. "I thought we were all living in the dorms together."

"Our tuition is free through our dad," Clara explained. "But not room and board. Plus, it's easier for us to live at home, because we don't drive. Or, you know, grocery shop or anything."

"But you don't have to do those things in the dorms," Bridget pointed out.

"Well, I'm probably going to be living at home too," Juanita said. "So that will be good. I can still drive you guys around in your minivan and everything, or maybe I can buy myself an old used car to get around to classes and work, and if it has the kind of backseat and leg room that you guys need, then I could even drive you around in that. Anyway, we can all hang out."

"Hey, I know," Bridget put in. "We could all share a house. Juanita and I can drive and shop, and you guys can help with stuff at home, and we can get furniture from Ikea and make our own decorations, and have parties—oh, this will be so fun!"

It actually did sound fun—a lot better than living at

home. More expensive, but at least we'd be getting a taste of independence. Maybe there was some way we could swing it. It had to be more realistic than my crazy art school dreams.

And maybe I could even try this ridiculous film school idea of Clara's; maybe I could make that work. People had been sending me a few clips, and some thoughts were starting to percolate around them in my mind. It was still pretty shapeless, but the seeds were there, and I was starting to see how film might be a canvas after all. I hadn't told Clara about any of this; I had watched all the clips with my headphones on, at times when she had her back to me and her mind focused on other things. I liked the idea of trying to surprise her.

But then I looked at Juanita, and her face was frozen in this sort of half smile, and there was so much sadness in her eyes that I thought she might be trying not to cry. And then I felt like I might cry myself.

"Not Juanita," I said. "You're leaving, okay? We're going to figure this out. I don't want to hear any more talk about you living at home next year."

She shook her head. "My dad did all these calculations. He just showed me last night, and he's right. It makes more sense if I take community college classes two days a week for the next two years, and work for three or four days a week. Then I can save money and I won't need so many loans."

"Where are you going to work?" I demanded. "Taco Bell?"

She looked down. "There are worse things in the world."

"But I just don't see the point. Yeah, college means loans, but it also means a higher salary, so you can pay them back. I feel like they're trying to bury you alive."

"No. They're just trying to be sensible." She gave her body an almost imperceptible shake, as if she were literally shaking the whole thing off. "Anyway, what's the deal with this art program? You really want to go to San Francisco this summer?"

"I really do." I'd spent a couple of hours looking at the program's website the night before. You picked two media and basically did art all day, six days a week, including some lectures and exhibitions. Some of their faculty had done this really mind-blowing work. I wanted it the way a little kid wants the candy at the supermarket checkout—with every molecule of my soul.

"The problem," I said, "is that Clara's too freaked out."

Clara sighed helplessly. "It's San Francisco. It's a dorm. It's nonstop art. There are so many things wrong with this. Too many things."

I grabbed her hand and twisted toward her, straining to see her whole face. But I couldn't, because she wouldn't look back at me.

"Just go to the interview," I said. "Just let me apply.

Come to the campus with me. That's all I'm asking for."

"That doesn't even make sense," she said, finally looking up to meet my eyes. "Why would you apply if you're not serious about going?"

"Just to see the place. Just to know. You have to give me this."

She drew away, folding her hands in her lap. "No," she said. "I don't have to."

I was conscious of Juanita and Bridget pointedly looking away from us as they munched on their sandwiches and celery sticks. No help at all, these two.

"Anyway," Clara said, "you'll never be able to convince Mom. And how will we even get there? She'd probably have to drive us, and she'll never agree to that."

"Oh, I can handle her."

"Really? How?"

I shrugged. "I'll tell her I'm not serious about going to the program. I'll tell her the interview's just an excuse to visit San Francisco and try something new. It's just a lark."

"So you're basically going to lie to her about it, the same way you're lying to me."

I grinned. "Exactly."

Clara shook her head.

I'd heard of conjoined twins who took turns making decisions, or doing the things they wanted. Like, on Mondays we do whatever you say, and on Tuesdays I get you back. Clara and I had never had a system like that. Usually we could just work things out, often with very little discussion. It was one of our magical qualities; just like we could walk, stop, and turn corners without talking about it, we could decide on most activities and priorities almost as easily. Two strong bodies, two strong brains, and more often than not, one will.

But every now and then we had to negotiate.

"What do you want?" I said. "In exchange for going to the interview."

"It has to be in San Francisco? I mean, don't they have an option where the interviewer can come to us here or something?"

I didn't know the answer to that, but it didn't matter. That wouldn't give me what I wanted at all.

"I could write your English paper for you," I offered. "Or we could schedule an extra five trips to the observatory. You can pick what we have for dinner every time Mom gives us a choice for the next, I don't know, the next year if you want."

Clara took a bite of her pesto chicken wrap and chewed it slowly. I was not exactly breathing, because I was afraid she would come up with something way worse than what I'd offered. Something like, *Don't go to the dance with Alek.*

Finally she put down the wrap. "No," she said, "I don't want any of those things."

"Come on, Clara, you have to work with me here. There has to be something—"

"I want to trade Halloween costumes."

I frowned. "What? Really? You want to be the Wicked Witch of the West?"

"Yes. I'm tired of always having the good-guy costume and letting you be the villain."

"But everyone will be confused," Bridget protested. "Hailey is always, always the bad guy. You'll be ruining your awesome tradition."

"That's okay," Juanita said. "It's about time they shook things up."

In our previous sixteen years of Halloweens, Clara had never objected to being the good guy before. And I had no idea why she wanted this now.

I pictured walking into Amber's annual Halloween party dressed as Glinda the Good Witch, all sparkly and smiley and so sweet that she could rot your teeth. What if Alek came to the party? Having him see me that way—wouldn't he assume that I'd chosen that costume on purpose? Alek was so serious and full of darkness; his art, it seemed to me, was all about destroying ridiculous images of cheerful, sunny perfection. It was all about being disgusted with the perfectly pruned flower gardens of the world. I couldn't let him think that a character like Glinda was what I admired, or what I aspired to. He would never take me seriously after that.

And then, also, what if he couldn't tell it was me, and not Clara, under that glittery blond wig? What if no one could? Clara would still be on the right, like always, but our costumes would be confusing, our hair covered up, and our faces indistinguishable—especially with the extra makeup. What if it turned out that nobody actually knew who was who?

On the other hand, what if I said no, and because of that I never got the chance to go to San Francisco at all? Ever, for the rest of my life?

"Hailey," Juanita said, "why are you even hesitating? This is an amazing deal for you."

I shuddered. "Yeah, okay. I'll do it."

13

Clara

True to his word, Max served three flavors of fresh popcorn on his deck, which was every bit as wide, comfortable, and splinter-free as he'd advertised. The house was up on a hill, and the trees and brush were cleared around it, leaving an expansive view of a clear, moonless, almost pornographically star-studded night sky. The one thing he hadn't said a word about was that Gavin and Josh were going to be there.

Gavin. And Josh. From the basketball team. Josh, who two years earlier had dumped Juanita for the despicable Lindsey Baker. And Gavin, who just eight months earlier, while dating Lindsey, had drunkenly confessed his love to Juanita in front of several classmates. It wasn't Juanita's fault, but people seemed to blame her anyway— even now, months later, when Gavin and Josh were dating Lindsey's two best friends, and for some reason no one seemed to have a problem with that.

Juanita was carrying two beach bags full of blankets and sweaters for the three of us—Sherpa-like, without complaint, as usual—and the minute she saw the guys, the straps slipped off her shoulder and a couple of blankets tumbled out.

She bent to stuff the blankets back down, hiding her face. Of course, she saw these guys at school every day. But outside of school, she'd been avoiding them for months.

"Hey, guys," she said to me and Hailey, not looking at Josh and Gavin, "I'm going to set our stuff down." She walked away, to where the chairs sat at the other end of the deck.

Josh and Gavin were unfazed. "Hey, Juanita. Hey there, Hailey and Clara," Gavin said, while Josh nodded and raised a hand in greeting.

As Juanita settled our bags among the deck chairs under the porch lights, a woman emerged from the house. "Hello, hello!" she cried. "I'm Max's mom, Julie. You must be those wonderful twins he was telling me so much about." She peered at each of us. "You're Clara, right? The astronomy enthusiast. And you're Hailey, and despite having the name of the world's most famous comet, you're an artist rather than an astronomer." Her smile was almost as huge and glittering as her son's. "I'm just so excited to meet you. I've heard so much. You both sound like amazing individuals."

Amazing individuals? Was I supposed to believe Max had said anything vaguely resembling that? The thought gave me an eerie, creepy-crawly feeling under my skin.

She held out her hand, and when I shook it, she gripped my arm with her left hand and gazed deeply into my eyes. She gave me the squirm-worthy feeling that she was trying very hard to peer inside my brain. After giving Hailey the same treatment, she said, "This is so lovely. The two of you have incredible strength. I can feel it."

"Aww, Mom, cut it out." Leaning in toward us, Max said in a loud stage whisper, "I promise, I won't let her read your chakras or investigate your past lives."

His mom waved this away. "Girls, please introduce me to your other friends."

She looked expectantly at Gavin and Josh, so we introduced them.

Juanita came back, and I noticed that Max's mom didn't grasp her arm like she had done with us, or call her an *amazing individual* with *incredible strength.*

"And are all of you astronomy enthusiasts?" she asked.

"Not really," said Josh cheerfully, "but we heard there's gonna be some shooting stars, and Clara's the expert, so I figured she could tell us which stars are shooting at us."

"Um, ah, hmmm," I bantered wittily. I was only 85 percent sure he was joking. It was hard to believe Juanita had once been smitten with this guy. But she had been. Very.

"Well, I'll just be inside if anyone needs anything," Max's mom said.

As everyone thanked her, Max stepped closer to me and

Hailey and said, "Sorry about my mom. She's weird with everyone."

I didn't believe him—she'd been a lot weirder with me and Hailey than with anyone else—but I smiled anyway and lied right back. "I thought she was nice."

"If you want to come and sit down," Max said, "any spot is good. We could push any two of the chairs—actually, no, wait. Here's the best spot, right here."

He pushed two of the reclining poolside chairs together, angling them to look right up at the spot where most of tonight's meteors would appear—between the Orion and Gemini constellations.

Unfortunately, Hailey and I were going to have to maneuver ourselves into the chairs while the three guys looked on. Actually sitting in them would not be a problem, but the process of getting into them would involve a lot of butt-scooting unprettiness.

I caught Juanita's eye. She looked down at the chairs, then back up at me and Hailey, and she seemed to register the problem, because she suddenly started asking questions about which chair she should choose, and whether she could move it, or did Max think it would be too heavy for her? All three boys sprang into action, turning their backs to us as they fought to help Juanita move a single lightweight deck chair.

Sophomore year, when Juanita had been dating Josh, she

had spent some time hanging out with him and his friends. As I watched Josh carry her chair, I thought about how she could have chosen to stick with that crowd if she'd wanted to. She could have been homecoming queen.

Max would end up in that group too, I supposed. And if he did turn out to be as nice as he was cute, wasn't it Juanita who ought to date him? If he was worthy, there was no point in her holding back just because of my unrealistic fantasy life.

While they were distracted, Hailey and I sat down, with Hailey fully on one chair and me sort of dangling at its edge. Then we hurriedly wiggled and scrunched ourselves across. Finally we both rested our weight away from each other, because if we rested it more at the center, where the chairs and our bodies met, there might be some danger of the chairs separating, and us falling through the center seam. Trust me, we've seen it all.

Meanwhile, the rest of them started working out who would sit where; they didn't talk about it, but I could see the hesitations, the back-and-forth moves, the hanging back, until finally it ended with us lined up thusly: Josh, Max, me, Hailey, Juanita, Gavin.

Josh grabbed a popcorn bowl from the table next to him, took a handful, and passed it down. "So," he said amiably, "I always get this mixed up. What is it that's going to land in Max's yard in a fiery ball of destruction? A meteor? Or a meteorite?"

"Meteor!" I shouted, pointing, because one of them had just shot across the sky. Everyone looked up, but too late.

"First meteor sighting of the night," Max said. "A point for Clara."

"Oooh, do we get a point for every one we spot?" I asked. "What do I get when I win?"

"Don't get too confident," Max admonished me. "I've never been beaten yet."

"That's because you've never played against me," I told him, surprised and a little pleased by my own boldness. "Come on, what's the prize? Better make it a good one."

Gavin laughed. "All these years in school together, and I never knew the twins had such a competitive side. I feel like I've been missing out."

The twins? Did he not know which one I was?

"Okay," Max said, "I'll tell you what, Clara. You and I are going mano a mano here, since we're the only ones who actually care. You're up for that, right?"

He cocked an eyebrow at me, and I nodded.

"All right then, here's the deal. The loser has to show the winner something new in the sky, up at the observatory. Could be something they've never seen before, or a different take on it, some fact they didn't know. Deal?"

Wait. Did he just say that we're going to the observatory together either way?

I tried to gather my wits about me. Behind Max, I heard

something—were the other guys snickering? I tried to ignore it.

"But—" The word came out as a hoarse whisper. Hailey elbowed me and nudged me with the back of her head.

I cleared my throat and tried again. "But how do I know what's new to you? How do I know if you already know it or not?"

"Hmm, interesting question," he said slowly, "because you kind of make it sound like you're expecting to lose." His grin was of dizzying splendor, and his voice was completely relaxed.

"Um, well." I cleared my throat again and reached deep for the sass that had been coming so naturally just a minute ago. "Of course that's not going to happen. But let me put it this way. How do *you* know what *I* don't already know?"

"I think," Josh said, "that you should both just focus on teaching *me* some stuff. Like, what are these meteors anyway? Where do they come from? I'm serious this time."

"You know, Josh," Juanita said, speaking across all of us from the opposite end of the row of chairs, "you could have Googled this stuff to avoid sounding like an idiot."

"Aww, come on, like you're such an expert?" he retorted. "You watch these mainly because Clara's into it, right?"

As they spoke, Max leaned in closer to me, and as I turned my face toward his, he whispered, "I'll just keep trying until I find something you don't know."

His face was so close to mine. Another inch or two, and I might have been able to feel his breath. But then he shifted away again.

"So, same thing," Josh was saying to Juanita, calling out across the rest of us. "I'm doing it for my pal Max. A show of support."

"Hey," Gavin shouted, "what was that thing that just flew by?"

"Another meteor?" I asked. "A point for Gavin!"

"No, no, not a meteor. Just right there. It went— Hey, there it is again!"

A tiny shadow had just swept through the sky, only a few feet above our heads.

"Oh crap!" Josh said, leaping from his chair. "It's a bat!"

The form disappeared, but a moment later it came right toward us—only to turn, sweep across the pool, and fly away again.

"Is it the same bat?" Gavin demanded. "Or a different one?"

A little way off, another dark little form flew between the trees.

"Max, man, your place is crawling with vampire bats," Josh said.

"It's not a vampire bat," I said. "It's just a little brown bat, looking for some insects to eat."

"I'm going after him," Josh declared. "Do you have a broom?"

"There's a fruit picker over there," Max said, pointing to a long stick with a sort of metal claw at one end. "But why not leave the bats alone? We're outside. It's their territory."

"Perfect." Josh grabbed the fruit picker and ran off down the hill.

Gavin laughed as he ran after Josh. "Max, you're shirking your duties, man. Leaving the bat chasing to your guests?"

"Let them go," I said. "The bats aren't going to hurt anyone. I just hope those guys don't actually catch one." But also, I didn't want Max to leave his seat, with the risk that he might switch to a different one when he came back.

"They seem like good guys apart from the bat chasing," Max said. "But to be perfectly honest, I'm not exactly sure what they're doing here."

I laughed. "What do you mean?"

"Well, they just showed up. They were saying something about playing video games. I guess they wanted me to go to one of their houses, or maybe an arcade or something. I'm not even sure. I told them I was staying here to watch the meteor shower and that you three were coming, and they decided to stay."

"Well," I said, "but you invited them to stay, right?"

He looked uncertain. "I don't *remember* inviting them."

Around the side of the house, Gavin and Josh shouted

to each other. I couldn't imagine what they thought they were going to do—stab the bats with the fruit picker?

Gavin reappeared at the edge of the light. "We need bigger weapons! Do you have a BB gun, or maybe an anti-aircraft machine gun of some kind?"

Max shook his head. "We're not the heavily armed types. Dude, it's time to consider diplomatic channels. Or, you know, just forget about them."

Gavin rocked back on his heels for a minute, looking up at the sky, then finally said, "Yeah, okay." He looked over at Juanita, then at me and Hailey. "So, I need your help."

"We're not going to help you chase the bats," I told him.

"No, not that. I've been trying to convince Max to join the basketball team. The season starts in a few weeks, so I want him on the team by Monday. Will all of you tell him how hot you find guys who play basketball? Please, help me out here."

"The problem," Max said, "is that being bad at a sport is never that hot. And I'm bad at basketball. Seriously bad."

"What you might not realize," Juanita said, "is that our entire basketball team is seriously bad. So even if you are as bad as you say you are, they can probably use you."

My eyes widened. Was she really picking a fight?

Gavin pointed right at Juanita, and I had only half a second to cringe before he shouted, "*Yes!* That's exactly right. *Thank* you! Our team sucks. We'll take anyone."

Max laughed. "That's very flattering. But what happened to all that crap you were trying to sell me earlier tonight, about my obvious natural talent?"

"Dude," Gavin assured him, "you're the tallest guy in the school. You'll be our star player. Juanita, you've been to some games. Tell him *exactly* how bad we suck."

Juanita said thoughtfully, "I think I might be a better judge of how the guys look in their uniforms. The Los Pinos guys looked pretty great in theirs. Oh, and ah, yeah . . . That's right. They creamed us."

"That's exactly right," Gavin said triumphantly as he flung his lanky frame into a chair next to Juanita, "and, Max, my man, we would be happy to train you up to that same level of suckage."

Josh rounded the corner, bent over his phone. "All right," he said to us without looking up. "Vanessa and Jasmine are coming over. Lindsey, too, I think. They were watching a movie at Lindsey's house, but I guess it sucked."

Max laughed. "Did you tell them about the bats?"

"Hell, no. Then they'd never come. I didn't even tell them the other girls were here." Josh swung himself into his chair as a bat flew over his head. Looking up at it, he said, "But I'm looking forward to seeing their faces when they get here, that's for sure."

I looked over at Juanita. I knew we should leave, for her sake. The last thing she needed was to see Lindsey. Or, for that matter, Vanessa and Jasmine—Josh's and Gavin's spawn-of-Satan girlfriends.

But she met my eyes and shook her head, as if to say, *We're staying.*

But that was just wrong. I couldn't put her through that. I leaned back, and as I tried to think of a good excuse to leave—one that would even convince Juanita—a brilliant light streaked across the sky. It was so bright and covered such a large swathe of sky that for a moment I was speechless.

When I spoke, my voice came out quiet and a little breathless. "Meteor."

"Meteor," said Max at the same moment, sounding equally awestruck. And then, a second later, "Jinx."

"You guys are, like, weirdly into this crap," Josh said. "What's up with that?"

Max looked thoughtful. "I don't know. It—it's hard to explain, right? I just . . . I look out there at the stars and I think—I feel . . ." He exhaled loudly. "I don't know."

My heartbeat started accelerating, the way it always does when I kind of want to say something but I'm not sure if it's the right thing, or whether I should talk at all. And I thought, *No, I should just stay quiet. No one will understand what I'm talking about. They'll look at me like I'm a—*

Oh yeah. They already do.

I cleared my throat. "Did you know," I said to Josh, "that

when you look at those stars, you're looking into all different parts of the past? That star over there"—I pointed to Bellatrix, the nearest star in Orion—"is two hundred and forty-three light-years away. We're looking at light from before the Declaration of Independence. But then when you look at that other star, down there"—I pointed to Alnilam—"that star's light has been traveling toward us since the early Middle Ages."

Josh looked skeptical. "Okay, and I should care because . . ."

"Because it's amazing," I told him, "that just by looking up above us, with no equipment but our own eyes, we can see such huge distances that we're actually seeing right into the past." I was gathering confidence now, and I tried to lean in Josh's direction, though I couldn't lean far, with Hailey behind me. "It makes you think about where Earth is in relation to the rest of it. It makes you feel how small we are. How small everything is that happens here. What a tiny, microscopic little window of time and space we ever see in our lifetimes. Can't you feel that?"

Josh shrugged. "Okay, but why would I want to feel small?"

I sighed, ready to give up, as Hailey and I leaned back together in our chairs. But then I looked at Max, and he was staring at me, and there was something both pleased and eager in his expression.

"It's not so much that you're small," Max said, looking at

me as he spoke, "it's that everything around you is small too."

I sat up again, pulling Hailey with me. "Right! It all seems so big, but it's just a blip in space-time. Less than a blip."

Max nodded, still looking at me. "Do you ever wonder about the creatures that must be out there on other planets?"

My breath stopped. I wanted to say, *I think about that all the time. I want so badly to meet them. I dream about communicating with them. The thought that we'll never find them in our lifetimes makes my heart hurt.*

But all I said was, "Well, yeah."

He said, "Do you ever wonder what they'd think about us?"

"What, are you worried about it?" Juanita teased him. "Like, whether the aliens will like your hairstyle? Will the extraterrestrials think you're cool?"

Max laughed. "No, kind of the opposite, right? Because how is an alien going to notice the difference between a cool haircut and a dork one?" He leaned toward me. "You know what I mean, don't you? I'm trying to come up with the words, here."

I took a deep, shaky breath. I had never really tried to express any of this out loud before. "Well, this might be different, but . . . whoever's out there, sometimes I wonder what constellation they imagine when they're looking at our sun. Like, maybe we look over at their star and see it as part of a great hunter's belt, and maybe they look over at ours and see it as part of some animal or shape that we can't even guess. And we could never see what they see, but it's still just as real."

Max's eyes had been on me the whole time I was speaking, and they stayed on me as he said, "I would kill to go into space someday. Far enough out to look back and see our whole planet. It would shift your whole way of looking at everything."

Hailey pushed her elbow into me, and I knew she wanted me to say something, but I couldn't. My mind was going in a million different directions at once, and it couldn't figure out where to land. My heart vibrated hard inside my chest.

I had never told anyone, not even Hailey, how much I wanted to see Earth from space. How much it hurt to know I would never be able to. What did it mean? How was I supposed to respond?

Max looked away. When he spoke again, his voice had returned to a slight stiffness. "Stupid, right?"

"No," I said quickly, "it isn't stupid at all." Not for him. Not for a healthy, able-bodied guy who loved the stars. In that moment I felt sure that he would find a way.

As I opened my mouth to tell him that, a bright flash of headlights whipped across us, and a car horn sounded, three quick blasts in a row.

Josh grinned. "Sounds like the girls have arrived."

14

Hailey

Like a trail of zombies, the dudes went shuffling out to meet Lindsey and her gang in the driveway. Clara leaned toward Juanita and said quietly, "We can totally go home, okay? I'll make up an excuse."

Clara was ridiculous. She was impossible. How could she not see how wrong a move that would be?

"What, because of Lindsey?" Juanita said. "No, I don't care. I didn't do anything wrong. I'm not gonna run from her."

"Good," I said, "because I think poor Max would be heartbroken if Clara were to leave." Not to mention the fact that it would give Lindsey more of an opportunity to sink her claws into him.

"Hailey, you're such a—"

"No," I said sharply. "Just shut it, all right? I am so sick of hearing that it's impossible. He likes you. I know he does. Juanita, will you tell her?"

Juanita looked at Clara. She seemed to be thinking it over. Unbelievable.

"See?" Clara said. "Juanita knows you're crazy, Hailey. Just because I like astronomy and he likes astronomy, it doesn't follow that he likes *me*."

"I don't know if he does or he doesn't," Juanita said. "But there is one thing I can tell you for sure. If we leave, he's going to think *you* don't like *him*."

"But that's good!" Clara said. "Don't you—"

"Sssshhhh!" Juanita waved her hands frantically in front of her, palms out. "They're coming!"

Max slid open the glass doors that opened from the living room out to the deck.

And moments later Lindsey, Vanessa, and Jasmine stood in front of us, staring down at us in our deck chairs, while the three guys stood by, all attention, like they were waiting for the mud wrestling to get started.

Lindsey stood right in front of me. She wore skin-tight jeans and a low-necked, clingy sweater, topped with a puffy red ski jacket that she'd left unzipped. Her hair, highlighted and flat-ironed to within an inch of its life, skimmed past her shoulders and onto the creamy skin of her throat and chest. For a moment, as I looked straight into her brown eyes, I could see her struggling with what to do.

And then her whole body sprang into a frenzy of excitement. *"Hailey!"* she cried out, sounding like I had just handed her a winning lottery ticket. "Clara! Juanita! I didn't even know you were all going to be here. What a great surprise! This is so *awesome!*"

She actually leaned down and started hugging us. I held my arms stiffly, torn between hugging her back and wriggling away.

Vanessa and Jasmine kicked it into gear quickly enough, with the same unnatural excitement and hugs.

Lindsey turned to Max and swatted his upper arm. "Max, you were holding out on us! You didn't even mention that our good friends were going to be here."

Max looked confused. "Um, I guess it was just lucky that it worked out."

"You know that Clara and Hailey and Juanita and I go way back, right?" Lindsey said to Max, still in that high, bouncy voice. "We've all known each other since the sixth grade."

This was true. Sixth grade had been quite a year, what with moving from a tiny little elementary school where everyone had known us since preschool, to a middle school with four times as many kids, many of whom had probably heard rumors about us but had never actually seen us, or anything like us, ever in their entire lives.

But to be fair, it's also true that until we reached middle school, Clara and I had never encountered the likes of Lindsey Baker.

The kids at our elementary school had gotten to know

us when we were little. Our mom had even arranged a series of playgroups, where she'd encouraged the kids and parents to ask questions and get it all out of their systems. And yeah, okay, a couple of them had at some point asked us how it worked when we went to the bathroom, which was embarrassing, but we'd just brushed it off, and they'd eventually dropped it.

Then, in the second week of sixth grade—in a new school, with dozens of new classmates—the old question returned. We were sitting in math class, watching the teacher write something on the board, and Lindsey was staring at me and Clara in the same dumbfounded way she'd been doing every day, with her mouth literally half-open. Then she blurted out, "But how do you go to the bathroom?"

And I looked right at her and said, making sure it was loud enough for the whole class to hear, "Lindsey, you're in sixth grade and you don't know how to go to the bathroom?"

And Lindsey's whole face just transformed into this animal fury. Back then she wasn't too attractive to begin with; her awkward stage was in full force. Her braces and frizzy hair didn't help. Scowling at us, she looked like some kind of wild beast.

But the next day, I guess she decided to investigate. Except she didn't just come into the bathroom and have a peek for herself. She brought in a whole platoon. She used a quarter to unlock the stall door, and there they all were, staring at us.

We sat at a diagonal to the toilet seat. I was facing forward, my pants down around my ankles, my shirt coming just to my waist. Clara faced backward, still exposed, though not quite as badly. And the area on our back—the spot where we're attached? I think they could see the whole thing.

I covered myself with my hands, but to pull up my pants would have meant standing up, not to mention taking my hands away from their job of covering me.

By then I'd had a few nightmares about being naked at school. Yeah, I know I'm supposed to be the tough one, but come on. I was eleven years old. Anyway, the reality turned out to be way worse.

I was half-aware of Clara behind me, shaking and crying, while I tried to convince myself that I wasn't humiliated, just pissed off. I tried, with limited success, to focus on how I was going to kick Lindsey's ass. Later. When my pants were on.

They all giggled and shrieked with excitement. I don't know how long they stood there laughing before Mrs. Barzetti started grabbing them by the shoulders and yanking them out of there. It felt like hours.

And then the whole school had to sit through a dumbass assembly on bullying.

At the time, I assumed that the assembly would back-fire and make everyone mad at us, since we were the reason they'd had to sit through all that garbage. But weirdly, it didn't work out that way. Instead, Lindsey actually got a bad reputation for a while, and not like the cool bad girl but just like everyone thought she was an asshole. And of course she was suspended.

But she didn't try to get revenge for any of that. She apologized, which I'm sure she was forced to do, but she cried when she did it and seemed like she actually did feel terrible.

So I guess in a way we forgave her. But it didn't mean we had to like her.

"Have we really known each other that long?" I asked now, mimicking Lindsey's saccharine sweetness. "I don't know, I guess you could be right."

"You know what," Max said, "I think we have some more chairs in the garage."

"No, no." Lindsey waved him off. "We're fine. I can sit wherever."

"I can share with Josh," Vanessa said, and she went and climbed into his lap. Jasmine did likewise with Gavin.

Max got up and gestured for Lindsey to take his chair. "Here, take this one, and I'll just go grab a blanket to sit on."

She put up a ritual protest, but Max said he wanted to head inside anyway to get some hot drinks started. Lindsey followed him inside, tra-la-la-ing about her angelic desire to help him with that.

As soon as they were gone, Vanessa slid out of her chair and walked over to Juanita. She dropped down onto the cold concrete and sat cross-legged as she leaned forward, resting one hand on the edge of Juanita's chair.

"You know," Vanessa said, loud enough for everyone to hear, "I just wanted to talk to you for a sec, because I'm feeling a teensy bit concerned."

Juanita looked at her.

"I'm not saying Lindsey is totally into Max," Vanessa said. "I mean, I don't know for sure. But she definitely thinks he's cute, and I know you heard her say that in econ." She pulled a strand of dark brown hair behind her ear and twirled it around one finger.

Juanita wrinkled her brow, managing to convey a combination of bewilderment, disgust, and not giving a damn.

"Of course I know you have a good heart," Vanessa went on, "and you would never step in there when Lindsey has already said that. But I wouldn't want anyone else to get the wrong impression."

Juanita kept staring at her.

"I mean," Vanessa clarified, "you came over here in the

middle of the night. And after what happened the last time? Some people might think you're up to no good."

Juanita threw up her hands. "*You* came over here in the middle of the night!"

Vanessa recoiled. "With a whole group of friends, including my boyfriend!"

"*I* came here with a whole group of friends!" Juanita said.

And Jasmine piped in, from her perch on Gavin's lap, "Yeah, you came here with *our* boyfriends."

Gavin guffawed. "Oh, so that's why you decided to ditch the movie and come over here, huh?" he asked Jasmine. At least someone was enjoying this.

Juanita scooted over to the edge of her chair and leaned way forward, right into Vanessa's face. "What am I supposed to say to you right now?" she demanded.

"Ah, how about, 'I won't stab my friend in the back'? Is that so hard?"

"My *friend*? My *friend*?"

Vanessa stood up. "Well, if that's the way you're going to be about it . . ." She brushed off her hands and flipped her dark hair over her shoulder. "I knew I shouldn't have bothered, but it doesn't even matter." She looked past Juanita, toward the house. "They're in there together right now. And Lindsey's so pretty, and so sweet. I'm sure he's asking her out right now."

"Or," Jasmine added, "she's asking him to the Sadie Hawkins dance at this very moment. And obviously he'll say yes."

The Sadie Hawkins dance. Of course.

I couldn't let this happen. Not before Clara got her chance.

I started sitting up straighter, pulling Clara with me.

"No," Clara whispered. "Drop it."

"I need to go inside," I said. "Right now." I started scooting us over toward one side of the chairs.

Clara groaned. I tried to pull us over farther, but she resisted. "Hailey . . ."

"What are you going to do?" Vanessa asked me. "Juanita's a big girl. She can fight her own battles. As she's proven time and time again."

Clara and I twisted toward her so smoothly, I couldn't tell who started the motion. "What the hell is that supposed to mean?" I demanded. "And what makes you think it's Juanita—"

"Hailey!" Clara said sharply. "Didn't you have some kind of needing-to-go-inside emergency?"

After a moment I said, "Right," and we scooted ourselves off the chairs together—slowly, awkwardly, but without any major mishaps—and hurried into the house.

The sliding glass doors opened into the living room, which was filled with leather sofas and dark wood furniture.

To the right was the open kitchen. Even as we stepped into the house, I could hear Lindsey saying from the kitchen, "Yeah, but have you been up to Devil's Ridge yet? You have to take the back trail at sunrise. It's unmarked but it's awesome. I can totally take you up there whenever you want."

Oh my God. She was going to Ironwoman her way into his heart.

I pulled Clara into the kitchen, where Max and Lindsey stood behind the large center island. Nine matching glass coffee mugs were lined up in front of them, along the edge of the island.

Max faced the island, arranging the cups so all the handles faced him—a touch of OCD, perhaps?—but he smiled down at Lindsey as he worked.

They both looked our way as we came in. Lindsey quickly returned her gaze to Max and sidled a little closer.

He didn't appear to notice. "Hey, Clara, Hailey," he said. "We were just getting some hot cocoa ready. Anything else I can get you?"

"Maybe we could help you," I said. "I'm sure you could use some extra hands to help carry it outside."

"Hailey," Clara barked at me, "the bathroom. Didn't we need a bathroom?"

"Oh, no," I said, attempting a breezy voice, "it turns out we don't. It turns out we're totally available to help with the hot cocoa." My eyes were on Lindsey as I said this, and my hands were smoothing the tips of my hair into sharp pink missiles, pointed directly at her.

"I don't know, Hailey. I've got a pretty bad headache," Clara said—a lie she'd used so many times before, half our school must have suspected she had a brain tumor. "I think I may need to go home and get to bed."

Max looked disappointed. "Oh, don't do that. Our meteor-spotting contest has hardly gotten started. Hey, you know, we've got some Tylenol, and I think some Advil right here in the kitchen cabinet." He went over to a cabinet behind him and started moving things around. He shook a bottle. "Yep, lots of both, and some Excedrin."

"Max!" Lindsey said. "Listen to you, being so sweet and accommodating. But you know, even though I totally wish they could stay, we should be careful not to push these poor girls too hard. We wouldn't want to undermine their health, keeping them up so much later than they're used to, even if they *are* good sports about it."

This was complete and utter BS. First off, how would Lindsey even know when we normally went to bed? And second, even if we did stay up later than normal, it wouldn't do us any more harm than it would do anyone else.

I remembered how, back in that sixth-grade bathroom, I'd made plans to kick Lindsey's ass. And I still hadn't gotten around to that. Maybe today was the day.

Of course, we weren't even the real targets of Lindsey's underhanded bitchiness. She was trying to get rid of us because she knew that Juanita was our ride, and if we left, Juanita would have to leave too. In Lindsey's mind, Juanita was the only possible threat.

Max looked quickly over at Clara, with an expression of surprise and concern. With the cabinet door still open, he turned in our direction. "Oh, ah—I—"

He seemed all confused about what to do or what to say. Maybe he'd actually noticed that Lindsey's supposed niceness was really a cover for being a full-on bitch? Or maybe he was at least trying to figure out whether that was the case? Well, I certainly hoped so. It's really annoying when guys are too moronic to notice that sort of thing.

Lindsey laughed and moved closer. "It's okay, Max! You're new here. Nobody expects you to know the twins as well as we do. And you are being so sweet to them. I have to tell you, I am totally impressed."

Wow. There were so many layers of nauseating to that, I felt like applauding.

Max shook his head, frowning at her, then looked back over at us. I couldn't blame him for not knowing what to say. I wouldn't have known either. I mean, she was making us out to be so pitiable, but the way she was doing it, how could you even call her on that crap?

"C—C—Cl—" He exhaled loudly, a frustrated sound, then started again. "Cl—"

"Not that you're doing it just to impress *me*, of course," Lindsey said, and giggled, interrupting him again as she let her fingertips brush lightly against his arm.

He pulled his arm away. "I d—d—d—*don't* th—th—th . . ."

He turned away from her and slammed his hand against the countertop.

Lindsey retreated a step back from him. She somehow frowned and smiled at the same time. "Max," she said, with a bewildered-sounding laugh, "are you all right?"

He was silent, leaning over the countertop, his back to all of us. Clara had her back to me too, and I wished I could read both of their thoughts.

From the other end of the living room, Max's mom trilled, "Is everything all right in here? I see you're making hot cocoa. How about some marshmallows?"

Max spun to look at her. He scowled and shook his head.

"Max?" Lindsey asked. "Is something the matter?"

He met Lindsey's eyes, and he looked furious, exactly like he'd looked back at the Sandwich Shack when he'd dropped those doughnuts and walked out.

And then his mother declared brightly, "We're all getting tired. It's so late! I know I can barely think straight, or keep my eyes open. It must be getting to all of us."

Max shook his head at her. "Mmmm . . . Mm—Mom!"

"Maybe we all need some rest," his mother said.

Max shook his head again. "Ssshh . . . Shhh . . ." He stopped talking and squeezed his eyes shut. His whole face had gone red.

Lindsey stared at him, then looked slowly at his mother, at Clara, and at me, before starting toward the sliding glass doors. "Gosh," she said loudly to no one in particular, "look at the time. It sure is getting late, and I'm pretty sure it's time for us all to get the hell out of here."

15

Clara

"Clara! Hailey! My girls!" cried Amber as we walked into English class on Monday morning. She leaned against the empty teacher's desk near the front of the room. "You're coming to my Halloween party this weekend, right? Oh my God, you *have* to. You two always have the best costumes."

"Of course we'll be there," I said. "We haven't missed one of your parties since the first grade."

The door opened behind us, and a jolt of adrenaline hit me as I turned to see who was coming in. But it wasn't Max. I forced myself to breathe.

"Well, not one of my Halloween parties, I guess," Amber said. "You *have* missed a bunch of my walkathons and charity book sales. But never mind." She waved her hand in front of her face, dismissing the complaint. "Did you know we raised more than eight hundred dollars at the last book sale? I thought that was pretty awesome."

"That's great," I said as I tried to remember what she'd been raising the money for. Amber had a lot of different causes. I suspected that she was always mentally tallying her list of "Things That Make Me a Good Person," and there was a strong chance that "Being BFFs with Clara and Hailey" fell under that heading.

"Anyway," Amber went on, "I'm so excited to see what you're going to wear on Saturday night. You won't tell us what it is, will you?"

I shook my head, trying to force a mysterious smile. My gaze darted again to the door, but it was closed. Still, I knew Max had to come in soon. I'd been anticipating this moment all weekend, and the hard knot in the pit of my stomach was starting to feel like an ulcer.

We had left his house at the same time Lindsey and her gang had, and he hadn't even come out of his room to say good-bye, though his mother had apologized profusely, going on and on about how tired we all must be. I had no idea whether he was angry, humiliated, or what.

I needed to see his face, his expression. I needed to know if he was okay. And whether he blamed me for what had happened.

From her desk Kim commented, "The one thing we know for sure is that it will be something where Clara's good and Hailey's evil. Like when they did angel and devil, or Batman and Catwoman. They're always so much better than my costumes. Amber, remember how last year my costume was so bad you almost kicked me out of your party?"

"I did kick you out," Amber corrected her. "You came in your real soccer uniform. That's not a costume."

"No, that was the year before. Last year I wore an old prom dress with fake blood on it, and you said it was okay."

"Oh yeah. Well, you should try to do better this year," Amber told her. "And no repeats!"

"Yeah, yeah, I know," Kim said. "I just wish I had a twin. Then I could come up with some great costume ideas too."

Hailey snorted. We headed for our desks, with Amber following behind.

"Don't be silly," Amber said, her voice pitched a little too high. "Clara and Hailey just happen to think of fantastic costumes every year because they have a talent for it. The fact that they're twins has absolutely nothing to do with it."

The thing about Amber is, she clearly has excellent intentions, but she terrifies me with her transparency. You know how some people have such pale skin that you can sort of look right through it, to the veins and blue tinge and changing colors underneath? And you realize that what you're seeing is the same thing that's going on behind everyone else's exterior too, but the only difference is that with these really pale people, you can see it.

With Amber it's not her skin that's transparent; it's her voice and her manner and her facial expressions. She is supersweet and loves us ever so much, but somehow you can see the strain that lies beneath it, the eagerness to be good, to be the kind of person who would be friends with us. And it always makes me wonder if she's showing us, without meaning to, what lurks beneath everyone else's skin.

Amber frowned at me. "Clara," she said with loud concern, "what's *wrong?*"

"Oh." I realized I had been scowling. "Um, nothing." I glanced at her as I settled into my seat. "I mean, I was just thinking that it sounds like our costumes are getting too predictable. But maybe this time we'll have a little surprise."

While we arranged our bags and got out our notebooks, the door opened, and I almost jumped at the sound; but a couple of guys who weren't Max walked into the room and went quietly to their seats. As the door started to swing shut behind them, a large hand caught it, and Max walked in.

I froze, torn between Idiot-Girl's desire to stare at him and the Cynic's need to duck under the desk and hide.

If he hated me, I wouldn't blame him.

All weekend my brain had been buzzing like a beehive in summer. Despite what I'd told Hailey and Juanita—and what I'd consciously, firmly told myself, too—the truth was that when Max and I had been talking at his house on Friday night, I'd felt such an electric surge of excitement, of connecting with him, that I'd half-hoped, half-imagined, even half-believed that maybe, just maybe, he might feel some hint of that charge on his end too. And yet, wasn't that just insane? Was I turning delusional, like my sister? Did I not understand what I was and how impossible my hopes were?

And then there had been the whole disaster in the kitchen. There he'd been, flirting with Lindsey, the second-prettiest girl in the school (after Juanita), and then something had happened and he'd turned into a quivering wreck. He'd stuttered worse than anyone I'd ever heard, right in front of Lindsey, who up until that moment had been throwing herself at him.

And maybe it had happened because of me. Because I'd been throwing myself at him too, after flirting with him at school and practically inviting myself over to his house. And then I'd put him in the awkward position of dealing with me in Lindsey's presence, when I wouldn't seem to take no for an answer.

And yet.

What if I hadn't imagined that connection?

What if he didn't hate me at all?

Standing in the classroom doorway now, Max met my eyes. Apparently Idiot-Girl had won, and I'd gone ahead with the staring.

For the longest time he seemed to have no expression at all. My heart beat wildly as I looked at him, waiting for something—a sign, a frown, a scowl, anything at all—that would let me know how he was, and where I stood. The seconds dragged on.

He hated me. Of course he did.

But then something twitched at the corners of his lips. And at the corners of his eyes. It was small; it was tentative; but maybe, just maybe, it was a hint of a smile.

And cautiously, slowly, as I filled with just the littlest bit of hope, I let my own lips curl upward too.

And there it was. The sparkle in his eyes. It still wasn't a full smile, but a quarter of a smile. Then a third of a smile. Three eighths of a smile. He held my gaze for a second, maybe two, and then he looked down, away from me, a hint of color rising up in his cheeks.

As he moved past me on his way to his seat, for a fleeting second his jeans brushed against my hip. I closed my eyes and took in a long, deep breath.

I was still a mess. I still had no idea what to think—about anything, really. But he'd given me three eighths of a smile, and that was a lot.

Idiot-Girl whispered, cautiously, *He doesn't hate me.*

And the Cynic didn't say anything back.

16

Hailey

After Clara and I were fully dressed in our Glinda/Wicked Witch costumes, down to the green skin and warts for her and the nauseatingly perky body glitter for me, our mom gave us a full inspection, while Dad stood back, faintly smiling. That was where he seemed to be a lot of the time, standing a little behind Mom, vaguely approving but with no real indication of what he was thinking about.

Like all of our Halloween costumes—and for that matter, all of our clothes in general—we'd bought these online, and then Mom had put them through some fairly elaborate adjustments to get them to fit us. In this case she'd adjusted them a second time, after we'd decided to trade, but she hadn't seen us in them since then. Her voice was a little stern as she said to me, "Hailey, that Glinda costume was not that revealing when your sister tried it on. What have you got stuffed in there anyway?"

The answer was her old argyle socks, but she didn't have to know that. I shrugged. "Well, how do you expect us to turn tricks if we don't show a little skin?"

Dad turned away quickly, looking vaguely embarrassed—so at least he'd been listening—but Mom just laughed. The last time I'd managed to shock her was when she'd been pregnant with us and the doctors had showed her our conjoinment on the ultrasound. The power of that shock had left her immune to all others, like if you heard a bomb going off so loudly that it deafened you.

We let her take a couple of pictures—she would print them out on our home printer and mail them to our grandparents, as usual, for fear that any type of Internet posting or even email might be intercepted by evil reporters—and then we shuffled into the minivan, with Dad behind the wheel.

As usual, we sat in the backseat, listening to the radio and looking out the windows. The sun was just going down behind the clouds, and the whole world had a pinkish glow.

"So," Dad piped up after a couple of minutes. "What's the story with this Max guy?"

I held back a laugh. Dad can seem so clueless half the time, you almost think he's got no idea what's going on. And then he asks questions like *this*.

"Um," Clara said. After a second she added, "What do you mean?"

"Well, you went over to his house last week, right? So what's his story?"

She shrugged, in a confused and useless display of fake nonchalance. "I don't know. He just moved here for his dad's work. We don't really know him that well or anything."

"Except," I said, "we know he loves stargazing. Constellations. And what was it? Schmidt-Cassegrain telescopes?"

Clara made a small noise of frustration.

"Well," Dad said, glancing back at us in the rearview mirror, "that sounds promising."

I smirked, but managed not to cackle.

"We're just friends," Clara bit out.

"I wasn't suggesting otherwise," Dad said, his tone easy and calm. I had no idea whether he really hadn't meant anything else or was just covering his tracks. "He sounds like a promising new friend. You could use someone to talk stars and telescopes with. Couldn't you?"

Again Clara shrugged, despite the fact that Dad couldn't see it as he drove.

"Also," I said—and maybe I was a little too revved up on pre-party adrenaline at this point—"we know that he's cute."

"We should take him up to the observatory sometime," Dad said, without necessarily acknowledging me. "Or out to the one at Chabot in Oakland. You know they've got a thirty-six-inch telescope? I think you'd get a kick out of it."

Clara looked out the window. I was pretty sure she had

only two things on her mind at this point: murder and suicide.

"That sounds like fun," I said.

"Really?" Dad asked. "*You* think telescope viewing sounds like fun, Hailey?"

It's kind of annoying that Mom and Dad can tell our voices apart, even when they're not looking.

"Yes," I said, "I do. Well, not telescope viewing so much, but going to Oakland. And bringing Max. I'm up for it. What do you think, Clara?"

I was needling her, partly. But also I was desperate to go anywhere outside of Bear Pass. If an observatory was what it took, I would do it, for sure.

She kept looking out the window.

"I think she's up for it too," I announced.

Clara elbowed me. "Could you just—please—could you . . ."

"Well," Dad said, "let's think about it, anyway, all right? I'd like to get you two out more. I think it's about time you had a few adventures."

"What about you?" I asked Dad. "Would it be fun for you, too? You barely get out of Bear Pass any more than we do."

"Yeah," he acknowledged, "it would be fun for me, too."

He pulled up in front of Amber's house. The sun had just gone down; a little of its light still filtered in above the horizon. Already cars lined the street all the way down the block. Most of the houses were decorated for Halloween, but none more than Amber's. Her whole front yard had been transformed into a haunted graveyard, with tombstones, skeletons rising out of the earth, and ghosts floating from wires between the trees.

"Midnight," my dad said as we stepped out onto the ramp. "I'll see you right here. One minute after twelve, if you're not inside the minivan, you both turn into pumpkins."

"Isn't it the minivan that should turn into a pumpkin?" Clara asked.

"The minivan," I assured her as we scuttled down the ramp, "is already no better than a pumpkin. A pumpkin would be a step up in coolness."

We waved good-bye and headed inside.

Just inside the front door, hordes of teenage werewolves, vampires, and sexy lady pirates filled the kitchen, all holding red plastic cups or cans of soda. Jack-o'-lantern lights were strung across the walls, and paper bats hung from the ceiling. People shifted around to let us pass. A couple of them nodded in our direction.

I just prayed to God that Alek wouldn't be here. Having him see me as sparkly sweet Glinda would make me want to bash my own brains in. This arts academy interview had better be worth it. I still wasn't entirely sure I'd gotten the better end of this deal.

Steam rose out of a big pot on the stove. I inspected it.

"Smells good," I said to Clara, raising my voice over the hum of conversations going on in the kitchen, not to mention the throbbing, spooky White Zombie music floating in from the living room.

"Hot apple cider," said a voice behind me.

Max.

I turned, angling myself so that Clara had no choice but to face him head-on. I could see him too, but I had made myself peripheral.

He was dressed as the Tin Man, from *The Wizard of Oz*. He had the whole costume, even the silly hat. It looked high-quality, probably a rental, but he hadn't bothered to paint his face silver, and his skinny wrists poked out from the not-quite-long-enough sleeves.

He said something that I couldn't hear over all the other voices and the music coming from the next room. Clara leaned in closer, pulling me with her as she cupped her hand toward him, straining upward toward his giraffe-like height.

He leaned down, raising his volume. "I said I like your costumes."

To me he said, "Hailey, that's amazing. That Glinda costume really makes you look so much like Clara." He laughed. "Okay, I know, I'm an idiot. But seriously, most of the time you look different. I guess it's the hair."

I touched my blond wig, looking up at him suspiciously. I felt like such an incredible dork in the sparkly wig.

"In a good way," Max said quickly. "You look beaut— I mean, the costume is great." Turning toward Clara, he said, "And your costume is superscary. Too bad I had to go and be the Tin Man, though."

Now, what was that supposed to mean? Was he worried that people would think we'd coordinated our outfits with his? Was he afraid of being associated with us like that?

I felt Clara stiffening and pulling back. I may have been frowning at him too. His voice became rushed. "I m-mean because you're the witch."

"Yeah," Clara said coldly, "I got that."

Behind Max, at the far end of the kitchen, a group of jocks passed through—Gavin and Josh and a couple of others, all dressed as vampires. Gavin looked our way and held up a hand in greeting. I nodded back.

I was pretty sure that wouldn't have happened before last weekend's meteor shower—the only time we'd ever hung out together outside of school. It wasn't like we were friends now. I didn't even want us to be. But we'd known each other since middle school, and it was weird to think that after all these years, there could still be this tiny little shift.

Max's hand brushed over Clara's loose black sleeve. "In the book," he said, "isn't there something about the Wicked Witch being responsible for the Tin Man's condition?"

"You mean having no heart?"

He shrugged. "I might be wrong."

"I don't know," she said. "I don't remember anything about stealing your heart, but I know you storm my castle at some point. Or infiltrate it."

I clapped a hand over my mouth. *Did she really just say that?*

There was this moment when they both seemed all frozen and red-faced, and I just knew that Clara was wanting to melt into a puddle on the floor. But then Max laughed. And after a moment, amazingly, Clara laughed too. Kind of a bubbly laugh, actually. Like maybe having her castle stormed wouldn't be so bad.

He cleared his throat. "S-s-so . . . *anyway*, I haven't forgotten about our bet. You saw more meteors, so I have to teach you something at the observatory."

Yes! He still wanted to go! Now I had to stop myself from clapping my hands and squealing with delight. But Clara, like a moron, just stood there not saying anything.

His cheeks turned pink. "I m-mean, if you still w-want to go."

"Um, yeah," Clara said. "Sure. Definitely. Only . . ."

Max frowned. "W-what?"

Clara said something, but it was too quiet; even I couldn't hear her.

Max leaned in, frowning, cupping his ear.

She said it more loudly. "I don't want you to feel like you have to do that."

Oh my God, what is she saying?

But she plunged on, as if she couldn't stop until she'd said every worst-possible-thing that she could come up with. "If you like Lindsey, hanging out with us might not be your best move."

Oh, I wanted so badly to scream at her, slap her, shout some sense into her. But I knew that I must not speak. All I could do was tear at my wig with both hands. And maybe stomp my foot a little.

Max cocked his head, looking down at us both at a quizzical angle. "What are you saying?"

Clara squirmed. Her voice came out squeaky. "Lindsey's nice enough, but she gets a little freaked out by things she doesn't understand. Like us, for example. And maybe even anyone who hangs out with us."

"I noticed that," Max said, with an uncomfortable laugh. "I mean, not so much about you guys, but the part about getting freaked out easily. When I started stuttering, she practically teleported out of there."

"Oh, I wouldn't worry about that," Clara said quickly. "I mean, if it was just a onetime thing, she'll probably—"

"It won't be."

"What?"

"It won't be just that one time. It will definitely happen again."

Well, I must admit, I hadn't been expecting that.

"Clara," he said calmly, "I was a special ed kid. I mean, daily speech therapy and full-day resource room for three years, because I was barely speaking at all. It's better now, but it's always going to be there. You have not heard the last of my stuttering."

"Special ed? Really? What was that like?" Clara asked. We'd never been in a special ed classroom; our elementary school hadn't had one.

He shrugged. "You get an interesting mix. One guy was in there because he was a biter and had violent tantrums, so that kept things interesting. Then there were these two really great, funny kids who were profoundly hearing impaired. Turns out I talk better in ASL than I do in English, so that was a bonus."

"Do you still know sign language?" Clara asked.

"Of course. I'm still friends with those guys, and they still can't hear."

There was a pause, and then they both started talking at once.

Max said, "So look, I'm not worried about—"

And Clara said, "Well, if you really think—"

Before either of them could finish, Amber appeared out of nowhere and tackled Clara in a giant hug.

"Clara!" she practically screamed. She grabbed me, hugging me too as she shouted, "And Hailey! I'm so excited to see you two! Your costumes are the best, as usual!"

Clara opened her mouth, but before she could say anything, Amber rolled right on through.

"Did you know," Amber said to Max, "that their mom actually makes their costumes for them? She's, like, the most amazing seamstress in the entire world."

Amber wore an elaborate eighteenth-century gown with a huge white wig, a glittery plastic tiara, white makeup, and a couple of fake beauty marks, and a deep, wide streak of blood across the neck, with more running down one side of her dress.

"Marie Antoinette," I guessed.

Clara quickly added the requisite, "You look so pretty!"

"Thanks, so do you!" Amber enthused nonsensically. "Hey, I've been wanting to talk to you about the Sadie Hawkins dance. You know I was one of the organizers, right? And I really want you guys to come. You know who I think would totally want one of you to ask him?"

"Um." Clara frowned. Max was standing right there; he could hear every word they said. Clara's desire to flee was palpable.

"Kevin Johnson!" Amber cried. "Wouldn't he be so perfect for one of you?"

We barely knew Kevin Johnson. He had never been in any of our classes, and we didn't have any friends or activities in common. He seemed nice enough. He was also epileptic, which was all very well, except that it was the only reason I could think of for Amber to suggest that either of us might want to date him.

On the other hand, this was the first time I could remember anyone suggesting that either of us might conceivably go on a date at all. Unless you counted Bridget, which I didn't. So maybe I should give Amber some credit for that.

When I glanced toward where Max had been standing, he had already slipped away.

Clara nudged me.

"I know," I whispered, "I'll think of some way to get rid of her."

"No, not that." She jerked her head toward the front entrance, and I followed her gaze.

"Oh."

It was Alek, walking straight toward us, and wearing the one thing that was sure to get him kicked out of Amber's party.

Black jeans and a plain black T-shirt.

17

Clara

My gaze darted back and forth between Amber and Alek. If she spotted him here without a costume, the best-case scenario was that she would merely throw him out a first-story window. Worst-case, she'd frame him as a North Korean spy.

"Amber," I said desperately, pointing to the opposite side of the room, "is that Tim? That is the best vampire costume I've seen all night. You must have helped him with it, right?"

She glanced over at Tim, who'd been her boyfriend for as long as anyone could remember. "No, he did that himself. It's okay, I guess," she said, before turning back to me. "Now, about the dance."

"Actually, it's taken care of already," I said.

Amber's eyes widened in surprise. But she was still looking right at me, and Alek was behind me. This wasn't good. I was going to have to play the disabled card. "I'm so thirsty," I said, "and it's so hard for us to get around the room when it's crowded. Do you have some sodas some-where?"

"Oh yeah, we've got coolers in the living room," she said.

I looked toward the hallway behind her. "I guess we could manage it . . ."

She put up a hand. "I'll fetch it for you. Diet Coke?"

"Perfect. And one for Hailey, too? Thanks, Amber."

I watched as Amber twisted through the noisy, thick-ening crowd. Even when Hailey and I were toddlers, we could never just slip and slide through the tiny gaps between people like other kids could, and I couldn't help admiring how deftly Amber pulled it off now.

On the other side of the room, Alek was talking to a freshman dressed as a sexy nurse. Although the girl was at least Alek's height, she had her head bent so low that it allowed her to giggle upward at him as she batted her big fake eyelashes. I couldn't tell whether Alek was flirting back.

He looked up, taking in the room for a minute, and then his gaze fixed on Hailey. He said something to the nurse girl and started walking toward us. I caught my breath.

He had to do a certain amount of twisting and nudging, but he was definitely coming our way, and he seemed to have his eyes on Hailey the entire time. They were more or less staring at each other.

Then Alek was right there, and he actually reached out and touched Hailey on the arm.

When people touch Hailey above the waist, I can't physically feel the sensations; our nervous systems are separate in our upper halves. I obviously can't read her mind either. But I swear, when he touched her arm, it was the closest I had ever come to feeling telepathic. I could feel the hairs stand up on my own arm. I could feel the adrenaline surge through my own bloodstream.

He leaned in toward her, on the side that was farther away from me, his mouth close to her ear. But I didn't have any trouble hearing him. "Hey, I wanted to talk to you. It's so noisy in here. Can we go outside?"

She nodded, while I quietly smiled to myself.

"But we've got to avoid Amber," Hailey said. "I can't believe you came without a costume."

"She's in the living room," I said. "If we go down that hallway on the other side, she won't see us, and we can pop right out into the courtyard."

Alek looked over at me, and something like surprise splashed across his face, then retreated. "Oh, hey, Clara," he said. It was almost like, for a second there, he had actually forgotten that wherever Hailey was, I was always there too. He said to me, "Do you want to c—" and stopped himself. Then he laughed. "You don't mind?" he asked me.

I shook my head.

"After you, then," he said.

"Actually," Hailey told him, "it's easier if you go first to break through the crowd."

"Oh. Yeah, right."

We followed Alek through the kitchen and down the hallway, which was crowded at the start but grew empty as we approached the bedrooms. Amber's room had its door standing open, and I saw some movement inside the room. I jumped in surprise, afraid Amber had somehow gotten past us and over to her room, where she would surely spot us. But it wasn't her; it was a couple making out, the girl leaning back against the wall while the boy leaned into her. I looked away quickly, wishing I hadn't seen.

Just past the bedroom, we went through a pair of sliding glass doors into a small courtyard.

We were around the corner from the main backyard. I could hear a few voices over there, and the low throbbing of music from inside. But this little nook was relatively quiet, and empty apart from us. The outdoor lights gave a soft yellow cast to the tiled patio and its table and chairs. The sky was dark except for a sliver of moonlight.

"I just wanted to ask you," Alek said as he pulled the sliding glass door shut behind him, "if you've thought about that summer art program."

I sensed Hailey's disappointment in the stillness of her body and the extra half beat she took before answering.

Though honestly, I didn't know what she had expected him to say. Had she thought he was going to open with a declaration of undying love or something? Or had she secretly wanted him to love the Glinda costume, which he had so far failed to acknowledge in any way?

"Oh, yeah, that sounded like it might be kind of interesting," Hailey said. "I haven't looked into it or anything."

This was a total lie. She had already spent hours poring over the school's website. Not to mention pressuring me into going down for the interview—though we still hadn't approached our parents about that. With any luck, they would refuse to let us go.

"Well, you know, I'm going down for my interview and portfolio review this week, and the deadline is coming up pretty soon. I was thinking if you want, maybe we could try to coordinate our appointment times. Or even, you know, if it's not convenient for you to go, I might be able to bring your portfolio for you. I'm not sure if they allow that, but I thought we could maybe ask."

Hailey's blond wig was starting to sag slightly to the right. "Um, yeah," she said, with convincing nonchalance. "I guess I could maybe think about that."

"It's no commitment, obviously," he said. "Well, just the application fee."

From around the corner came the low hum of guys talking and laughing in the main backyard. Michael

Jackson's "Thriller" flowed out of the living room's stereo
system—one of the old standards that had been on Amber's
Halloween mix since her very first Halloween party, back
in first grade, when her mom had still been choosing the
songs for her. I crossed my arms and looked down, trying
to absent myself as much as possible from Hailey and Alek's
conversation.

"What do they want to see?" Hailey asked. "For the
portfolio review?"

Alek started telling her the details, which I was pretty
sure she already knew.

More voices came from the backyard now, and I recognized at least one of them—Max. He was talking to some
other guys. It sounded like Gavin, and maybe Josh.

"I know you'll get in," Alek was saying to Hailey.
"There's no way they won't love your stuff."

Hailey said, "Well—"

"Wait," he interrupted. "Don't say no. I also wanted to
show you something I'm working on for it."

He pulled out his phone and tapped the screen a couple of
times. As he did, I could hear Max and the other guys joking
around in the backyard, around the corner of the house. A
voice that sounded like Josh's said, "Delicious, juicy watermelons." This was followed by raucous laughter.

Alek held his phone out to Hailey, showing her something on the screen. I started trying to peer over at it but

got distracted as Gavin said, "Seriously, Max, you haven't hooked up with any girls since you moved here. What's your story?"

"No story," he said.

Hailey stared into the screen of Alek's phone; their heads were bent close together. But then I felt her stiffen, and her head jerked back, away from him.

"Not that I've heard about you hooking up with any guys, either," came another voice from around the corner— Tim?

"I like girls," Max replied. His voice sounded casual, but loud enough to be perfectly clear above the lightly taunting laughter of the other guys.

"What's the matter, then? No girls at Bear Pass are hot enough for you?" Josh said.

He made it sound like Max could have his pick of any girl at the school. Which was probably true.

Hailey said something to Alek, but I wasn't listening, just straining to hear every word of the other conversation.

"I didn't say that," Max said, sounding unconcerned.

"All right, then tell us. Who's hot? If you had to pick."

There was a brief silence, then more laughter.

Alek said, "Hailey, no, that's not—"

"Then what the hell?" Hailey said sharply.

And then from around the corner, Gavin said, "I know. I know who Max goes home and dreams about at night."

Who? I was desperate to hear the answer, and I was also equally desperate *not* to hear the answer.

"I don't think you do," Max said. His voice was still calm, but maybe too calm. Or too controlled. The words were enunciated with great precision.

"So you admit it!" said Josh. "You do have *dreams* at night."

"I nnever ssaid I wasn't human." He didn't quite stutter on this, but some of the consonants were just a little drawn out.

Alek said something to Hailey, his voice quiet but urgent. I felt Hailey's resistance, but I didn't want to know anything about it. I could only think, *Shut up! Shut up and let me listen!*

"It's not that hard to figure out," said Gavin. "I know exactly who strips down every night in Max's dirty mind."

There were a few loud whoops. Hailey and Alek both turned their heads in the direction of the noise, as if by instinct. They were both quiet now.

Against my will I pictured Lindsey in her cheerleading uniform, performing a striptease in front of Max. I supposed all those guys were picturing the exact same thing, with the only difference being that they were presumably a lot happier about the image than I was.

Then Gavin said, "Problem is, one girl at a time isn't enough for this guy. He's planning to double down, this one is. And I do mean double, and I do mean down. A sweet little blonde and a pink-haired vixen, all rolled into one sick package."

And everything grew quiet. Not just in the backyard. But in the courtyard, too. The only sound was Rihanna's voice floating out faintly from the living room stereo. *I'm friends with the monster that's under my bed.*

Hailey and Alek were still looking toward those voices, listening. It seemed to me that none of us were breathing.

And then Max said, without a trace of laughter in his voice, "Dude, you are disgusting."

"Hey, I'm not into judging," Gavin said. "Whatever you're into. Dudes, trannies, Siamese twins. It's all good."

I could feel Alek looking at me. And I could feel Hailey looking at Alek. I pulled my arms tight around myself and tried not to look anywhere at all. I had never wanted so badly not to exist.

Max's voice was firm and perfectly controlled. "I am not a pervert."

Pervert?

I could feel every inch of my own skin. And most of all, that ridge near the bottom of my lower back where I came together with Hailey. The ridge that made me not just one of the girls in the senior class, to be evaluated as hot or not, leered at or asked out or sneeringly dismissed, but something else entirely.

Pervert.

"Come on," Josh said, laughing. "Who wouldn't go for an automatic three-way with identical twins?"

And Gavin: "Talk about two for the price of one. You know, there are four watermelons, but I heard that between the two of them, they've only got one—"

There was a brief scuffling noise, followed by a screeching sound that might have been metal scraping against concrete.

Then something heavy and solid slammed against the side of the house.

The next voice I heard was definitely Max, but a version of Max that I had never remotely encountered before.

"Dude," he said—not shouting, but absolutely clear above the music, and without a trace of a stutter—"if you ever. Say that perverted crap. Again. I will smash your face. Against this wall. I will break your arms. You will never. Play basketball. Again."

18

Hailey

We all stood there, not looking at one another—me, Clara, Alek. My mind raced every which way, like a tweaking jackrabbit:

- They were just a bunch of Decepticons. Their puny thoughts were insignificant to me.
- Or, they were right about everything; they were just speaking truths I didn't want to hear.
- Just a week ago, at Max's house, these assholes had pretended to be all friendly and relaxed, and I'd thought that maybe they weren't so bad.
- I'd been an idiot.
- They were giving voice to Alek's secret thoughts.
- But was Alek Max in that scenario, determined not to be a pervert? Or was he Gavin? *Two for the price of one.*
- Max was the biggest jerk of all.
- Clara liked him, and she couldn't turn that off in a flash. She couldn't choose to not care.
- Neither could I.

Alek was standing there, hearing it. What was he thinking?

I should say something to Clara.

Alek should say something to both of us.

What was he thinking?

What was he thinking?

Then Amber appeared out of nowhere, gaping at us. Had she heard everything too? Would she be the one to start saying stuff to make us feel better? She would say all the wrong things. I would have to slap her. I would have to scratch her, and then Clara would have to pull her hair. It would turn into a giant catfight.

I giggled. It came out in a kind of gasp, and I realized that I hadn't been breathing. Maybe I was getting giggly from the oxygen deprivation.

Everyone stared at me.

I shut up.

Amber turned to Alek. "Sorry," she said, "but that's not a costume. You're outta here."

"Oh yeah, sorry about that," he said. "I didn't have time to find one."

"No excuses," she said. "You've gotta go."

He frowned. "You're not serious."

She raised her eyebrows.

"Um, Alek," I said, "Amber doesn't know the meaning of not being serious."

"That's right," Amber agreed, oblivious to the insult, "and if you don't get out of here, I'm going to sic the dogs on you."

We all looked around. Amber didn't have any dogs.

"Okay," he said, holding up his hands, "I'm gone."

He slipped away.

We stood there. I was still reeling, punch-drunk. I didn't have a grip on the situation. But there was one thing I knew for sure.

"Actually," I said, "we have to go too. Clara has a headache."

Behind me I could feel Clara trembling, her breath coming out in short, shallow bursts.

"We told Juanita and Bridget we'd see them here," I told Amber. "Will you tell them we had to go?"

"Of course. But can I do anything for you?"

I shook my head. "Is there a quick way out of here, without going through the house or the main yard, so we can just get out front and call our dad?"

She frowned at me for a moment, but then nodded. "Sure. Let me show you where the gate is."

19

Clara

I have no idea what it feels like to be alone, but the middle of the night is when I can come closest to imagining it. Sure, I can feel Hailey's back pressed against mine, I can hear her breathing, and I'm conscious that I don't have the freedom to get up and move around. But at least I can't feel her mind humming along beside mine. My mind, for once, is on its own.

And what do I do with that mental freedom? Mostly I use it to wallow in old topics that Hailey got tired of talking about years ago. I think, for example, about the Hilton twins, and why they weren't allowed to get married.

Violet and Daisy Hilton were pygopagus twins, which means they were conjoined back-to-back, like me and Hailey. When we were little, Mom sometimes told us stories about the Hilton twins' talent and charm, but she left a lot out, which we learned only when we got hold of a full book-length biography in middle school. Hailey and I passed it back and forth until we were both finished reading, but I was the only one who read it multiple times.

Born almost a hundred years before us, Violet and Daisy were abandoned by their unwed mother, who saw them as monsters, her punishment from God. Then they got adopted and turned into a traveling vaudeville show, without being given any choice about it. My ultimate nightmare—dancing onstage for the freak-ogling crowds, night after night.

What gets me about these twins is that Violet actually found someone who wanted to marry her, and she wanted to marry him, too, but the authorities wouldn't give them a marriage license. Violet Hilton and Maurice Lambert went all around the country trying to get that license, and of course Daisy was always along for the ride, which was why again and again they were turned away. Everyone with power said that a conjoined twin getting married was immoral and indecent. Because, of course, whatever went on between Violet and Maurice, Daisy was always going to be right there with them.

Violet and Maurice finally gave up, but not without getting a lot of press coverage, and Maurice Lambert was soon known throughout the land as a pathetic freak—a man with a conjoined-twin fetish.

All of this happened a long time ago. In many ways the world is completely different now. And in many other ways, it isn't.

Sure, there might be another Maurice Lambert out

there somewhere right now. A guy who would want a girl with another girl attached to her back. But what kind of guy would he be? What would need to be wrong with him, to want a thing like that?

If a guy ever did like me—or Hailey—would he have to be, by definition, a pervert?

These are the kinds of questions that I try to answer in the middle of the night, while Hailey slumbers peacefully beside me.

Some nights are longer than others.

In the shower that morning I scrubbed myself raw. I wanted to remove every last atom of that green witch makeup. If I took off a few layers of skin in the process, fine. I only wished I could scrub my ears so hard that I could erase everything I'd heard in the last twenty-four hours.

When I looked down at my arms, my hands, my belly, I thought, *Disgusting.*

It was true. I was disgusting. A mutant. Had I really forgotten that? Had I imagined, in some fleeting moment, that there was anyone in the world who wouldn't be horrified at the thought of touching me?

I knew I wasn't supposed to absorb Max's words like this. My mom had explained it a thousand times. The way we view ourselves has to come from the inside, not from the reflection that we see in other people's eyes.

But sometimes it seems to me that reflections are all we have. Without them, we could never see ourselves at all.

We took turns getting dressed. Hailey wore black pants with a snug, low-cut, velvet maroon top—it clashed with her pink hair, which I would have told her if she'd asked—and I wore jeans with a lavender button-down shirt. She wore a necklace of rough, chunky metal beads on a leather string, and I wore a dainty leaf-shaped pendant.

Sometimes I don't mind the way Hailey dresses, because it sets her apart from me and allows me to have my separate self by default, without having to do anything but stay bland. But on this particular morning, her top and her necklace made me angry. Her tight shirt, with that expanse of creamy white flesh above it—she had succeeded in scrubbing off all the glitter—made me feel exposed. Her necklace appeared to be made out of rusty old gears or bits of things picked up in shop class, and it looked like at any moment it might tear at her skin and make her bleed.

"Why do you have to wear that thing?" I demanded as I waited for her to apply her makeup. "It's going to give us tetanus."

It was the first time I'd spoken all morning. Hailey jumped, and her lip liner went skidding across her cheek. "What thing?" She rubbed at the lip liner with the back of her hand.

"You know. That ugly necklace. Where did that even come from?"

She looked down at it. "I ordered it online, remember? You saw me open the package on Friday."

"Well, it's ugly."

She raised her eyebrows, stared at me in the mirror, then shrugged. "Yours is pretty."

She finished with her makeup, and we turned so I could get a good look at myself in the bathroom mirror. Despite all my scrubbing, I saw now that there was still a streak of green running along my hairline on the right side.

"Damn it!" I bit out. "It's never going to come off. Maybe I should just leave it."

Hailey opened a drawer and pulled out a bottle of makeup remover and a cotton ball. "Get it off now," she said, holding them out to me, "or you'll feel weird all day."

"You don't think I'm going to feel weird all day anyway?" I snapped.

Hailey looked at me. Her phone, which was sitting on the bathroom counter, giggled—her standard ringtone. She glanced at it, but she didn't do anything.

Even though Hailey hadn't said a word, I kept arguing with her anyway. "How could I ever have a day where I don't feel weird? They used to put people like us in the circus! We go around this town, acting like everybody here accepts us, like they all think we're just one of the gang, but it's never been true."

It had been a long time since I'd talked like this out

loud, but suddenly I felt so energized, I knew I should have been shooting my mouth off all along.

Hailey put the makeup remover and the cotton ball back into the drawer. She shut it hard. "You know, you're not the only one who had a crappy night. The party, Alek, those goddamn—and then I barely slept a wink, and you were lying there snoring."

"I'm the one who was awake all night," I protested. "You were asleep! Nothing bothers you!"

She gave a short, loud exhale. "Yeah, right. Nothing bothers me. Sure. That's what you have to tell yourself, right? Because your head is so crammed with your own problems, if you tried to make room for mine, your brain would burst open at the seams."

I stared at her in the mirror. When I found my breath, I managed to gasp out, "What are you so mad about? What did I do?"

"Nothing." She shook her head. She took in a long breath, so deep I could almost feel it in my own lungs. "It's not even you."

Quietly I said, "Then why won't you tell me what happened with Alek?"

"He's out of the picture," she said. "And by the way, I think Mom's trying to fatten us up again. I smell bacon. We should go see about that."

20

Hailey

In the kitchen, our mom was indeed frying bacon. She wore a bathrobe; her hair was unbrushed, her face still puffy with sleep. She barely looked up as we walked in. Clara took two mugs from a cabinet and handed them to me, and I started pouring us coffee.

"Hey, Mom," I said, "how's it going? How were the trick-or-treaters last night?"

Mom looked up at me with a pained expression. "The trick-or-treaters were very cute," she said. "Not as many as last year. But very cute."

"Okay," I said. "Well, what's wrong?"

"It's those twins. Remember the ones we saw the news story about? The little girls they were separating for no good reason?"

No good reason. Like staying fully attached through the chest and abdomen forever would be totally copacetic. I rolled my eyes.

Mom looked down at the bacon. In a subdued voice, she

said, "Well, the surgery went okay, and they were both doing fine, or so it seemed, but now the littler one—well, she didn't make it. She just—" She looked up at me. "She died!"

"Oh, I'm sorry, Mom." I patted her on the shoulder.

"Well," Clara said, "that's too bad. It really is."

But the truth was, we didn't know these little girls. Of course it was very sad for them and their family, but it didn't make sense that Mom was so upset. She was on the verge of tears. She acted like every pair of conjoined twins in the world was a part of her inner circle. And every twin who died was not only a tragedy, but also evidence that all of her own choices had been the correct ones.

Clara and I took our coffee cups to the table in the dining nook adjoining the kitchen and sat down. As we sat, Clara made a slight twisting motion away from me that was just a little different from normal, and I felt an unaccustomed pulling at the lower back, in the place where our flesh came together. It didn't hurt, and it was over in a moment, but something about it made me catch my breath.

An image flashed into my mind. The image that Alek had showed me the night before, on his phone's screen. The vision that had come from his mind, and that should have stayed there, locked away. But it had invaded my own brain now, and I didn't know if I would ever be able to get it out.

"What's wrong?" Clara said quietly. "I feel like you're not breathing."

It was true. I caught my breath, drew it inward in a shudder.

I felt her looking in my direction, but not too far. Not twisting enough to draw Mom's attention.

"I'm fine," I whispered.

But I wasn't. All night I'd been feeling this weird thing that I couldn't name, an *offness*, like there was a giant piece of me that didn't fit into the rest. Or a piece that wasn't fitting because it was pulling away from the rest, not in a clean break but in a jagged, messy rip that had maybe just begun.

Lying awake all night while Clara slept—at least that was how it seemed to me, though she denied it—had only made it worse. Hour by hour, minute by minute, I'd been dropping further into this dark hole that kept getting bigger all around me.

The worst of it was that I could never tell Clara what had gotten under my skin. Bad enough that she had heard those awful guys in Amber's yard. She didn't need to know the other thing, the thing that I had seen.

Keeping a secret from my sister was like holding some large, bitter foreign object in my mouth. It felt crazy and wrong, and I wasn't sure how long I could manage. All our lives, I had kept almost nothing from her—how could I?—and that was part of the beauty of being us. But I had to try.

"You're going to ask her about San Francisco today,

aren't you?" Clara whispered. "Is that what you're so wor-ried about?"

San Francisco. God. All those hours of lying awake, and I'd barely even thought about San Francisco.

All those years of telling Clara she was wrong. Telling her there was nothing to fear. That it was all right to be a freak. Telling her, and telling myself too, that I didn't care.

I'd been lying to her, and lying to myself. I kept saying that I didn't mind being a freak, but the truth was that I just never fully believed that we *were* that freakish. Never fully believed that the people around us didn't accept us and get us and know us for who we were. Or that new people couldn't quickly learn to do the same.

From where we sat in the dining nook, we could see Mom at the kitchen stove, flipping the bacon slices back and forth with a pair of tongs, staring down at them, prob-ably still thinking about that damn dead baby.

Dad stumbled in, looking barely awake, in his pajamas and with his salt-and-pepper hair sticking up at a lot of weird angles.

When we'd called him the night before, asking him to pick us up early from the party, he hadn't asked why. I knew he could tell that we were both upset. But all he said was, "Everything okay?" And we both said, "Yes!" with uncon-vincing brightness. Then he asked if there was anything he could do for us, and we both said, "No!" in the exact same way, and we got into the minivan, and he said, "Radio?" and we nodded, and he turned it up loud enough that there was no more pressure to say anything at all. And I appreciated that.

Now he went over to Mom and kissed her on the forehead, then watched her for a moment before asking her, "What is it?"

"Nothing." She shook her head, and actually sniffled a bit. "It's just those babies they were separating. One of them died. It's just hard to hear, you know? To think about it."

He pulled back, looking at her carefully. "You all right?"

"Of course I'm all right," she said, her tone turning irritable. "It's their mother who isn't all right." She flipped a slice of bacon, then added, apparently as an afterthought, "And their father. Why am I the only person in this house who seems to be bothered by any of this?"

"Of course I'm bothered," Dad said. "That's very sad for that poor family."

"It's more than sad. It's a travesty, the way the doctors push the families to do this. They don't give them all the information. If it wasn't for— If I had listened— You would have just— It's just wrong."

"I know," he said gently. "We did the right thing. You were right. You were right from the start. And our girls are fine."

Clara whispered to me, "Do you want me to ask her for you?"

San Francisco. After everything that had happened, now Clara *wanted* to go? And she wanted to bring it up *now*?

"What the hell?" I whispered back. "Are you pranking me?"

"We had a deal," she whispered, "and we're sticking to it." And then she called out brightly, "Hey, Mom, we have something we want to ask you about."

Mom looked up.

Clara started explaining the summer art program and the interview, and how I didn't really want to go but wanted to see if I could get in. It was just an adventure, Clara told her, like I'd planned to say all along. Just a lark.

"So do you think you could give us a ride down there sometime next week, if we can get an appointment?" Clara asked.

I didn't understand what was happening.

My phone giggled again. I shut it off, powered it down completely. There was nobody I needed to hear from today.

The bacon sizzled loudly in the pan.

"San Francisco?" Dad said. "You should make a whole day of it, if you're going. There's so much to see. Maybe I can find a way to go with you, at least for part of the day."

Mom shot him an angry look. "I don't see the point," she said, turning back to me and Clara. "If you're not actually going to go this summer."

Clara went through the whole explanation again. It

was just for fun, she said. "So you're free on Wednesdays and Thursdays, right?" she asked.

Mom didn't even look at her, but she carried a platter of pancakes over to the table. "We had a lot of leftover candy bars from last night," she said, "so I chopped some up and mixed them into the pancakes."

"Perfect," I said. "Here I was afraid that my belly might look flat all day."

"There's also a bowl of mixed berries," Mom replied.

Dad looked back and forth between Mom, Clara, and me before speaking. "You should do this. Even if it's nothing but the interview, it will be a great experience for you. And if we can't make it work with my schedule, then you three can just go, and we'll all go back together on a weekend and see the sights."

"I don't know," Mom said as she laid the bacon out on a paper-towel-lined platter. "San Francisco has all those hills. I haven't driven there in years. And the minivan . . ." She looked worried.

"Well," Dad said, "I think you'll be fine. But if you really don't feel comfortable, or if you can't find a time on Wednesday or Thursday, then I'll take them. I'll cancel classes and office hours if I have to. I know you don't like to cancel yours, since it's your first year teaching and you're still proving yourself. And that's reasonable."

Mom's eyes widened, and for a second I thought she

was going to start shouting at him. But she just cleared her throat and said in a steady voice, "They're talking about this whole summer program. Six weeks. That's an awfully long time. We would have to find an apartment to rent."

Just yesterday I would have said she was wrong—that six weeks was nothing. But today I wasn't as sure. Last night had left me feeling exposed, stripped down in a way that I wasn't sure how to fix. Could we honestly wander around among strangers? For six weeks?

I cleared my throat, pushing these thoughts down into the cold cellar of my brain. Fearful thoughts were not for me. Those were Clara's job.

"We might be able to live in the dorms," I said. "That's something we can ask about at the interview."

Now Mom looked really alarmed. Standing there with the platter of bacon in her hands, a thick lock of hair falling into her eyes, she demanded, "But where would *I* live?"

"I think we can manage it on our own," I told her, willing myself to fully believe this. "It would be a great experience for us."

"That's an interesting thought," Dad said. "You know, I bet you'd do just fine in the dorms. I bet that would work really well."

Mom set the bacon down on the table and dropped into her chair. "But I thought what we talked about for the summer, what we agreed on—"

"You keep saying 'we,'" Clara said sharply. "You know, you don't always have to speak in the first person plural. Some of us have to. But you don't."

"Clara," said Dad as he came over to the table, "your mother is just trying to think through all the ramifications. You don't need to take that attitude with her. It's not constructive."

"Right," Clara said. "And refusing to let us out of a ten-mile radius is constructive? Refusing to even take us to this interview, when we know perfectly well you've got nothing else to do that day? What are *we* so afraid of, Mom?"

Now Clara was the angry one? The adventurous rebel? I dropped my head into my hands. I wanted to crawl back into bed and finally get the sleep that had eluded me all night.

Mom pinched her lips together and served herself some pancakes from the platter, while we all watched her. Finally she said, "What *I* am afraid of is that you girls don't understand what you're getting into. You've never been on your own. You've never lived in a house where everything wasn't set up especially for you, where you didn't have someone to cook for you and reach the high shelves and drive you around to appointments. You've never—"

The doorbell rang.

We all looked at one another.

Dad said, "Anybody expecting a visitor?"

We shook our heads.

He went to the front door. There was some murmuring, and then Dad said in a loud, friendly voice, "Of course, come on in."

After a pause he added, "No, we were just having break-fast. We've got plenty. Come have some pancakes with us."

I looked at Mom and at Clara, and I could see that nei-ther of them had any idea who was at the door.

But I was pretty sure that I knew exactly who it was. I clutched my phone, where it lay silently on the table next to my plate.

Dad came back into the dining room, trailed by the very last person on earth I wanted to see.

Alek. And *now* he was wearing a costume.

21

Clara

Alek had a hatchet planted in his head, and about a gallon of blood flowing down through his dark hair, onto his face, and even splattered on his T-shirt, which for once was white, not black. But he still wore his usual dark jeans and black sneakers.

"Hailey," said Dad cheerfully, "this young murder victim tells me he's a friend of yours. I'm assuming he's been up all night, with that hatchet in his head."

"I've never seen him before in my life," Hailey muttered.

"Great, great, perfect," said Dad, either oblivious or deliberately ignoring Hailey's surliness—it was hard to tell with him. "Alek, was it? Sit down. There's a spot for you right there. I'll get you a plate. Do you drink coffee?"

Alek shook his head. As Dad trotted off to get the plate, Alek approached the dining table, but he didn't sit down, and he didn't seem to notice me or my mom. He looked only at my sister. "Hailey," he said, "I'm sorry."

She didn't acknowledge him, and my mom just stared

at him in confusion, so it was left to me to ask, "Did you seriously go home last night and put on the hatchet and the blood, and then go back to the party?"

Alek's eyes widened, and he drew back. "What? No! Of course not. I put this on when I got up this morning."

"What for?" I asked.

"It's an apology!" From his tone, I gathered that he had thought this was obvious. "Hailey was so ticked off at me last night. She wanted to kill me with her bare hands, and I get that. I deserve it. I *encourage* it!"

This guy was seriously odd, I thought. And in almost the same moment, another thought struck me, clobbered me really, with a force that almost knocked me cold: a guy this strange could be serious, *really* serious, about liking Hailey.

I would never have a chance with a nice, normal guy like Max—and I did still think of him that way, even though I wished I could hate him now—but Hailey might have a chance with a weirdo like Alek, assuming that he didn't turn out to be a bona fide murderer.

And I would never have a chance to live a nice, normal life, but that wasn't what Hailey wanted anyway.

All this time I'd been holding on to the idea that the life we'd planned—or rather, the life our parents had planned for us, and that we'd accepted—was the best that either of us could hope for. But maybe that wasn't true for Hailey. Maybe it was true only for me.

Maybe she was right, and I really had failed to make room for her in my overcrowded, self-centered brain.

I glanced at Hailey, who sipped nonchalantly from an empty coffee cup, and then I looked back up at Alek, who was staring at Hailey with a pained expression. As weird as he was, he didn't seem like a psycho killer to me. And nobody had ever turned up any actual evidence of that, had they?

"What is she so mad about, anyway?" I asked him. "What did I miss?" Maybe if he would explain it to me, I could find some way to get it straightened out.

"Nothing!" said Hailey, with a menacing look at Alek.

He looked confused. "You were there," he reminded me. "You don't know?"

"I . . . wasn't really listening. I was a little distracted."

As soon as I said it, I wished I hadn't; it was like pulling those guys' voices right into the room with us.

Dad reappeared, with an empty plate for Alek and a steaming mug of coffee for himself.

"Hailey," said Mom, "should we ask your friend to sit down?"

"I'm not really that hungry," Alek said, looking at Hailey. "I just wanted to apologize. And to make sure that you being mad at me isn't going to stop you from applying to Golden Gate for this summer."

The way Hailey scowled up at Alek through all that

dark eyeliner and mascara, she actually looked a lot scarier than he did. "Of course I'm still applying. What did you think, I was doing it for *you* or something?"

Dad set the plate down in front of Alek and lingered at the edge of the table, not too far from Alek, looking back and forth between him and Hailey.

"Well, good," Alek said. "I guess that's it then. Except, um . . ." He took a deep breath, looking down at his hands, and then finally back up at Hailey. "Well, what about the dance? Are we still on for that, too?"

Hailey bugged her eyes out at him. "What, are you kidding me? No, we're not going to the dance, you fraudulent frog-faced Frodo!"

My dad, perhaps belatedly realizing that he ought to play the role of bouncer, took a step toward Alek.

"Honestly," I said to Hailey, "what did the poor guy say to you last night?"

Alek backed slowly toward the door, his hands held up, palms out, as if to show that he had no weapon. Other than the hatchet in his head. "I didn't say anything."

"It's not what he said," Hailey confirmed.

Alek stopped and pulled his phone out of his pocket.

"Put it away," Hailey said.

"I just wanted to show your—"

"I said, put it away!"

He said, "She was mad because I—"

Hailey stood up abruptly, yanking me with her, and my leg slammed into the edge of the table. By the time we were four years old, we had learned not to do stuff like that.

"Hailey!" I snapped. "Seriously!" But I knew she could feel the impact, just as much as if my leg belonged to her.

"Alek," she said, "get out of here, and don't you ever bring that up again. To either of us!"

"But you don't understand. It wasn't a wish! All those paintings I do, they're not—"

She pointed at the door. "OUT!"

Dad gestured toward the front door, making a sweeping motion with one arm, as if urging Alek in that direction; and finally Alek followed him to the door and walked out.

22

Hailey

At 1:24 a.m. Clara nudged me awake. "Bathroom. Sorry."

I groaned but clambered out of bed with her, groggy from the deep sleep I'd been in. We trod quietly down the carpeted hallway, leaving the lights off.

As we passed our parents' bedroom, we heard some muffled sounds. Couldn't tell what they were. Did not want to think about it.

But on the way back from the bathroom, the sounds were a little louder, and I realized what it was: Mom was crying.

Without discussing it, Clara and I paused in the hall-way.

I heard Mom's voice through the door, too quiet and muffled for me to make out the words.

Then Dad. "They're going to be fine. They're only asking us to take them for the interview. That's not asking so much."

Mom said something, but again I couldn't hear.

"Well," Dad said, "would that be the end of the world?"

My heart rate accelerated. What could he mean? Was he talking about letting us go for the summer? For the whole six weeks?

I pressed my shoulder against Clara's in the dark. Reminded myself that it didn't matter what Dad said. Between Clara and Mom, there was no way a thing like that was going to happen.

"I know," Dad said, his voice clear through their thin wooden door. "Of course. You were right about not separating them. You were probably right about that, and you were probably right about raising them here. But—"

"*Probably?*" Mom demanded, her voice louder now.

I grabbed Clara's hand. I hadn't even known that it was Mom who had insisted on these things, these choices that they'd made for us. They always put up such a united front. But I should have known, should have been able to tell that the front they put up was always hers. He was always the one who went along.

"Probably," Dad said evenly. "All those things I said back then, about the things they might miss out on, that's all still true. So it's hard to say. But even assuming that you were right—"

"I *was* right," she said forcefully. "I *am* right. If it weren't for me, you'd have had them separated, even if it had left us with only one of them."

This knocked the wind right out of me. And out of Clara, too. I could feel it.

"Maybe," Dad said. "I don't know what I would have done. I needed time to think about it. I needed a few days to be sure. You convinced me, and you were right, and I've never looked back at that part. The part about living up here isn't quite as clear to me."

"This is about you," Mom said, a sharp edge entering her voice. "This is about what you gave up for them, isn't it? You'd like to think they would have done just as well in LA, so you could have had the career you planned."

"No, Liza. No. Come on. We've talked about this. I don't regret any of that. I like Sutter. I like being able to focus on the actual teaching. Not every minute of it, obviously. But on balance it's turned out to be good for me, even though it's not what I originally thought I wanted. Anyway, you gave up a lot more than I did."

"No," she said. "As soon as we saw that ultrasound, I knew I would give up work. So moving up here didn't matter for me in that way. And I do like it here."

"Me too," he said. "And I know there have been a lot of advantages for the kids. But things change. They're nearly grown. It's up to them now."

Yes. Yes. Please.

"But this is what we always planned," Mom said, her voice rising in shrill desperation. "This is what we agreed on."

"You and I agreed," Dad said. "They didn't."

"If they leave Bear Pass," Mom said, "then we could leave too, if we wanted. Are you sure that's not what this is about?"

"I'm sure," Dad said. "I'm not saying I wouldn't like to travel sometime, but we can do that even if they stay. I'm not looking to move or change jobs. Unless you are. I promise."

Mom started crying again, or maybe had been crying all along.

Clara squeezed my hand. Pressed her shoulder against mine. But I knew she must have been feeling something very different from what I was. I wanted so badly for Dad to make Mom understand that she was wrong—wrong to limit us, wrong to think that she still knew what was best for us in every situation. But what did Clara want? To be held carefully, forever, in this cocoon?

"I know you're scared," I could hear Dad say, through the door. "I get that. I do."

"And you're not?" Mom demanded.

"Maybe I am. Yeah. Thinking where this could all lead. I'm just not sure that's a good reason to hold them back."

"I've been scared for so many years," Mom said, her voice raw. "Do you know how exhausting it is to be so worried about so many things, for so long? All the things that could happen to them. Even now."

There was a long pause. *Did* he know? Did *I*? No. I didn't know, couldn't know her fear, her need to protect us. What that felt like. I could only guess. And maybe Mom couldn't know what it felt like to be me, to feel like I was suffocating here and needed so badly to break away.

But wasn't it her job to try? Wasn't it?

And then my dad's voice came through, as clear as if there'd been no door between us at all. "Liza. I'm sorry. But I think you have to let them go."

"I *have* to? *Have* to?"

A much shorter pause this time, and then, "Yeah. I think you do."

When I was finally sure that Clara was asleep, I pulled out my phone and started looking through all the video clips that everyone had been sending at my request.

Art school wasn't going to happen. Leaving Bear Pass wasn't going to happen. But some kind of change. That had to happen, even if it happened right here, in place.

If I was going to apply to Sutter's film school, I had to send in a sample film by December 1. That gave me just less than a month, and all I had done was collect some material. I had some general thoughts and ideas but nothing coherent; basically, I had no idea where I was going with any of this.

Luckily, I already had around thirty clips to start

working with. I'd put out the call to a few friends, but the files were coming in from unexpected places too. Even people I no longer wanted to speak to, like Gavin and Josh.

I'd glanced at a few of these clips before, but I was always rushed, trying to hide them from Clara, and always with the sound off. Now I reached carefully for a pair of headphones and took my time, still lying on my side and barely moving so I wouldn't disturb her.

A new clip had just come in from Juanita a couple of hours before, with a message attached.

What are you doing with all this? Film project for that art school in SF?

I answered quickly.

No, for Sutter film school.

Since it was the middle of the night, I didn't expect any response to this until morning. But before I could even open the clip, I got her reply.

Good. Ironic if I stay in BP and you leave.

I rolled my eyes and replied.

You're not staying. What are you doing awake?

Same as you, I guess. Don't you think a house together sounds fun? Like Bridget was saying?

Of course I did. The truth was that these two ideas—trying out film school and living in an apartment with friends, instead of at home with our parents—had given me a surge of hope about the near future. Where these coming years had looked so grim and suffocating, without any space to grow up and out of our old enclosures, now they were offering at least a taste of change. Enough to seem like a time when maybe, in some small way, a little bit of me could bloom.

And if part of me also felt just a smidgen of relief at the idea of staying, well, it didn't matter. Nobody even had to know.

I responded to Juanita. *Superfun. Wish you could be there. We will miss you when you're off at Harvard and we're partying at Sutter.*

Ha-ha. Can't get rid of me so easily.

Shut up and go fill out your FAFSA.

Already done.

I stopped and thought. Could she really not scrape together the cash for even one or two college apps, without her parents interfering? I wasn't sure about the mechanics of how you paid, but I supposed you might need a credit card or a bank card so you could pay online. Maybe actual cash was beside the point. Though there must be some way you could use cash. Should I offer to pay? Ask Mom if we could loan Juanita the money?

I opened a browser and typed in *can't pay college application fees.*

A minute later I sent Juanita a link to a website describing how you could get the fees waived if you couldn't afford them.

She responded after just a couple of minutes.

I don't qualify. Anyway, it's not the point. My parents could pay the fees if they really wanted to. They just don't want me getting my hopes up.

I nodded against my pillow, though she couldn't see me. I probably should have known that.

I know you don't believe me, she wrote, *but I'm okay with this. It makes sense in the long run. Starting at a four-year college is money down the drain.*

I closed my eyes. I had this weird claustrophobic feeling, like the three of us—Juanita, Clara, and me—were trapped in a tiny dark cave together and we were never going to get out.

But then I thought of the house. Living on our own with Juanita and Bridget. No Mom to take care of us or tell us what to do. Of course she would call every day and text us constantly and stop by without warning. But we still wouldn't be living at home, right under her wing.

I opened my eyes and felt like maybe I could see a little sliver of light just shimmering into view on the horizon.

Will it really work for us to live together? I typed out, feeling half-sick with the selfishness of my hope—my weakness in letting Juanita give up on her own dreams and stay here with us.

No, I reminded myself, she wasn't giving up. She was just postponing. And who knew? Maybe that was all I was doing too. Maybe eventually Clara would agree to let us, too, move away from here and on to other things. When she was ready.

Not too much money? I typed. *Or too far from the community college?*

I think it will work. Still a lot cheaper than four-year college, and I'll have flexibility to work a lot at the same time.

Do you promise to transfer to four-year after?

When I have the credits. I promise.

I nodded again, looking into the darkness but seeing something bright inside it. Feeling my lungs expanding with new oxygen. Maybe all of this wasn't so terrible. Maybe this place, this tucked-away part of the mountains, could really be an okay place to live and study and begin to grow, for all of us. For now.

Okay. Good night, Juanita.

Good night.

I opened her video clip. It was from Halloween two years earlier, when Clara and I had been Batman and Catwoman, posing for the camera with a series of goofy postures and expressions. That made me smile.

I scrolled through the others. Mostly, everybody had sent clips of me and Clara doing obvious, everyday things. There we were, walking down the school hallway, in our sort-of-funny, not-that-graceful little shuffle. There we were at our desks, always together but always turned away from each other.

There we were in the girls' bathroom, the main one next to the school library, angling back and forth as we took turns washing our hands in the scratched-up little sink, each of us looking up into the mirror under the subtly vibrating, blue-tinged fluorescent light. Always feeling each other's presence but mostly just seeing ourselves.

Me, leaning in toward the mirror to examine a blackhead swelling up through my makeup, while behind me you could see Clara in a forty-five-degree profile, distant, just far enough away and just blurred enough by the video's middling quality that it smoothed out her skin and obscured her flyaway hairs, making her seem like an almost flawless version of me. You could see my blackheads, but you couldn't see hers.

Come to think of it, I've never seen hers.

And farther back on the screen, Vanessa's reflection caught just at the edge of the mirror, a glimpse of her walking out of the bathroom, removed from us just enough to look as glossy and smooth-edged as a Photoshopped girl in a magazine.

Vanessa pretty much always looked like that. But then again, when had I ever stood face-to-face with her, leaning in until I could see her from just an inch or two away, as I did with myself at the bathroom mirror every day? When had I ever inspected Vanessa's pores?

Not that she would ever allow me to.

Not that I had ever thought to ask.

But even Clara. Even my own twin, who was never apart from me, whose legs and feet were like a part of my own body—even now I could feel the sheets, cool against the skin of my sister's legs. But even with her, there were close-up things about her that I couldn't see, and things in her mind that I would never be able to feel. And as for me, there were things about myself that I would never be able to see directly, as others did. Things that I could only see through the limited, distorting lenses of cameras and mirrors.

I watched the clip again, and then I watched it a third time.

23

Clara

I wanted to stay home from school on Monday, but Hailey wouldn't let me. As we walked to our first-period English class in the early morning fog, I kept my head bent low, unwilling to meet anyone's eyes. I could hear groups of kids talking, whispering, laughing. Even with my head down, I couldn't avoid seeing what seemed like dozens of couples holding hands or walking arm in arm, their hips pressed into each other.

My brain knew that none of this had changed since last week, but my stomach didn't know it. My stomach believed that all the whispers and not-quite-heard conversations were about me. My stomach was sure that all the other students were staring at me and Hailey and thinking, *Disgusting. Horror show. Get away.* And that was why my stomach was clenched and nauseated.

I really did feel sick enough to stay home, but I understood that it wasn't a virus. I was just sick of being myself, and that wasn't the kind of thing you got to stay home for.

I stared at my shoes as we walked into class, and I managed to get out my things and arrange them on my desk without ever looking up.

I knew when Max walked in, and when he passed by me on the way to his desk. My peripheral vision couldn't avoid him entirely. But I didn't look up. All through class I was focused on not looking his way, and also trying not to think about him—though this was laughable, because he was all I was thinking about.

I wanted to hate him. I wanted to believe he was an idiot, a bigot, a complete and utter asshole for talking about me the way he had. For *thinking* of me the way he did. I would have given anything to have believed that, if only I could.

Without discussing it, Hailey and I lingered a couple of minutes after class, taking longer than necessary to put on our jackets and pack up our bags. But when we finally walked out, with my head bent as low as it would go, the first thing I saw in the hallway was Max's giant sneakers.

I sucked in my breath, and barely stopped myself from looking up.

"Hey, Clara. Morning, Hailey." His voice was easy this morning. Whenever his voice was relaxed, it was deep, warm, and low-pitched, with tones that were somehow vaguely soothing, even now. After all those things he'd said about me, his conscience apparently wasn't bothering him enough to cause him any tension at all.

I stopped walking, my head still down, but Hailey stepped forward, pulling me along. Max fell into step with us. Hailey stopped.

She drew in her breath to speak, and I silently urged her with my mind, *Don't tell him off. Don't tell him off. Please be quiet. Just ignore him. Just keep walking.*

If she told him that we'd heard him talking about us at the party—if she even hinted at it—our humiliation would be so much worse. And it was already more than I could handle.

I looked at her and quickly shook my head, though I knew there was a fifty-fifty chance she would just ignore me.

After a moment Hailey said, "I forgot something. I dropped a pencil. We'll see you later." She turned us back toward the classroom, and I felt myself breathing again.

There was a pause, and when Max spoke, his voice wasn't quite as low-pitched as it had been before. "All right," he said. "I'll s-see you later, then."

That afternoon we were walking to the Sandwich Shack and had almost arrived when Max caught up with us. "Hey, Clara, Hailey," he said, nodding as he fell into step with us, his voice once again just as easy as it had been that morning. "Braving that bad coffee again?"

I watched my feet as we walked. I couldn't think what to say. How could I just make him go away?

"We go there every Monday," Hailey said.

We all kept walking.

Max cleared his throat. "So, what did you guys think about that physics homework?"

We had arrived at the Sandwich Shack's front doors, and he moved forward and pulled one door open, then stood waiting for us.

I forced myself to look up at him. "Were you, um, planning to stay? Because we . . ." What excuse could I make? I was so desperate to find some diplomatic, creative, and clever way to get rid of him that my mind had gone completely blank.

"We're meeting up with our friends," Hailey said, "and there's going to be so much girl talk, you'll get sick if you get within twenty feet of us."

"Oh." He was still standing there, holding the door. "Um, okay." He turned, peeking inside. "I was thinking of maybe just grabbing a snack? And then I'll go?"

I sucked in my breath. My face was as low as I could make it, but probably not low enough to hide how red it was. It was unbearable. I twisted away from Max, which forced Hailey to look at him straight-on.

"Just go to the convenience store," she said. "It's right across the street."

I caught my breath. She had basically just told him that he couldn't even come in. Any hope of dodging him subtly was gone.

He let the door swing shut, but he didn't leave. "Wow. Okay," he said. "Um, sorry, but what's going on? Did I do something to piss you off?"

I looked up, even though I knew my face was still red. "It doesn't matter. Can you just go? Can you just please drop this and stop trying to pretend that we're friends or something?"

He stared at me, his brow wrinkled with what might have been confusion or annoyance, his cheeks turning slightly pink.

He stepped forward. "I'm m-missing something here. You know, what you s-said on Halloween—and what I s-s-said—maybe I should have explained—"

I drew back, taking Hailey with me. "It doesn't matter." My voice came out so squeaky and quiet, I couldn't even understand myself. I cleared my throat. "It doesn't matter," I repeated, "what you said on Halloween. Just leave us alone, all right?"

I brushed at the corners of my eyes. I looked around, hoping that no one else from our school was near enough to witness my little episode. We stood right at the edge of the main road outside our school. Various classmates were bound to be driving by, and there would usually be a few walking, though I didn't see any right then.

Finally I looked back at Max. His face had gone from

pink to red. "W-wait a second," he said. "What are we talking about?"

"We're not talking about anything," Hailey said quickly. "Just leave my sister alone. Leave us both alone. We just want to go in there and drink some bad coffee and eat some chips and talk with our friends. All right?"

"About Halloween," Max said. "We were talking about Halloween."

I tried to look up at his face, but I got only as far as the slightly frayed hem of his jeans. "We're not talking about Halloween," I said.

"I only talked to you guys for a few minutes," he said. "I don't think I did anything terrible. I know it ended a little abruptly, but I figured I would see you again later, at the party I mean, but somebody told me you guys had left early. . . . And that was . . . That was after I came in, after . . ."

A silence fell around us. Behind me I heard a couple of cars go by, but thankfully, there were still no other pedestrians.

Hailey took my hand. To Max she said, "Just let us go in. You're blocking our way."

"But I'm worried now," he said.

I drew in a deep, shuddering breath. "Max, for God's sake," I said, addressing myself to his big, long-fingered hands. "Why do you keep talking to us in public? Don't you realize that anybody at all could be driving by right now and see you here with us? It's like you *want* people to call you a pervert."

I bit my lip, my heart pounding as I realized the implications of what I'd said. But maybe it was for the best. Nothing else seemed to be able to shut him up, to make him go away.

He didn't say anything. When I finally looked up at his face, all its color had drained away.

"Holy shit," he said.

"It's all right." I finally managed to look him in the eyes, and I held my voice steady. "Nobody asked you to be a pervert. Nobody asked you to be disgusting. If you think I was asking—"

"Clara! I can't believe you had to hear that crap those assholes were saying about you. And Hailey. Both of you." He took a step toward us, and Hailey and I stepped back.

He stopped, looking at us, then looked down. "I had no idea you heard any of that. God, I still want to pound their faces in." His fists were clenched, and he started to raise them, then stopped. He was looking somewhere over our heads. "They've known you all these years, they've hung out with you, and then they talk about you like you're . . . I don't know, exotic sex toys or something. What the hell is the matter with them?" He looked at me. "Did you know they were like that?"

"Jesus, Max, you're the one who said I was disgusting! You're the one who said you're not a pervert!" I clapped my hands over my mouth as I realized that I was shouting.

Hailey reached back and held my hand. Hers was damp and shaky, and she didn't say a word.

"I said *you're* disgusting?" Max demanded. "What? Did someone say I said that? They were lying if they did."

"Max, for God's sake, I heard you say it!"

He moved in, and before I could draw back, he grabbed my arm. "You did not. When did you hear me say that?"

"At Halloween. They said—they said—and you said that was disgusting. I heard you!"

"I said *they* were disgusting. They *are* disgusting. They're worthless piles of crap for talking about you that way. You thought I said *you* were disgusting?"

I pulled my arm away from him, looking up at him warily, my other hand still gripping Hailey's. "So I'm not disgusting, but the idea of—the idea of—well, thinking of me like that. That's what's disgusting." My heart was jackhammering away at my chest wall, trying to burst out as I said, "Right?"

He stared at me. His lips were parted slightly, and some wild, insane part of my mind created an image, a stupid, ridiculous image of me throwing myself at him, grabbing him by the shoulders and pulling myself up onto my toes and kissing those lips, that almost-open mouth.

"That's not what I said." He shook his head. "It's not what I meant. But, Clara, I'm not saying . . ." He closed his eyes, and though he didn't take a step or shift his position, I thought I could see each molecule of his body pulling itself back from me ever so slightly, by no more than the width of an electron or two.

"It's not that you're disgusting," he said, "and it's not that the idea of you is disgusting. I'm not saying that at all. And you're so nice, and so interesting, and I really do like talking to you. But . . ." His voice trailed off. He had angled himself away from me now, and he looked off someplace, out at the horizon.

"But," I said softly. "Of course."

Behind me Hailey let out the quietest and saddest sound I could ever imagine.

Max looked down, his gaze almost meeting mine for a moment, but then sinking all the way down to the ground. "You do understand, don't you, Clara?"

My heart had stopped beating. My lungs were empty.

"Of course," I said, or maybe just whispered, or maybe didn't really say at all.

Just one kiss. If he would give me one kiss before he vanished, before the fantasy of him vanished. The fantasy of him, or anyone like him, ever seeing me as just one individual girl like any other—as just myself. And liking what he saw.

And what if I were normal? I wanted to ask. *What if it was just me, standing here on my own? Would I be good enough then?*

"Oh no, you're crying," he said.

"No I'm not."

I blinked rapidly and brushed my fingertips over my lashes, which were barely even damp.

"It's not like I can't see myself," I said. My gaze had fallen back down to the frayed hem of Max's jeans. "I know what I am. I don't know why we're even talking about this."

"N-no, d-don't say it like that. It's j-just m-me. I just don't happen to—but I really—it's just kind of r-random, right? Feeling that way or not."

I couldn't be having this conversation. How had this even happened? It seemed I had somehow admitted that I had a crush on him, but I'd never meant to admit it, was sure I hadn't said the words, and yet somehow it was out there.

I wanted to run away. I wanted to vomit. I wanted to faint and wake up somewhere else, in a world where Max didn't exist.

But I looked up at him, and through my tremors I met his eyes and said, "No, it's not random. It's a lot of things, I guess, but some of it is physical attraction, and you're never going to feel that."

Max blinked, and he opened his mouth as if to speak, but no sound came out. What could he possibly say?

It was time to leave. I would never be able to look him in the eyes again, let alone have a normal conversation. I was throwing myself at him, even as he pushed me away. I was a big wet puddle of pathetic, and all I wanted now was to seep into the ground and disappear.

Except that wasn't true. I wanted something else. I wanted information.

Because even as most of me seemed to drown in this moment, one small part of me was looking beyond it, into a long hazy future, and probably a lonely one, where someone like Max could never be a part of my life. But was that only because I was conjoined, or would it have been true anyway? Were there other things about me that made me unwantable? That was the part I couldn't answer.

And as I stood there breathing rapidly, feeling Hailey hold herself so still and silent behind me, my anchor and my shackle and my security blanket and my life's companion, I found that even stronger than my need to run away was my need to know.

So I looked up at Max and said, "I'm not going to keep

bothering you, but just tell me the truth, just this one time, okay? Just tell me, if I weren't conjoined, would it make any difference?"

He looked at me for so long that time and space seemed to open out between us, a chasm as vast as the future.

Finally, looking into my eyes, he said softly, "Honestly? I have no idea."

24

Hailey

I've seen a lot of movies. I've watched a lot of TV. It's not like I don't know what the San Francisco skyline looks like. It's not like I've never seen the Bay Bridge. But it turns out real life is a whole other thing. Actually looking right up at those white suspender ropes on the bridge, and across the water at the whole city. Shining under pure sunlight, as if to say, *Fog? What fog? Don't go telling me how I'm supposed to be.*

And the freeways. And then the crowded city streets. All those cars. All those pedestrians. Being right in the middle of so much reality. My blood just started buzzing.

We drove all the way through the city and out toward the ocean, through rows of narrow houses and small apartment buildings. Pretty Victorians gave way to featureless midcentury rectangles, houses that a preschooler might build with a stack of blocks.

The Golden Gate Arts campus itself—which was so far from the actual Golden Gate Bridge that you couldn't even

see the damn thing—consisted of several plain, squat buildings surrounded by green grass and trees. At the edge of
the parking lot, a dirt walkway surrounded the grass, and
a pair of garbage and recycling cans overflowed with old
coffee cups and fast-food containers.

As Mom pulled into a parking space and turned off the
minivan, a couple of college-age girls got out of a nearby
car, laughing as they collected their jackets and backpacks
and portfolios from their backseat. They wore tight black
clothes, their hair was dyed black, and their eyes were circled
with thick black eyeliner.

All at once I wasn't sure how I felt about any of that,
and I almost regretted my own thick eyeliner. Was I just a
poseur? Were they?

Maybe at art school my makeup and clothes would look
like an awkward, pathetic attempt to fit in. The thought
made my chest feel tight and heavy inside.

I peered toward Clara. "You ready?"

She nodded in this sort of sped-up, hyperactive way,
like she wasn't so much agreeing as having a minor, terror-
induced seizure.

I pulled open the minivan's door, and we scuttled down
the ramp.

I could smell the ocean, but I couldn't see it. Garbage
and exhaust fumes mixed with the salty ocean tang, all of it
startlingly unfamiliar.

The two girls, laughing and teasing each other, stood beside their small, faded-brown car, the doors still open.

One of them glanced our way, and she stopped laughing. A confused look crossed over her face.

"What?" said her friend.

Mom was closing up the minivan, my portfolio under her arm. Clara and I stood there waiting, and maybe we looked like two girls who just happened to be standing really close to each other, or maybe we didn't.

The second girl quickly scanned us and turned away. "Um, *anyway*," she said pointedly to her friend, and she sort of laughed, but you could hear her discomfort.

The minivan beeped, and then Mom was next to us, ready to go.

We started toward the walkway, which meant we were also walking toward those girls. They took turns glancing nervously in our direction. As we passed by them, I could feel them turning toward us more and more, unable to resist the pull.

"Oh my *God*," one girl stage-whispered to the other just a moment after we passed.

"Have you *ever*?" asked her friend.

Of course she hadn't ever. There are just a handful of us alive throughout the world. We kept walking. I told myself that the shakiness I felt was coming from Clara's body, not from my own.

Behind us their voices got louder. "They must be, like, Christian Scientists."

"You mean Scientologists?"

"I don't know. Whoever it is that doesn't believe in medicine. You know, like surgery? To separate them? Hello? Or maybe an abortion?"

I started turning toward them.

Clara grabbed my hand. "No! Come on. Just keep walking."

My mom nudged me. "Hailey. It doesn't matter."

But it did. Not what they thought, but how we responded. Whether we cowered away or pushed through it. That mattered.

I knew we weren't really going to come here for the summer, let alone in the fall. Clara could never handle it. Sutter would be hard enough for her, with all those new faces; I couldn't ask her to tackle an even bigger environment, a place where there would be new faces every single day, day in and day out, with no chance to ever catch her breath and relax. Not yet; not anytime soon. But I did have to convince myself—and convince her, too—that we could at least get through this one day without falling apart.

And I had to convince myself that the trembling that I did feel in my own body now was pure rage, and nothing else.

I strained toward the bitchy girls. Clara tried to pull me away, but I yanked myself around and planted my feet, holding my ground.

"And which religion is it," I demanded loudly, "that requires that every child be lobotomized on her third birthday?"

The girls looked at each other nervously. They didn't make a sound.

I said, "You don't know the name of your own religion? Oh, I'm sorry, was that information stored in your frontal lobes?"

One of the girls looked at her friend and said, "Let's get out of here. This is some seriously weird crap, and it's giving me the creeps."

They hurried away. As the adrenaline faded, I didn't even know whether to feel like I'd won or lost.

"All righty then," Clara said, her voice shaking and straining toward lightness. "We freaked out the freaks at an art school in San Francisco. We're probably the first people ever to accomplish that. Maybe there's a special prize for it."

I forced a smile. "One can only hope."

So I feel weird admitting this, but growing up in Bear Pass and never going anywhere else, I had only ever seen a handful of Asian people in real life. Bear Pass is just really, really white. I don't know why. Maybe it's because we're near the snow line, so the people turn white for camouflage, like polar bears.

Anyway, when the admissions lady came out to meet us in the waiting area, and she turned out to be Asian, there was this interval where I was so distracted by trying not to pay attention to her Asian-ness that I forgot to even notice how she was trying not to pay attention to our conjoinedness. It was like this mutual game of everybody trying to act like we were totally used to one another and we absolutely didn't care or even notice what anybody looked like anyway.

She spoke with Mom for a minute, pleasantries were exchanged all around, and then Clara and I followed her toward the interview room while Mom stayed behind. A few other kids were waiting nearby, some with a parent and some without, and they all played the game too as Clara and I stood and shuffled through. It wasn't that they didn't stare, but they tried to hide it. They stared furtively, peeking up at us and then looking back down at their phone screens or their Golden Gate brochures, then peeking again. And none of them said a word.

About half of them were wearing thick black eye makeup, just like mine. It really bugged me. I felt like they'd all stolen something from me. Like they'd ripped off a layer of my clothing and left me awkwardly exposed.

As we followed the admissions lady, we passed by an elevator. I was hoping we might get on it, because I'd never been on one before, or at least not that I could ever remember. A young guy in jeans and a T-shirt punched the button to go up, and there was a little dinging noise, just like I'd heard on TV. But we walked right by. I stared back wistfully for a minute, wanting to know what it would feel like to ride up into the air. But then the admissions lady—Judith was her name—asked me some question, and I had to turn away.

I didn't even have much time to soak up all the art that filled the hallway. The walls were covered with paintings, drawings, photographs, and mixed-media collages; in the center of the walkway was a series of sculptures, some semi-realistic and some abstract, inside Plexiglas boxes. Student artwork, I supposed. Still, it was the closest thing to professional art I'd experienced in real life. Most of what I knew about the current art world came from following artists, students, and galleries online.

In the interview room Judith had us sit on a little sofa. There was an easel on one side of the room, and she set my portfolio next to it, then took out one of my paintings and set it on the easel. She was wearing a snug, retro-fifties-style dress and bright-red high-heeled pumps, and this getup seemed to make her movements a little awkward—the bending down, the stepping backward to have a better look. It was hard to tell with all her makeup, but I guessed that she was only a few years older than us, so maybe she was new to the job.

The way we were angled on the sofa, I couldn't really see what she had put up on the easel; only Clara could. So, without discussing it, Clara and I stood up and turned so that I could see.

Judith turned to us with a look of alarm. "Oh, please! You can sit."

I hesitated for just a second before explaining, "Um, I can't really see if we sit."

"Oh." She looked flustered. "Um, wait. I can move the easel." She picked it up and shuffled over awkwardly, struggling to stuff the easel into the tight space between her desk and the sofa.

"It's okay," I said. "We'll just stand."

So we stood there while she went through the paintings and talked about why she loved them. She would look each one over for half a minute and then start burbling away. As she worked her way through, her praise kept getting more and more effusive, even though I had put all my favorite pieces near the front. By the time she got to the pencil sketches at the back, she was practically calling me the greatest living artist in the world.

I enjoy praise as much as the next person. But this was so hollow that instead of making my pride bubble up, it just sank it like a stone in my gut.

"But do you have any suggestions for me?" I asked. "Any ideas for making my work stronger?"

"I'll leave that to your professors when you get here," she said. "And now please, if you'd like to sit, we can talk about you and your plans."

She proceeded to babble away about why Golden Gate Arts was the earth's greatest resource for burgeoning artists such as ourselves. (She seemed to think that Clara and I were an artist team.) Listening to her, I had the feeling you get with infomercials, where part of you is deliriously excited to try this amazing, life-changing new product, but another part is pretty sure you're being had.

After a while she did ask some questions about life in Bear Pass, but every time I tried to steer the conversation toward my art, she would swerve off in another direction, talking about what an asset I—we?—would be to the Golden Gate Arts community. How challenging and invigorating we would be.

Struggling against that heavy stone in my gut, I tried asking, "Do you want to know about my influences?"

After some vague response Judith started praising me and Clara for our courage and leadership, two traits that she had apparently invented for us out of thin air.

"Do you want to know about my goals?" I tried, and then she went off about how everyone could learn so much from those who had lived through uncommon struggles.

"Yes," I said, exasperated, "I suppose I *would* be interested in meeting someone like that."

Judith cocked her head to one side and narrowed her eyes at me.

"Of course," I added, "I probably wouldn't even ask them about their uncommon struggles, unless they were the ones to bring it up, because they would probably be so sick of talking about it, they would be like, 'Oh please, can we just talk about anything else? I would rather talk about the molecular structure of table salt than talk any more about my uncommon struggles.'"

Judith's mouth was open now. And not just a little bit.

Clara held her face in her hands.

"I mean," I clarified—briefly deluding myself that this was a gesture toward politeness—"that's how I *imagine* that person would feel. I have no way of actually knowing."

I could see what I was doing, how I was trashing this interview, throwing it away and stomping all over it, but I couldn't bring myself to care. I'd had so little hope of really coming for the summer anyway. And now I wasn't sure if I wanted to. If they wanted me this badly, and if the reason they wanted me was not so they could teach me about art but so I could teach others about courage and leadership, then what was the point?

I watched as Judith struggled to form her mouth into a smile. "That is so interesting," she said, her voice both bright and cold. "I think you will find that Golden Gate will provide just the nourishment you need for those fascinating ideas of yours to flourish."

25

Clara

When we stepped out into the building lobby after the interview, I was surprised to see that Mom wasn't waiting on the bench where we'd left her. It was a relief to have an extra moment to ourselves, without her watchful eye or her worried questions.

"Can we go outside?" Hailey asked me. "I need some fresh air."

"Mom's going to freak if she can't find us. She's probably just in the bathroom."

"Just for a minute," Hailey said. "We'll be back before she is."

We started down the hallway. I drew in a breath and forced myself to say out loud the sentence that had been repeating itself in my mind all morning, like one of those terrible pop songs that you can't get out of your head, no matter how much you dislike it. "If you want to come this summer, we can."

My voice came out squeaky, but audible.

Hailey stopped abruptly, causing us to lurch awkwardly. "You're serious?"

I nodded. "And if you want to come back next fall . . ." I sucked in my breath. "I'd be willing to think about it."

Hailey twisted her body and her head, trying with all her might to look at me. "You'd think about coming to *art* school? What the hell are you talking about? You hate art!"

"Yeah. I don't know." We started walking again; we turned a corner and started toward the building's outer doors.

My own dreams were all impossible fantasies. So if Hailey had a chance at the things she wanted, no matter how little appeal those things held for me, how could I stop her from trying?

"I've just been thinking," I said, "if it's something you really want, then at least I—"

I stopped abruptly, because there, right near the big pair of heavy glass doors, was Alek.

He stood a few yards away, with his back to us, and he didn't see us. He had a bunch of paintings lined up along the backs of some chairs, which in turn were lined up along one of the lobby's long gray walls. He switched the order of a couple, looked at them for a minute, and then started putting them into his portfolio, one by one.

There was a half-burned cottage, familiar from art class at school.

A shadowy charcoal drawing that I thought might be a self-portrait, the head bowed low, the dark smudges around it looking vaguely like wisps of smoke.

And then something else that I had never seen before.

"Come on!" Hailey whispered fiercely to me. "Let's go!" She tugged on me, trying to pull me around and away from Alek.

"Wait!"

I resisted her, turning back to look at Alek's painting. He had picked it up and was getting ready to put it into his portfolio. It was partially obscured by his arms and hands, but still, I could see plenty.

It was a painting of Hailey, but her hair was such a pale pink, and so wispy and loose around her face, it almost could have been me. Her face was pale too, as if all the color had been drained from it, and she was staring straight ahead, wide-eyed, her mouth slack. She wore light gray pants and a cream-colored boatneck top, which was more like something I would wear in real life, not her. Everything about her in the painting was pale and washed out, except for one thing.

She was alone—entirely alone. And where I should have been, there was nothing but blood. Streaming bright red from her back, and pooling behind her in a mass of darkening, deepening shades of red, it was everywhere, a massive amount of blood, more than she could afford to lose.

His back to us, Alek shoved the painting into his portfolio, clasped the case shut, and swung it over his shoulder
as he turned around.

"Oh!" He jumped with surprise when he saw us there.

And that was when I started screaming.

26

Hailey

While Clara shrieked like a crazy person, I stormed toward Alek, shouting as Clara stumbled along behind me.

"I told you I never wanted to see that painting again! I told you to destroy it!"

"All right, all right, I put it away! See, look, it's gone!" He gestured at his portfolio, where he had tucked the painting away.

At the other end of the lobby, three or four people stood still, staring at us openly. Most of the other people we'd seen had been much more furtive, but I guess shrieking tends to get a whole different level of attention than just Walking While Conjoined. Good to know. A woman in a pencil skirt and silk blouse rushed past them, coming in our direction.

"I didn't know you were going to walk up behind me like that," Alek said. "I was getting it ready for my portfolio review. And I'm sorry, but it's one of my best pieces."

Oh, how I itched to slap him.

"What do you mean, you told him to destroy it?" Clara

demanded. "I've never seen this painting before. When did *you* see it?"

"That's what he was showing me on his phone on Saturday night, at the Halloween party. I didn't want you to know about it."

It was my fault. If I hadn't wanted to go outside, we never would have walked into that lobby. I wished I could rewind that part. Or go back further and make sure that Alek really did destroy the painting, and the photographs of it too. Clara would never be able to unsee that image now, any more than I would.

The woman in the pencil skirt had reached us. "What's wrong?" she asked. "Is someone hurt?" She didn't seem surprised by the sight of conjoined twins, or maybe her surprise at that was just subsumed by the alarm about our yelling and screaming.

"We're fine," I lied.

A couple more people had come into the building, and they joined the ones who were already there, all staring our way.

"Are you sure?" the pencil skirt woman asked.

"We're fine," I repeated. "No one's hurt."

After one more drawn-out searching look at each of us, the woman nodded and walked away. She stopped near the small crowd that had gathered at the other end of the lobby, and it looked like she said something to them. They all looked at us, and then they quietly dispersed.

Was that how it would be if we came here for the summer? Would people periodically gather to stare at us, then get broken up and sent away by some staffer?

Before my imagination could start spinning out of control, I pushed the whole thought away. Of course we weren't coming for the summer anyway. I didn't even have to consider whether I could handle it, or how it would feel for me. Those things didn't matter, because it was Clara who couldn't deal. It was her fear that we wouldn't be able to push through. It would be cruel to even try. That was it, I told myself; I was just looking out for her. That was all I needed to know.

"I need to sit down," Clara said. "I need some fresh air. I need something to eat. I need to go home," she babbled, her face turning paler by the second. "I need to get out of here. I need privacy. I need to be outside."

Alek grabbed her arm, then looped it around his own shoulder. "Let's just get her over to these chairs," he said.

"No," I told him, "we need to get outside."

Alek glanced at his portfolio, sitting there on the empty chairs. I had dropped mine at the other side of the room. We left them both where they were; Alek opened one of the big glass doors and led us, in a sideways shuffle, out the doorway to a concrete patio surrounded by grass.

"The grass," I said, and we went there and sat down.

Clara leaned forward into her knees, holding her head in her hands.

"Lean against me if you want," I said. "It's okay."

"Why are *you* so calm?" she demanded, as if I'd done something wrong.

"Oh, Clara . . ."

Alek hovered over us. "Can I get you something? Do you need something to drink? Food?"

"We're fine," I said. "I think you've done quite enough."

"This doesn't normally happen," Clara said. "Hailey, don't make it sound like this happens all the time. How do you know we're going to be fine?"

Alek said, "Look, I told you, I'm really sorry about—"

"You're not sorry," I said, cutting him off. "If you were sorry, you would have destroyed that painting like I told you."

"But it's so sad!" he protested. "You see that, right?"

"All I see," I said, "is that you used a repulsive image of me to try to promote yourself in your application, even after I told you not to."

But the truth was, I saw other things too. I saw that Alek, the one guy who I'd ever thought might like me, didn't like the real me at all. He liked a different me—a grotesque fantasy version. A me without Clara. But there was no such thing. I didn't know who that person would be—the person I would have become if I hadn't been attached to her, if we hadn't been part of each other—but I knew it wasn't me at all.

"Wait. Hold on." He sat down in the grass, in a spot where he could face both of us. Behind him a concrete walkway cut back through the grass until it met a small concrete-covered square, where a group of students walked by, two girls laughing at something that one of the boys said. None of them even glanced in our direction. Farther back more walkways led to a series of other buildings, which were maybe three or four stories tall. This place was bigger than I had imagined it. Also uglier.

Alek said, "I understand what you're saying, but I couldn't bring myself to get rid of my best work. It's the saddest thing I ever made, and probably the scariest."

I closed my eyes. Did he really think that was the point? His pride in his artistry was the most important thing?

"You're an artist, Hailey," he said. "You know how it is when you make something and it's like a piece of you, a better piece than you even knew you had."

"I'm an artist," I agreed, "but I'm a person first. And if that's a better piece of you, well, I don't even know what to say."

"This is coming out all wrong," he said. "I'm obviously not saying it's a good thing. It's what I was trying to tell you before. The things I paint are like, I don't know, maybe my nightmares or something."

I opened my eyes and assessed him coldly. "Seriously? *That's* supposed to make us feel better?"

But maybe it did make me feel better. Maybe it could. Depending on what the hell he thought he meant by it.

On the walkway behind him a couple more students walked by. None of them looked our way.

I went on. "So you're telling me that when you go to sleep at night, you have scary nightmares about English cottages burning down. You're telling me *that's* what wakes you up in a cold sweat. That, plus *me* all covered in—" I stopped, choking on my own words.

Clara finished my sentence. "Blood."

She was still shaky; I could feel it. God, how I had wanted her never to see that painting. That fantasy of her gone, turned to nothing but a pool of blood. And me, what—free?

Asking me to be free of Clara was like asking me to be free of being a girl. If he didn't like me as I was, then he didn't like me, period.

Alek gave a sad imitation of a smile, his eyes downcast. "I don't mean it quite that literally."

But he was saying that it wasn't a fantasy. It was a nightmare. But why was he having nightmares about me at all? And why this nightmare?

He looked at me searchingly. "Hailey. Can I tell you something? Please?"

I let out a loud, hard sigh. "I think it would be better if you didn't."

Clara shook her head. "Actually, I want to hear what he has to say."

Alek cleared his throat, looking back and forth between us. I gave him a curt nod. "Fine. Go ahead."

He rested his elbows on his cross-legged knees, and his eyes searched the clouds for a minute, as if trying to locate his thoughts there. "Um . . . Okay. So when I was ten, my parents took me to Southern California. We went to Disneyland, and then we went to this little beach town in Orange County. The beach was amazing. And the ocean. I freaking loved it. And one day they took me into this Thomas Kinkade art gallery that they had there in the town. And I just fell in love with those paintings."

I scoffed, thinking this was some twisted joke, but Alek went on. "No, I'm dead serious. I thought they were the most beautiful things I'd ever seen. I don't know why. They weren't like anything I had ever seen in real life, all those little cottages and flower gardens. But there was something about them. I felt like I could stay in that gallery all day, staring at those pictures."

"Are you telling me your paintings are an homage?"

Alek shook his head. He looked down at his hands, took a breath that sounded shaky, and went on, in a voice that had flattened into a monotone, as if he were reading from a script. "Then right after the gallery, my parents took me out for ice cream, and instead of letting me get a single scoop like normal, they let me get this giant hot fudge sundae, and just when I was starting to eat it, they told me my dad had cancer."

Cancer. In all the crazy rumors that I'd heard about Alek and his family, no one had ever mentioned cancer.

"He lived for a year and a half," Alek said. He took another long breath and met my eyes, and his voice seemed to float into something more like pain, but still a distant pain, a thing he was holding far away from himself. "He was in treatment the whole time. It was not a good year and a half. And it ruined ice cream forever, I can tell you that much."

A loud silence seemed to reverberate through my ears. Looking down at my knees, I murmured, "And Thomas Kinkade."

"And Thomas Kinkade," Alek agreed. "It ruined a lot of things."

All those pictures he had drawn back in middle school, of men killed by monsters, vampires, wild creatures. The men always struggling heroically, and always losing the fight.

"I'm so sorry," I said. "I didn't know."

Alek cleared his throat and sat up a little straighter. "It was a long time ago. The point is, I didn't want you to think this stuff is some kind of sick fantasy where I'm into the gore and I think it's cool or something."

I whispered, "But that picture . . ."

"I don't know," he said. "I guess it started with me wondering about it, you know? I mean," he added quickly, "not wondering about you bleeding to death or anything, but wondering about, um, about separation. Why you hadn't ever done that, and whether you ever would. But then I felt—" He stopped abruptly, looking away. After a moment he said, "Well, it seemed wrong to even wonder about it. Like I didn't, um, have the right. And that was when I got this image."

I didn't know what to say. I didn't want him to have ever wondered about separation. But wasn't I being unreasonable, to ask that much—to ask for him never to have even thought about it? And here he was, backing down, admitting that he didn't have a right to have thought about it at all. And claiming, maybe, that this was the whole point of his painting.

But maybe he did have a right.

If he liked me. If he liked me the way I liked him. Then maybe that was enough to give him the right—not to ask for this, not even to wish for it, but just to wonder.

Was that it? Was it possible that he liked me that much?

Silent, waiting for my thoughts to collect themselves, I breathed in the familiar scent of grass. All my life I'd been sitting on grass. But even when I was little, I'd never rolled down a grassy hill, like I'd seen other kids do, or done a somersault or a cartwheel across a grassy field. I had always really wanted to do a cartwheel.

Alek stood up abruptly. "Okay, well, I guess I just wanted to explain that. Are you waiting for someone? Should I wait with you?"

I shook my head. I knew there were things I should say to him, but I didn't have a clue what they were.

27

Clara

"We could do it, you know," I blurted out, while Alek still hovered beside us on the grass. "We could talk to a surgeon. At least call someone. Set up an appointment. Get their opinion."

"Oh my God," Hailey said. "You cannot be serious."

I closed my eyes, and behind my eyelids I could still see it, the image of Hailey bleeding out, without me. It shook me with its wrongness. I was revolted.

And yet.

And yet there was something else about it too. A terrifying sense of freedom. A sense that if only she could survive that moment, she would be able to walk away a new person, and then she would be able to walk *toward* so many things that she never could have before.

And a small voice whispered inside my ear, *But what if she wasn't bleeding and alone? What if we both came out of it healthy and whole?*

And in the background of that whisper was an image of Max.

But I couldn't tell which voice was behind this little audiovisual brain campaign. Was it Idiot-Girl, or was it the Cynic?

"Mom and Dad would never sign off on that," Hailey said.

"We'll be eighteen in a few months," I said. "We'll have the right to do what we want." I hesitated before adding, "And you mean Mom wouldn't sign off on it. Maybe Dad would."

"No." Hailey shook her head. "I don't care what he thought when we were babies. He wouldn't sign off on it now."

"Would it be dangerous?" Alek asked. He sat back down in the grass.

I looked at him, trying to figure out what he was thinking. Why he was asking.

"Yes," I said. "It would be dangerous, and I hate dangerous things. But if we did it . . ."

I stopped. How dangerous was it, precisely? What were the odds that we would both make it through? What were the odds that one of us would? And if just one of us did, which one would it be? I didn't know the answers to any of these questions. With our situation being as rare as it was, I wasn't sure if the answers even existed.

I cleared my throat. "If we both made it," I said, "then all those things that are dangerous now would turn into safe things. Hailey could go to art school and just be like any other normal student. She could travel without having to worry about people staring or screaming or giving her a hard time. I know she wants to go all over the world."

I imagined her off at art school while I went to college somewhere else. I would talk to her on the phone, unable to see her, unable to feel her physical presence, her skin, the sensations in her legs and feet. The thought gave me a dizzy, nauseated sensation.

But then I pictured her at the top of the Eiffel Tower, beaming out at the view that she had always wanted to see. I imagined her touring the Louvre, spending hours there, studying the paintings. Climbing its broad staircases straight up, with grace and confidence. And holding a hand that wasn't mine. Maybe Alek's, maybe someone else's. But a hand that she had chosen.

"And you could get a PhD and become a professor," Hailey said, "and I wouldn't slow you down. Right?"

I tried to picture that. I saw myself in a dorm room with a roommate who wasn't Hailey, a stranger. Sleeping alone in a twin bed, without the sound of Hailey's breathing beside me, as strange a thought as not being able to feel the breath moving in and out of my own body. Lying on my stomach or my back—two things I'd never done.

And I saw myself in the middle of the vast and empty desert, surrounded by telescopes that peered into the far corners of space, searching for radio signals, for proof that we're not alone, but finding the same thing that my predecessors had been finding for years—nothing but silence.

"But to answer your question," Hailey said, "yes, it would be very dangerous."

"Well," Alek said, "don't get too carried away with the idea that everything else would turn safe if you did it. The rest of us don't always feel safe all the time either, you know?"

I studied his face. How could he not feel safe, walking around in that perfectly normal, solitary body? He could go anywhere he wanted and just blend in, like it was nothing.

I waited for the meaning to sink in, but instead I kept picturing him slow dancing with Hailey in the high school gym, surrounded by other couples, without me. And a mass of confused feelings started to well up in me again, good ones and bad ones so intertwined and knotted together, they would be as difficult to disentangle as—well, as our entangled small intestines.

"The surgery has a lot of risks," Hailey said. "That's why they didn't do it in the first place. Not that the surgeons didn't want to, but our parents wouldn't let them. Mainly because our spinal cords are conjoined through the lower section. It's a rare complication. Once you involve the nervous system, separation surgery gets really dicey."

"There have been a lot of conjoined twins born since

us," I said. "It seems like the surgeons are getting better all the time."

"But how many with our exact complications?" Hailey asked. "And then, also, we're so old now. They like to do it on older babies, or toddlers. Sometimes they might do it on four-year-olds. We're basically fully grown, like adults. They never separate adults."

"They separated the Bijanis," I said.

"They tried to separate them," Hailey corrected me, "but both twins died in surgery, so I'm not sure how that helps your argument."

"The buh-who-whos?" Alek asked, his gaze darting back and forth between us.

"Oh, sorry," Hailey said. She explained that Ladan and Laleh Bijani were Iranian women who had been in their twenties when, in 2003, they'd finally found surgeons willing to undertake the risky surgery to separate them. They had been warned, and had fully understood, that the surgery might kill them—and it had.

"But they were conjoined at the head," I said. "Even their brains were involved. It was much more dangerous than us."

"But the spinal cord," Alek said. "That sounds like pretty serious stuff."

"The truth," Hailey said quietly, "is that we don't know how dangerous it is. Nobody can tell us exactly what chance we'd have of being okay. Pygopagus twins with major involvement of the spinal cord and the gastrointestinal system, operated on in the last ten years? That's not the kind of thing that anybody has meaningful statistics on."

"Fully grown pygopagus twins," I added.

"Right," Hailey said. "I don't think that's ever been done before. So who knows? It could kill us or paralyze us, or who knows what else. Honestly, even if it was nothing that catastrophic, I'm pretty sure there's a good chance of some complication that would make us less healthy than we are now. Considering that right now we're totally fine. And then there's the money. You think that's covered by our HMO?"

"I'm sure there's a way," I said. "People do it all the time, and they're not all rich. They get it paid for somehow."

I glanced over at the building that we'd just exited, and jumped; my mother was coming out the door. She was only a few feet away. Surely not within hearing distance. I hoped.

Moments later she stood in front of us. "What happened to you? I was waiting and waiting for you to come out of your appointment. I finally asked someone, and they said you were already out. Didn't you know better than to run off like that? Didn't you know how much that would scare me?"

Belatedly her head snapped in Alek's direction. "What are *you* doing here?" she demanded.

Alek had stood up as she'd approached. "I'm sorry about that," he told her. "I didn't realize you were waiting for them inside."

"It's not your fault," Hailey told him.

"Was he bothering you again?" my mother asked, looking back and forth between me and Hailey.

"No," Hailey said, "he's not bothering us. It's a long story."

Alek backed up slowly. "Um, I'll see you around, okay?"

He was looking at Hailey, but she didn't respond.

He looked at my mom, but she was looking at Hailey.

And then my mom's head snapped up and over to the right. "Oh no!" she shouted.

A girl at the end of the concrete walkway was holding up her phone like a camera, pointing it at us. My mother's brain apparently had some internal sensor that set off an alarm if anyone pulled out a camera within five hundred feet of us.

"You put that away!" my mother shouted, walking toward her.

The girl, looking alarmed, slipped the phone into her pocket. "Sorry," she said, "I was just—"

"No!" my mother answered, as if she were rebuking a small child. "Did you take a picture?"

"No, I didn't take one yet," the girl assured her, palms out. She looked scared. "Honestly. I'm sorry about that. I promise I won't."

Hailey leaned toward Alek. "Mom's in rare form. You may want to take off."

He nodded. "I'll see you tomorrow, right? At school? Unless you think we can still make it to art class this afternoon?"

Hailey shook her head. "I have some shopping to do," she told him, half-whispering as Mom continued to harass the hapless camera girl. "I've got to buy a dress for the dance."

I caught my breath. So we were going to the dance after all. I hated the thought of going, hated the idea of being on the dance floor in front of all our classmates, but if it meant that Hailey and Alek really did have a chance, then I could find a way to get through it.

Alek looked surprised for just a second. Then he smiled. "Any particular color tie you want me to buy?"

"Black," she said. "Black will do just fine."

28

Hailey

"So," I said as the minivan pulled out of the parking lot, "we need to stop at the mall to buy a couple of dresses."

I tried to make this sound like the sort of normal, casual thing that I might say on any ordinary weekday. Never mind that we had never been to a mall in our lives. Mostly we shopped online.

"Don't be silly," Mom said. "It's November. You don't need any dresses in November."

"I meant formal dresses," I explained patiently. "For the Sadie Hawkins dance. I'm going with Alek. And I thought Clara just might want to tag along, so she'll need a dress too."

Mom didn't answer. I gave Clara a sidelong glance, worried that she would side with Mom, but she didn't say a word. In fact, if I wasn't mistaken, she was smiling faintly.

"Yes," she said, "I think I'd like to get a dress for that."

I didn't understand what was going on with Clara today. But at the moment I definitely liked it.

"Absolutely not," Mom snapped. "You are not going to any dance with that boy, Hailey. And I do not want you spending any more time around him."

"Really?" I gave a short, bitter laugh. "Why, what did he do to you?"

Mom glowered at me in the rearview mirror. "That was the same boy who came to our house all covered in blood the other day. You were angry at him. You were telling him to leave. You sounded like you never wanted to speak to him again. And now you're going to a dance with that boy? I don't think so."

"Alek," I said. "His name is Alek, not 'that boy.'"

"Well, you're not to talk to him anymore," Mom said. "He's bad news. I can tell."

"Oh, you can *tell*," I spit out. "That's a good one, Mom."

"Hailey!" Mom turned around to glare at me over her shoulder.

"What do you want me to say?" I demanded as she turned her attention back to the road. "'Gee, Mom, sure, I'll stay away from this guy because you don't like the look of him.' Because that's what you've taught us all our lives. That's what you've preached to the whole town, right, that if someone looks weird, you should definitely avoid them? You know, he's the only one who— Oh, forget it."

"What?" Mom demanded sharply. "The only one who what?"

I shook my head. There was no point trying to explain.

No, that wasn't it. It wasn't that there was no point. It was that I didn't want to. I wanted to hold this feeling inside myself and not share it with her. Not even share it with Clara. I didn't want to try to put it into words, even for myself.

Mom looked at Clara in the rearview mirror and asked, "What was she going to say?"

"I can't read her mind, Mom," Clara said bitterly. "You should know that."

Mom gripped the steering wheel tightly, her knuckles white. "I never said it was based on how he looked. It's the conversation that went on at our house. I don't want any more of that sort of thing going on."

I stared at my reflection in the window, then decided to try a different tack. "What if I went with a different boy? Then could I go?"

"To the dance?" Mom exhaled sharply. "Why do you need to go to this dance so badly?"

"I'm just trying to figure out your exact policy on dating," I said. "Am I allowed to date other boys, as long as they're not Alek?"

"I'm sure you could go to this dance without a date," Mom said. "They allow that, don't they?"

"Why won't you just answer the question?"

There was no response.

"Well, look. One way or another, we *are* going. If you and Dad won't drive us, we'll get Juanita or Bridget to drive us. You're not going to physically stop us from leaving the house, are you?"

Mom hit the brakes, hard. It took me a second to realize that this was because we'd arrived at a traffic light.

We sat there, silent, as the light stayed red. And stayed red. And kept staying red.

Up until now my mother had never expressly forbidden us to date. But I think she had assumed it would never come up.

When we were little, Clara and I sometimes played with baby dolls. We would pretend to bathe them in a little doll bathtub, push them in a double stroller, and take them to the "beach" at one end of our living room. And sometimes we would talk about "when we're mommies someday."

I'm not sure exactly how old we were when Mom started to quietly shut the fantasy down. It seems to me that when we were little, she would smile when we talked about what we would do with our babies someday and what we would name them, and then later she stopped smiling, and later still she stopped meeting our eyes.

But maybe that's not even true. Maybe she had always had that same pinched, closed-off look when we brought it up, and it just took us a while to notice.

As we got older, we stopped talking about being

mommies or getting married when we grew up. Our mom was always carrying on about how normal we were and what normal lives we could lead, but I think we both began to understand that she didn't actually believe this. Or maybe in some ways she did, but not in others.

And it wasn't that I wanted to marry Alek anyway. It wasn't that I wanted to have his babies.

Did I want that someday, with someone? It was hard to say. There were so many uncertainties behind that question, so many far-flung unlikelihoods and questions buried deep inside it that it was like a tangled knot of yarn that I'd set aside, pushed deep into a corner of the closet of my mind. I didn't know what I would want someday, or what might be possible.

But I knew what I wanted right now. I wanted to dance with Alek. I wanted to feel his hands on my arms, my waist, my skin. And I wanted him to look at me again, the way I had caught him looking at me a few times now, when he thought I hadn't noticed. I wanted him to look at me like that, and to do it even when I was looking back.

The light turned green.

"Clara," Mom tried as the minivan pulled forward, "you don't want to go to the dance, do you? You've never been interested in that sort of thing, and just because Hailey has this forceful personality—"

"No," Clara said, "she's not forcing me. I agreed to it."

"You *want* to go?" Mom demanded incredulously.

Clara shrugged. "What I want is for Hailey to go. And I'm willing to go with her."

"Well, I'm not willing—"

"Mom," Clara said, her voice quavering just a little, "we're almost eighteen. You have to start letting us make our own choices."

Mom didn't answer. She just kept driving. But a minute or two later, when I looked up into the rearview mirror, I saw that she was silently crying.

29

Clara

Late that night I whispered into the darkness, not even knowing for sure whether Hailey was awake or not. "I want to talk to a surgeon."

I felt Hailey's quick intake of breath, and then the absence of any breathing at all. Finally she said, "I truly did not think you were serious about that."

"Well, I was."

Her voice turned sharp. "You're afraid of walking down a city sidewalk. You're afraid of going to a dance at our own school. But you're not afraid of elective surgery that might very well kill us both?"

I breathed in her anger. I held it in my lungs until I could speak. "I didn't say I wasn't afraid."

She made a frustrated noise, half groan, half wail. "Clara, honestly, you can't be this in love with Max. You're going to cut us apart on the off chance that he might start liking you then?"

"It's not Max."

"I'm sorry, that came out really mean, but I just—"

"It's not Max," I repeated more forcefully. "I want you to go to art school, Hailey, and I don't want to come with you."

"Oh, Clara," she said, her voice quiet and sad, "we don't have to go to art school. I've always known that wasn't going to happen."

"But I want you to. I want you to have the life you want."

"And what about you? What would you do then?"

"I don't know."

I would have to go off to college somewhere, I supposed, since I would have no excuse to stay back in Bear Pass. I would have to learn how to live on my own—without Hailey, without my parents, without my familiar landmarks. The whole idea made my stomach churn painfully. I had to try not to think about it, though. Had to focus on doing the right thing. The right thing for Hailey, and maybe for myself.

"Caltech?" Hailey suggested. "Berkeley?"

My chest tightened, and my throat felt dry. "I haven't given it that much thought."

"Well, we couldn't go anywhere right away," Hailey said. "If we actually got surgery, I'm sure the procedures and recovery would take up our lives for a good long time before we could move on."

I hadn't thought about that. But it was almost a relief—a waiting period.

"You know," she said, "you really don't need to keep

worrying about all this. We can go to Sutter. I'll apply to film school there, and the painting program too, and it will be fine. I've been thinking a lot about it, actually, and I'm okay with it. Hopefully we can live with Juanita and Bridget. But even if we have to live at home, it's still okay."

"I don't believe you, Hailey. I don't believe that would be okay for you at all."

"I still think," she answered gently, "that this is kind of about Max."

I could still see him looking down at me, a sadness in his clear blue eyes that was maybe not quite pity but close enough. *Honestly? I have no idea.*

"It's not about Max," I said.

"You're talking about a huge decision," Hailey said. "You're talking about risking your life and changing everything. And it's the first time you've ever told me that you want this. Are you completely sure it's not about Max?"

"God, Hailey, would you just— I just— It's not him, but any other guy I ever— This is what I'm always going to be to everyone who looks at me, ever. And I'm sorry, Hailey, I'm not trying to make you feel bad, and maybe it's different for you, but I'm afraid I'm going to be lonely for the rest of my life."

Out of nowhere a sob wrenched my body. I covered my face in the darkness.

I had thought I was suggesting surgery for Hailey's

sake, so she could go off to art school and pursue her ambitions. I had never meant for the conversation to take this pathetic turn.

Hailey leaned a shoulder against me, the back of her arm brushing mine, her skin surprisingly warm. Her foot touched the bottom of my calf, and I could feel the pressure of the touch in my own leg, but I could also feel it in her foot, in the nerve endings that transmitted their information up through her body to the base of our spine, and from there up to both of our brains.

She said, "We might be the least lonely people in the entire world."

"I know," I said, forcing myself to breathe normally, even as the tears still flowed. I knew the truth of what she was saying; I accepted it as a fact; but I couldn't feel its weight any more than I could feel the weight of the Earth's atmosphere pressing down against me. It was just a part of my existence.

"I know," I said again. "But don't you want someone to look into your eyes from the outside and just love you for who you are, for all of you?"

She didn't answer.

After a minute I said, "And it's not only that. Other people just do what they want to, you know? They just get up and go. They don't have to negotiate every move they make. They don't have to compromise."

Hailey gave a short laugh. "Well, which is it? You want love, or you want freedom?"

"I want both," I said, and the anger that I'd breathed in from her began to grow inside me. "I want both, and if we stay together, I don't see how I'll ever have either one. Or how you will either."

"You're willing to die for that, Clara? We're only seventeen. We haven't even really started our lives yet. We don't know what we can have and what we can make happen. Are we not going to give ourselves a chance?"

"But that's what I'm saying. That's what I want. I want a chance."

"But I mean a chance at life as ourselves, Clara, without tearing ourselves apart."

"That's not what it is. We can still be ourselves. We can be more ourselves, if we're not standing in each other's way. Cutting ourselves from each other isn't the same as cutting ourselves apart. It doesn't make us any less of who we are."

"Doesn't it?"

I couldn't answer. Really, how could I know what it would mean to separate ourselves from each other? How could I know whether I would still be myself or not, without her?

She sighed. "Well, anyway, it doesn't matter, because it would kill Mom and Dad. We can't do that to them."

I thought about Mom in the kitchen, watching those

video clips, nearly in tears over those baby girls whom she'd never even met.

I imagined our parents sitting in a hospital waiting room like all those parents in the news clips, waiting for their conjoined twins to be separated, hoping that they both might survive. I tried to imagine how that would feel for them, but of course I couldn't imagine it at all.

"It's not even a question," Hailey said. "Not when you think about it that way, right?"

"We don't even know what the odds are," I said, so quietly that I could barely hear my own voice.

"Clara, they've shaped their lives around us. Mom sacrificed her career, and Dad basically did too, compared to what he could have done."

This was true; he'd given up a tenure-track position in UCLA's English Department to move up here and teach at a place that nobody had ever heard of. This was not the life he'd once been destined for.

And Mom—if we'd been regular babies, regular twins even, would she have kept working? If she hadn't needed to spend so much time taking us to those childhood medical checkups, to physical therapy and the occupational therapy that we used to do when we were small; if she hadn't needed to spend so much time at our school, creating a path for us there, and running all those playgroups to get people used to us, and modifying our house, and forever readjusting all those clothes that we kept outgrowing, would she have been a tenured professor now too?

Hailey went on. "Not to mention all the other places they might have wanted to live or things they might have wanted to do. They could have signed up for the surgery when we were babies. It probably would have made their lives easier, no matter how it turned out."

My heart ached. What could I say to that?

"Clara?" said Hailey. "Tell me you'll forget about this. Okay?"

I didn't answer.

"Clara?"

"Okay," I said quietly. "Okay."

But I lay there blinking in the darkness, my mind zinging all around.

And finally, when I was sure that Hailey was asleep, I pulled my phone under the blankets and searched for the name of the surgeon who had separated those twins in San Francisco. With just a little bit of detective work, I found his email address, and I sent a message.

And when that was done, I found that I could sleep.

30

Hailey

As we opened the front doors of the high school gym, I heard the shrill, unmistakable voice of Lindsey Baker. "Seriously, are you kidding me? I can't be hungover tomorrow, and you guys can't either. It's our first game, and it's Los Pinos. We have to crush them!"

She stood near the back of the gym's front entryway, beside a cluster of blue and silver balloons. Vanessa, Jasmine, and two other girls surrounded Lindsey, all wearing dresses so tiny that they couldn't possibly intend to sit down in them. They wore elaborate hairdos with little sparkly gems and glitter, and masks of thick makeup. As we walked in with Alek, they all turned to stare.

Well, let them look. We looked good.

Back in San Francisco, I had eventually convinced Mom to take us shopping. We had gotten through the mall without causing anyone to faint or scream—not even Clara!—though nearly everyone had stared at least a little, often followed by an all-too-obvious looking away, hushing of children, or speedy exit. A few had made comments or asked questions, most of them sounding well intentioned, a few less so. I'll grant you, the whole thing had been about as pleasant as having them pelt us with rotten fruit. But, per the agreement that we'd made just before arriving, we had all steadfastly ignored them. It had been a compromise between my strategy of screaming at them like a fishwife and Clara's strategy of fainting like a Victorian lady.

Most important, we had found the perfect dresses, and Mom and her sewing machine had made them look great on us.

I wore a long black gown, strapless and formfitting, flaring out slightly at the bottom, plus elbow-length black satin gloves and strappy sandals with a chunky three-inch heel. My hair was freshly hot pink and sleek, my makeup dramatically glamorous.

Clara's outfit was a combination of "contrasting good girl" and "don't upstage the contestant." She wore her hair in a French twist, her makeup softer than mine. Her dress was creamy white, sleeveless, draped, and she wore white chunky heels. Neither of us had ever worn heels before, but we'd spent some time practicing at home, and we were only a little bit shaky now.

And then there was Alek. In a black suit, black shirt, and black tie, he was devastating. As we walked in, he actually took my hand. His felt so warm and strong, I felt like I wanted him to hold on to me like that for as long as possible.

"Hey, Lindsey," I said, trying to be friendly. "Does basketball really start tomorrow? I didn't know that. You have some new cheers for it?"

She gaped at me, almost as wide-eyed as on the first day she'd seen us, back in sixth grade.

"Soccer," Vanessa said, looking me up and down with a vaguely confused scowl. "Girls' soccer. We're not cheering. We're playing. Soccer starts in November. Basketball doesn't start until December."

"Oh, right." I probably should have known that.

Lindsey grabbed Vanessa's arm. Though she was staring at my hand—the one that was clasped in Alek's hand—and looking positively frightened, she was plainly talking to Vanessa when she said, "Hey, didn't you have something to show me? Inside? Right this second?"

Vanessa followed Lindsey into the gym proper, the other girls streaming behind them, though two of them turned to stare at us as they went.

"Well," Alek said when they were gone, "that could have been worse."

I narrowed my eyes at him. "You sure you're not worried about it? You sound a little worried."

We had talked on the phone the night before, and he'd assured me that he didn't care what anyone thought about him coming to the dance with me, didn't care what they said to him or how they acted. "I'm used to weird looks and rumors anyway," he'd said then, but I wasn't sure if he really knew what he was getting into. Or if any of us did.

He smiled now. "I'm not worried. I was never worried. I admit I'm a little relieved so far. But not worried."

I nodded; it might not be logical, but it was basically the same way that I felt myself. "Let's walk in slowly, to give them a head start," I said. "Which shouldn't be a problem in these heels."

Inside, the gym was decorated in an underwater theme. The collapsed bleachers were hidden behind some kind of gauzy fabric, with cutouts of fish, shells, and mermaids; in front of these a few cardboard cutouts of coral stood propped up on the floor. The back wall featured a huge mural of a sunken pirate ship, while layers of blue and silver balloons covered the ceiling. The overhead lights were off, but smaller blue and white lights shone down along the edges of the room, partially illuminating the dance floor.

Beneath it all, I was sure I could detect, however slightly, the leftover smells of sweat and stale popcorn.

A DJ in one corner, set up with a laptop and a sound system, played a slow song. Only two couples danced. Others clustered in groups around the edges of the dance floor, or near some small tables at one side of the room. Some of the tables were already piled with evening bags and red plastic cups.

As we walked through, I could feel people's eyes on us—watching us but always quickly looking away as soon as they thought we were noticing their stares.

Our classmates didn't usually act like that. But we didn't usually have a date. Funny how such a little thing could turn us back into strangers and freaks, right here in our hometown.

I gripped Alek's hand more tightly. He held mine firmly but not in a tight squeeze. He really did seem relaxed. I could tell Clara was a little more rattled, but she didn't say anything. She was trying.

"Let's go put our things down," I said.

As we headed for the tables, I spotted Juanita talking with Amber, Tim, and Kim, and I waved to them. This was a surprise, because just that morning Juanita had told me that she wasn't coming to the dance.

Juanita hurried over, her face flush with excitement. She was wearing a dress that she'd worn to another dance the previous spring, but of course it looked amazing on her.

"What happened?" I asked. "You decided to come at the last minute?"

"Yes! I just decided, like, an hour ago." She grabbed my hand, and then she grabbed Clara's, too. The three of us formed an odd shape, but both Clara and I could face her, more or less.

"You guys," she said, with a little bounce on her toes,

"I had the best afternoon, and it made me so excited that I had to come out and dance with all my friends. I got some financial aid estimates, and I went over them with my parents, and they agreed to let me apply to all of the four-year colleges on Pletcher's list. Nothing is for sure until we get the final offers, but, you guys, I think they're going to let me go!"

"Oh my God!" Clara shouted, and she threw herself into Juanita's arms in a giant bear hug, twisting me away from both of them. "I'm so happy for you!"

I was glad I was facing away from them. I felt shaky and flushed, and in an instant, tears had sprung up into my eyes. I rapidly brushed them away, hoping that no one was looking in my direction or noticing my reaction.

I was happy for Juanita. Thrilled for her. This was what I'd been wanting, what I'd been pushing for with all my might.

So why was my whole body trembling? And why did I have to concentrate so hard on steadying my breathing? On holding back the tears that suddenly felt like they wanted to start overflowing?

As soon as I was sure that I wasn't crying, I twisted toward her. "Congratulations," I said, giving her a big hug too. "That's wonderful news." I breathed in through my nose and blinked a couple of times. "What do you think it was that changed their minds? Was it just getting more information?"

"I think so. I've been researching and gathering stuff, but then I—"

Clara drew her breath in sharply, and Juanita interrupted herself midsentence to ask, "What is it?"

Clara shook her head. "Nothing, sorry. Go on. So you decided to show them?"

"Yeah, but—seriously, Clara, what's wrong?" Juanita asked. She started looking around the room, and I followed her gaze. It took a minute before I spotted the issue.

Near the back wall, beside the refreshment tables, Gavin was tossing popcorn at Josh, one kernel at a time. Josh was bobbing and weaving to catch each piece in his mouth. And right next to them, watching but not smiling, was Max.

31

Clara

I tried not to look toward Max, but I couldn't help it. In his perfectly fitted black suit, white shirt, and blue tie, he looked so handsome and so fully formed, as if those last traces of boyishness had, for the moment, disappeared. Even as Juanita and Hailey resumed talking about Juanita's college plans, and I tried haltingly to join the conversation, my eyes kept going back to him. My brain couldn't do anything about it.

I couldn't tell if he was hanging out with Gavin and Josh or if he just happened to be standing near them. He had seemed so genuinely angry about the way they'd talked that night, at the Halloween party, I hadn't thought they would be friends again so soon. Or maybe they'd never actually stopped being friends? I tried to remember if I'd seen them together recently at school, but I drew a blank.

He looked in my direction, and I turned away immediately, reflexively. Hailey and Juanita were laughing about something; I smiled, pretending that I'd heard them.

Then I looked back at Max.

He was still looking at me.

But then Lindsey walked up to him, and he turned toward her, smiling.

I flinched.

Lindsey leaned in close to Max, beaming up at him. She said something, and he nodded and followed her out to the dance floor, gazing down at her with the slightly dazed expression of a guy who had been drugged by his own testosterone.

They were here together, then. I shouldn't have been surprised. I really shouldn't have.

But I was.

I forced myself to look away, not wanting anyone to see me staring. Bridget was walking toward us with her date. As tiny as ever in a pair of ballet flats, she wore a gauzy green dress that made her look like a brunette Tinker Bell. Her date—a blond, shaggy-haired guy named Dan—towered over her.

We scuttled in their direction, and as soon as we were close enough, Hailey, Juanita, and Bridget started complimenting one another on their dresses.

"You look beautiful too, Clara," Bridget told me. "I bet every guy here is wishing you were his date." She looked at Dan, and when he didn't say anything, she whacked him in the arm.

He laughed. "You've got me in a tight spot," he pointed out. "There is no possible thing I can say to that."

Bridget had asked Dan to the dance only a few days earlier, and I had thought her choice seemed almost arbitrary; but as she gazed up at him, blinking her eyes and seeming to harness a smile that wanted to be a giant grin, I realized that she actually liked him.

"Of course, I meant every guy except you," she told him. "But you know what? You should definitely dance with Clara."

He looked uncertain.

"That's okay," I said quickly. "I don't want to dance."

Bridget looked at Hailey and Alek, who seemed to be conferring quietly together. Bridget leaned in toward me. "But what if *they* do?" she whispered loudly.

Amazingly, the slow song segued into an even slower one.

"Clara," Hailey said, looking out at the dance floor, "I think . . . we . . ."

I nodded. "All right."

Max was out there with Lindsey, his hands on her waist. Josh and Vanessa joined them, and Jasmine pulled Gavin toward the dance floor. A few other couples had begun dancing too.

Bridget nudged Dan, tilting her chin in my direction.

After a very noticeable pause he said to me, "I'd love to dance with you!"

"Um . . ." I supposed I would have to go out there, one way or the other. Better to dance with a semi-willing partner than to be on the dance floor with Hailey and Alek behind me, and me just looking out at the crowd—at Max and Lindsey, really—as I swayed, with nowhere even to put my hands.

I nodded. "All right."

Alek took Hailey's hand again; Dan walked beside me and a little behind as we approached the dance floor. A handful of couples swayed together. Bright little spots of light twisted around them.

I looked up at Dan, not sure whether I should mention that I'd never done this before. There were so many strange things about this moment. I'd never danced at all, let alone with a guy, and in front of other people. I'd never been to a school dance, even just to watch and linger on the sidelines. And then there was the question of how Dan felt about the whole thing. I didn't even know how he felt about Bridget, let alone about dancing with her freak friend.

He took my right hand in his left, while his right hand moved toward my waist. Hailey, of course, was just to my left, although she was turned almost completely away from me. Alek had taken her hand already, and Dan had to go under their hands to place his own hand on my waist. More awkward still, my waist was inevitably so close to Hailey's that his hand had to wedge between us, the back of his fingers brushing against Hailey's waist.

There was a moment of charged awkwardness, but then he accomplished the task and smiled at me, and all four of us began to sway to the music. Or at least, theoretically to the music. I felt clumsy and deaf, with no connection to the rhythm whatsoever.

"You used to be in my history class last year," Dan said. "I remember you're a real brain, right?"

I looked up at him, trying to figure out what to say to that.

"No, it's okay," he assured me. "You are. You should own it, girl."

I laughed. I remembered Dan from that class. Most of the time he had seemed to be either asleep or focused on drawing curvaceous female superheroes in his lined note-book, but then every once in a while he would open his eyes to make some comment like (to our fifty-year-old female teacher), "Dude, why are you still teaching that Vietnam was a draw? Was this textbook written by Henry Kissinger?"

"Yeah," he said now, "I always wished I had brains like you, but I can only learn stuff I care about. The rest of it just goes right by me."

"Well, that's probably true for everyone," I said. "Or at least, if we do learn the stuff we don't care about, we just forget it the next day."

He had started shuffling his feet to the music, and behind me I could feel Hailey moving too. I tried to follow.

And tried not to wonder whether everyone else in the room was staring at us, quietly laughing at our clumsiness, or feeling disgust at the sight of us touching these boys.

"Nah, it's a defect," Dan said cheerfully. "It's attention deficit hyperactivity disorder, otherwise known as 'failing to give a crap.' That's why I'm not going to college. But you are, right? I bet you're going to Berkeley or Oxford, or, I don't know, the Sorbonne or something."

It was strange how his words created a flutter inside me, something like excitement mixed with fear, even though his guess was so far off the mark.

My mind started its stupid slide show. There we were, me and Hailey at art school, her excited but me standing next to her easel for hours with nothing but audiobooks to occupy me. Or there was me in a wheelchair, attending physics classes in rooms full of science geeks, with nary an artist or a strand of pink hair in sight.

"We're going to Sutter," I told him, and the flutter collapsed into a limp little nothing and died.

He pulled his head back and went all bug-eyed. "Oh, no way. You're staying here in BFE? Why would you want to do that? You and Hailey are both, like, total geniuses. You could go anywhere."

I shook my head. "We're not geniuses. We might share a house with Bridget next year, and maybe Juanita. It's going to be fun, I think."

We were moving now. I did my best to follow Dan's movements in front of me and Hailey's behind me. I tried to focus on the music's rhythm, tried to feel it in my body, but it wasn't reaching me; not even close.

I glanced around, sure that everyone around us must have been looking at us with horror, or at least amusement. But everywhere I looked, people were just dancing.

Slowly, we all turned. Remarkable. I didn't trip or fall. None of us did. It took a few beats, but we made it a good ninety degrees.

And then my heel came down on something, and almost in the same moment that I felt it, I heard the wail.

32

Hailey

Startled by the shriek, I took one lurching step away from it, and my foot stomped down on something. Josh's foot, it looked like.

At almost the same moment, Clara collided with Alek, and then Dan crashed into both of us, pushing us forward so that my face got shoved into Josh's shoulder.

Josh grasped my elbow and steadied me. "You all right?" he asked.

I nodded, looking at him warily, unable to forget for a second how much I hated him.

Beside us Lindsey kept letting out these little shrieking gasps. She seemed to be the source of the original wail, which had startled the rest of us so much that we'd caused this pileup.

"Oh my God," Clara said. "Lindsey, did I step on you? With my heel? I am so, so sorry."

"It really hurts," Lindsey whined, her shrill voice piercing right through the music. "It hurts so bad. Oh, holy crap, we're playing Los Pinos tomorrow, and I'm crippled. I can't walk."

As if to demonstrate, she hopped up and down on one foot, while the blue and white lights circled around her and the music kept throbbing.

"I'm so sorry," Clara repeated. "I didn't mean—I never thought—"

The blue and white lights blinked off, and Clara looked up in surprise.

Through the music Lindsey muttered something that sounded like, "Sure you are."

"Jesus, Lindsey, come on," I snapped, my voice pitched loud enough to be sure she could hear me over the beat. "You're so full of shit."

Unfortunately, somewhere near the middle of this statement, the music suddenly went silent. My voice rang through the whole gym, clear enough to be heard by everyone at the entire dance.

The overhead lights came on.

Lindsey stared at me, her face as stricken as that of a little girl who's just been excluded from a birthday party. "Why do you hate me so much, Hailey?"

Nobody was dancing, nobody was talking. All through the gym they all just watched us.

"Seriously?" I asked. "You're asking me that?"

"Yes." She looked at me steadily, still balanced on one

foot. Her brown eyes were outlined in black, the lids covered in glittery shadow. Her pink-glossed lips trembled slightly, so that she looked both glamorous and fragile. "I'm finally asking."

Clara grabbed my arm. "Hailey, please," she hiss-whispered, "just let it go."

I pulled my arm away and took a step toward Lindsey. "We could start with the fact that you've been a raving bitch to us for the past six years."

She shook her head, swaying slightly on her one high-heeled foot. Then she steadied herself with the toe of her other foot, but she winced in pain as she did it. "But that's the thing," she said. "I haven't been. At all."

I squinted at her. "Really? You haven't been a bitch to us? Then what do you call it when you bust into the bathroom stall and take pictures of us going to the bathroom to share with the whole school?"

She shook her head again. Actually, she had never stopped shaking it the whole time I'd been talking. "There were never any pictures. I did bust into the stall, and what I call it is a very bad, very stupid, very bitchy sixth-grade prank that happened six years ago, when all of us were eleven years old."

Clara sucked in her breath and then exhaled, a long, slow, shaky sigh.

"Also," Lindsey added, "I call it a thing for which I have

apologized multiple times, for which I have sincerely asked your forgiveness, though I've never gotten it, and for which I have been punished by the school, by my parents, and even by a few months of social ostracism back when it happened. I call it a thing for which I have done my time."

Clara touched my arm, but I didn't know what she was trying to tell me. To be strong? To know that Lindsey was twisting everything to her own advantage?

Or maybe just the opposite of that?

Alek stood beside me, tense and wary, watching me. Was he concerned for my feelings? Or worried about what I would do? Dan had backed up a few feet, as if uncertain about whether he should stay or go.

Max stepped forward and rested one hand on Lindsey's smooth bare shoulder. "Come on," he said. "Why don't we get you a chair? And then I'll find you some ice for that foot." He didn't look in my direction, or in Clara's, even once. In fact, he had his body angled away from us, like he was determined not to glance our way.

But Lindsey didn't take her eyes off me.

I felt like the floor beneath my feet was tilting just a little, not enough to make me fall down or even stumble, but enough to make me feel unbalanced and strange, and like I didn't know how to hold myself upright quite properly anymore.

Because I was feeling like maybe Lindsey was right.

Like maybe we'd been hating her for almost no reason, all this time. I mean, other than her disgusting high-pitched voice and her fakey-fake cheerleadery cheer and her vastly over-highlighted hair. Like maybe we—I—had been the actual bitch, and not her.

Maybe.

But then she said, glaring a little, "For the past six years I have been nothing but nice to you. I have made a huge effort to be just as friendly to you as I am to everyone else."

And I responded reflexively, without stopping to consider my words. "So you want an award? What's the level of difficulty on that?"

She held up her hands in a helpless shrug. "When you keep giving me dirty looks and whispering about me behind my back? Harder than you might think."

Max touched her arm. "Come on. Let's sit down, okay? The sooner you ice that foot, the better your chances of playing tomorrow."

She looked up at him, and after a moment she nodded and followed him away.

Neither one of them looked back.

33

Clara

"She's not hurt that bad," Alek said. "She's totally playing it up." We stood in the middle of the dance floor. The music had come back on, bright and blaring, though no one was dancing. A blue circle of light snaked festively across the nearly empty floor.

"God, I hope so," I said. "Isn't she the star of the team or something?"

Lindsey and Max made their way over to the tables and chairs; he held something that might have been ice, wrapped in a cloth napkin. Three girls trailed her, and one of them looked our way with a bitter scowl.

"Maybe we should get out of here," Hailey said.

We scurried out to the lobby; Alek came with us, looking almost as relieved as I felt. A middle-aged woman stood near the outer doors, her dark blond hair pinned up in a twist. I didn't recognize her, but she didn't appear surprised by the sight of us. And that, of course, was the beauty of Bear Pass.

"Just a reminder," she said to us, smiling, "if you decide to go outside, there's no reentering. And it's pretty early still, so you may want to think twice."

Great. I'd forgotten about this policy, which was aimed at stopping kids from going outside to drink or get high in the middle of the dance. Now Hailey would insist on going back in.

She hesitated but then said, "Oh, what the hell. Let's just go."

"I'll get your bags." Alek disappeared back into the gym.

The mom at the door eyed us. "I hope you girls aren't planning to drink or do any drugs tonight. I hope you're being careful."

I expected some sarcastic retort from Hailey, but she didn't say a word. Lindsey's tongue-lashing seemed to have left her strangely subdued.

I felt a little weird myself, having heard Lindsey say those things. Hailey might be the vocal one, but in my mind I'd hated Lindsey too. And yet everything that she'd said was true. I racked my brains but couldn't think of one unkind thing she'd done to us, large or small, since that day in the sixth-grade bathroom. Sure, maybe she looked at us in a wary, almost fearful way sometimes, but it probably wasn't much worse than the way we looked at her.

Finally Alek returned, and we managed to get outside. The air outside felt brisk but not really cold; the campus was empty and covered in moonlight. Hailey and I had each brought a wrap, and we pulled them around our shoulders.

Just down the hill from us was the football field. We had been to a night game once, and I remembered being amazed at how bright the field looked beneath the stadium lights—a circle of light, almost as bright as daytime, its grass a brilliant green despite our ongoing drought.

But tonight the stadium lights were off, and an enormous full moon glowed overhead. Beneath it the football field was clearly visible, but without the harshness of the artificial lighting, it seemed almost like a part of nature.

"Take my jacket," Alek said to Hailey, "and then your sister can use both of your wraps."

"Good idea."

She pulled off her soft black wrap and handed it to me; I pulled it over my shoulders. As she slipped on Alek's jacket, I felt it against my arm for a second. It was warm and not quite soft, but subtly textured, and it had a very slight scent that reminded me of Alek. I couldn't decide whether I liked that or not.

"I wouldn't worry about Lindsey," Alek said. "She really is a bitch. Everybody knows that."

"Well," Hailey said quietly, "everything she said was basically true. I feel pretty bad when I look at it that way. She rubs me the wrong way, but she's not actually mean to us. Other than dating the guy who should be with Clara."

"Hailey. Please. Shut up." My fingernails dug into her arm.

Alek raised his eyebrows, looking interested. "Max? What's the story there?"

"Hailey's just being ridiculous," I said. "There's no story."

"I still see him looking at you," Hailey said.

"So what? Everybody looks at us."

Though, this wasn't really true, not here in our home territory. Not usually. But it had been true tonight.

I realized, to my great embarrassment, that tears had sprung up in my eyes.

We stood just above the football field, looking down at the bleachers that gradually descended to the field farther down the hill.

"Let's sit," Hailey said, and we took the two steps down, filed in, and sat down in the top row of bleachers.

As we sat, Alek reached for Hailey's hand, and for just a fleeting moment as he took it, his fingertips brushed against her thigh. It had to have been an accident. But I could feel it, and I could feel the shot of warmth run through her bloodstream to mine.

"Actually," Alek said, looking at Hailey but somehow making it clear that he was speaking to both of us, "I think I've noticed that too."

I swallowed. "Noticed what?"

"Max looking at you. Maybe he likes you."

I shook my head. "He doesn't. He told me."

"Well, maybe not. But you never know. Some people just don't know what they want. Or they're scared, or too worried about all the wrong things."

"Do you think that's it?" Hailey asked him. She sat close to him; I could feel her knee brushing against his. "You think Max is scared?"

He shrugged. "I don't really know the guy. I'm making wild guesses."

"And what about you?" Hailey's voice dropped to a hush. "Are you sure you're not scared?"

Oh my God. What is she saying?

I couldn't speak for Alek, but I, for one, was terrified.

"Nah," he said. "Why should I be?"

"We're two girls." She was almost whispering. "We're never apart. They're going to call you a freak. In fact, they're probably saying it already."

"It wouldn't be the first time. And I'd rather be a freak than a coward."

There was a strange pause as we all took that in. What did it mean, exactly? Was he trying to prove some point to someone, coming here with the two of us tonight?

But then he answered the unspoken question. "What I mean is, I'd rather do what I really want to do, no matter what anyone thinks. And that's exactly what I'm doing."

I had promised to disappear tonight. I had to try to not even be here. I had to distract myself, to make my mind go somewhere else, to be anywhere but here.

I looked up at the moon. All its features were so clear and visible, so distinct in its full light. All right, there was something I could do to occupy my thoughts, to pull myself away from this moment. I could spot and name the lunar craters. Copernicus, that was my favorite. Aristoteles. And over there was Humboldt. I searched for Picard.

Try as I might, though, I couldn't distract myself enough not to notice what was happening behind me.

I could feel the silence. I could feel the space between them gradually shifting, their bodies and then their breath drawing closer.

And I knew the moment his lips brushed hers, because a burst of electric heat that must have started at her mouth took no more than an instant to run straight through her whole body and into mine. I could feel the voltage at the base of my spine and everywhere below it, in all the shared parts of our blood and nerve fibers and flesh.

And it ran right back up from those shared places, straight up through the rest of me, and I felt my face growing flushed, my whole body growing warm and tingling, and I thought, *This is wrong. I'm not supposed to be feeling this. I'm not supposed to be a part of this. I'm supposed to not even be here.*

But I was there. I was there completely.

And Alek was there too, even though Hailey was a con-joined twin, a freak of nature, no closer to normal than I was. Alek was there anyway, and he was kissing her, and not just once.

I knew they were still kissing, because I could feel the heat still stirring throughout my blood. And I couldn't help it. I wanted.

Not him. Not Alek.

Not even a boy, really; not even a kiss.

Or yes, okay, I wanted those things, but also a thou-sand other impossible things, and maybe a few possible ones too. I wanted to take off in a rocket ship; I wanted to bungee jump in the moon's Apollo Basin and go for space walks in the asteroid belt. I wanted to be the one to finally discover a radio signal coming from another planet, and I wanted to study with real astronomers and find out all they knew. I wanted to parachute over the Grand Canyon, and when Hailey climbed the Eiffel Tower, I wanted to be there with her.

But mostly what I wanted, as Hailey went on kissing Alek, was this feeling of blood rushing through my veins. This surge of life, of energy, like something in the world was calling out to me, and my body was answering. It was something that I almost never felt.

I pressed my hands against my face and closed my eyes,

286 • SONYA MUKHERJEE

and I felt the moonlight washing over my closed lids, and the heat of Hailey's desire washing through my veins, and I saw, finally, that this just wouldn't do.

All this wanting inside me was not going to go away. I couldn't turn it off. Something had been flickering to life inside me for years now, and it was growing steadier, and hotter too. If I tried to keep it buried much longer, I was going to go up in flames.

Deep in the middle of the night, as Hailey slept, I quietly picked up my phone. Earlier in the day I'd gotten an email from the surgeon I'd contacted about separation— or, technically, from his assistant—offering to set up an appointment. If I set up a time, just to talk to him and get his thoughts, with no commitment at all, how could Hailey say no?

I turned on the screen, and my messages opened right up.

Except they weren't my messages.

They were unfamiliar messages from Gavin and Josh, and from Amber and Kim. They all had attachments.

I must have switched phones with Hailey. But why on earth would she have all these messages from Gavin and Josh? Didn't we hate them?

I opened the first one from Gavin and clicked on the attachment. It was a video taken just a couple of hours earlier, at the dance. It showed us on the dance floor, moving awkwardly, out of time with the music. We looked even stranger than I would have guessed. Our gait looked more awkward and uneven than it had felt at the time. Maybe the high heels we'd been wearing had made it worse than normal, but it hadn't *felt* that much worse.

Behind me Hailey muttered, "You're keeping me awake. Put down your damn phone and go to sleep."

I didn't answer.

"Oh, fine," she said. "Then I'll check mine too. Any good gossip come up in the middle of the night?"

She turned on her phone screen.

Except it wasn't hers. It was mine.

The video I was watching ended.

The room was very quiet. I heard the low clank of the furnace, and a tree branch outside, tapping gently against our wall. I couldn't hear my breath, because I wasn't breathing.

"Clara?" said Hailey, pushing herself up with one arm. "Are you setting up an appointment to get us separated?"

"Hailey?" I said, ignoring her question. "Why has Gavin sent you seventeen videos in the last six days?"

34

Hailey

"Oh, that," I said, straining to keep my voice casual, as if that would somehow convince Clara that this whole thing was no big deal. I coughed and cleared my throat. "I was going to tell you."

I leaned over to my bedside lamp, pulling Clara with me, and switched it on. Without needing to discuss it, we propped our pillows behind us and sat up in bed.

"Are you friends with Gavin now?" Clara asked. "Are you having an affair with him?" she added, her voice rising. "Do you keep giving me roofies so I'll black out while you go at it with him?"

I snorted. "Doesn't he wish. No, dork. I just asked some people to help me out with a project, and for some reason Gavin and Josh keep sending me stuff for it too. I didn't ask them to." I hesitated before adding, "But I haven't told them to stop."

"Seriously? You're getting help from *them*?"

"Ah, yeah." I grimaced into the dark. In the face of

Clara's anger, I was suddenly unsure whether I should feel bad about this or not. "I guess I figured that they owe us, right? Just for their general assholeishness? So they *should* do something to help out." This sounded like a plausible explanation, and as I said it, I thought that yeah, this was probably true. It probably was my real reason. Or one of them, at least. Still, I felt compelled to add, "Plus, some of the stuff they sent me is pretty useful."

"What kind of stuff? What kind of project are we talking about anyway? And how have you managed to do all of this without me knowing about it?" Her voice was shrill with anxiety.

I thought for a second. How to explain the whole thing? "Um, well, maybe I should just show you what I have so far."

I leaned over to the nightstand again, pulling Clara with me, to grab my laptop. It flashed through my mind that this was the sort of thing that would seem weird to other people, how we had to always move with each other and be moved by each other, how I couldn't even reach for something without dragging her along with me. But to me it was as natural—and almost as unconscious—as having to shift my own body parts as I moved.

I opened the laptop and selected the video that I'd just begun to stitch together.

I felt weird showing this to her, or to anyone. It was so far from complete. It was like fragments of thoughts that I'd thrown together without really making sense of them. I didn't know what Clara would think, or how she would take it.

It started with the video of me and Clara in the school bathroom, the one where I was leaning into the mirror and looking at my blackhead. It was close up, and in the mirror you couldn't necessarily tell that we were conjoined. It was almost like there was just someone standing really close to me for some mysterious reason.

Then there was one of Juanita leaning into a mirror at home, examining her front teeth, which were not perfectly straight but had a very slight overlap. The video was so close up that you couldn't even see her whole face, or how beautiful she would look if you were just a few inches farther out.

Then Josh trimming his nose hairs; the camera here was so close up that you couldn't see much beyond his nose. He had sent me that one himself. It was too bad I hated him so much, because the fact that he'd sent me this was actually kind of awesome.

In the next sequence the camera was a little farther back, the moments a little less private.

Lindsey and Vanessa putting on their makeup together in the girls' bathroom off the school gym, laughing and having fun, even as one of them remarked, "God, I hate my hair so much!" and the other one said, "I have the ugliest nose. I wish I could just chop it off."

Amber, straightening out her clothes as she arrived at school, looking around almost furtively as she did so.

Kim, putting on her lip gloss in class.

Me and Clara sitting in the same class; in this one, because the focus was on our faces and shoulders, you still couldn't really tell we were conjoined. Clara was running her hands through her hair, smoothing it down.

A close-up of a pale thigh, with blue veins clearly visible through the skin, and tiny dots at each hair follicle.

Then a hand with a spray bottle, spraying that leg until it appeared perfectly smooth and lightly tanned.

And then the camera pulled even farther back.

Me and Clara walking down another school hallway, in the weird shuffle that felt so natural and normal when we were doing it. On video it looked a lot more awkward than it felt.

The cheerleaders all lined up, doing a choreographed dance with perfect timing.

Josh dribbling a basketball down the court, fast and graceful, a beautiful performer on display.

And then the screen went blank.

"I don't understand," Clara said. "What's the point of all this?"

"It's not done yet," I said. I felt a little nervous and defensive, because when I'd tried to watch it through her eyes, it had seemed even further from being complete than it had when I'd last watched it by myself. Incomprehensible, maybe. Nonsensical.

"It seems a little chopped up, right?" I asked. "A little random? I'm trying to figure out how to pull all this together, so you'll be able to see the point. The close-ups and the faraways. How different they are. There's something I'm trying to get at, but—well, you know I'm not very good at explaining this stuff in words."

I stopped, trying to think of how else to put it, but I ended up saying rather lamely, "It needs to be longer anyway. Two and a half minutes."

"Needs to be? What are you talking about? What are you doing this for?" She was almost shrieking.

"Well, remember you said I should apply to the film department at Sutter?"

"Jesus, Hailey! *This* is what you're planning to send them? You're going to exploit us and play the conjoined twin card for film school at freaking Sutter? You couldn't make a real film and rely on your actual creativity?"

Trying not to be stung, I said evenly, "It's not only about being conjoined. That's just a piece of it. Plus it's not finished. I'm trying to build toward something smarter than what I have now. I'm just groping my way toward it, but that's what I always do."

"Couldn't you do something else, Hailey? Is this even necessary? I mean, is it even hard to get in?"

"I don't know," I admitted. "I guess I mostly just thought it might be fun to give it a shot, see what I could come up with. Maybe create some extra options. But I don't have it figured out. I might not even send it in."

"You're damn right you're not going to send it in. What happens when someone at the admissions office decides to post this thing on YouTube?"

I threw up my hands. "I don't know. What does happen? Someone sees us? People outside of Bear Pass find out that we exist? Is that the end of the world? Is the sun going to explode in a giant supernova if someone actually sees us, for once?"

I hadn't meant to say any of that, but now that I had, I didn't regret it.

She wiped at the edges of her eyes. "That's not even what's going to happen to the sun."

"*What?*"

"It's never going to be a supernova. The sun. That's not what happens."

"Oh my God, Clara."

"I know. I know that's not the point. But you make it sound like you *want* this to end up on YouTube. Is that what you want, Hailey? Is that what you're secretly hoping for?"

I was as stunned as if she'd slapped me hard across the face. "Are you being even halfway serious right now? You think I would do that?"

294 • SONYA MUKHERJEE

"I'm not saying you would put it up on the Internet on purpose. But you know you want us to move away from here, Hailey. You've been looking for ways to push me into that. Maybe somewhere in the back of your mind, this is another way to do it. Get us exposed to the world anyway, and then there won't be any point in hiding, right?"

"Clara," I said, every muscle in my body tight and tense, "honestly, you're crazy. This is the opposite of that. This is about trying to figure out if I can make the film school thing work, so I can maybe learn something new and expand inside myself without having to leave at all. This is me making peace with staying where we are. This is you winning."

Quietly she said, "But what if I don't want to win?"

35

Clara

"What do you mean?" Hailey asked slowly. "You don't want to win? What does that mean?"

"Why do you think I contacted that surgeon?" I asked her. "Because I don't want to force you to stay here with me forever. I'm not trying to keep you prisoner here in this tiny little town that you hate so much."

"Oh." Her voice became more muted. "So you're just giving up. I was hoping you meant that you actually *wanted* to leave."

As she said that, a strange thing flashed through my brain. It was as if Hailey and I were sitting together in a tiny, sealed capsule floating in outer space, and she had unexpectedly opened its door. And all at once I could see the vast universe all around me, a dark, freezing vacuum, awash with the distant fire of uncountable stars; and I could feel the eerie weightlessness of being untethered from the only world I had ever known, and I didn't know whether the breathlessness that I felt was awe or terror, and I didn't know if I should jump out through that capsule's door or slam it shut.

"I don't know what I want," I said. "It's just—well, do you ever feel like you're trapped in a tiny box and you're running out of air?"

After a long minute she said, "You're telling me you feel that too?"

I thought of last night's kiss, and even now I felt something thrumming inside me. Or maybe I was feeling it thrumming inside Hailey. It was hard to know. Whoever it belonged to, I could feel it just the same, hot and strong and impatient, and increasingly claustrophobic.

But what was this thing that had me tied up and trapped? Was it that band of flesh that connected me to Hailey? Or was it something else?

What would it even mean to jump through that capsule door, if I could find the guts to do it?

"Don't you ever want to be free of me?" I asked.

There was a long silence, filled with nothing but the sounds of our almost-synchronized breathing. Almost synchronized, but not quite.

"I want to be free," she said finally. "But not free of you."

My chest tightened. "Free of Bear Pass, though," I said. "You hate it here, for some reason."

I remembered Juanita saying, *Sometimes I can't think about anything but busting the gates and getting out of this place, once and for all.* They both seemed to see something terrible here that I didn't see.

And now Juanita was getting out.

"No. I don't hate it here," Hailey said now, her voice tight and harsh with emotion. "Sometimes I think I do, okay, yes. But how would I know? I don't have anything to compare it to."

"It's a good place," I said, "if you think about it. It's beautiful and peaceful and serene, and the people here have been good to us. Not every single person, not every single minute. But overall? They've been kind of amazing to us."

I was thinking of what Lindsey had said at the dance, about how she had been nice to us for the past six years. Not that one day in the bathroom stall, but ever since. It was true. And yet she was probably the person I liked least in the entire school—or she had been, until that night at the Halloween party.

I still didn't know what to think about Gavin and Josh and their friends, and the way they'd talked about us that night. But in all these years it was the only time that I'd heard anything like that. And even they had been nice to us the rest of the time. Was it possible that even they, like Lindsey, were just jerks some of the time—thoughtless, insensitive, showing off their stupidity for their friends— but not really evil or hateful at their core?

"You're right," Hailey said. "It's been a good place

to grow up. I guess I don't notice that very much. And I should." After a moment she said, "What I'm agreeing to is to stay here for now. To go to Sutter for at least two years, and probably four. I guess I'm hoping that after that, you might start wanting to try something different too."

But the truth was, that wanting was inside me already, pressing up hard against my fear. A hunger for something new. Sand between our toes. City noises in our ears. The rush of an airplane lifting off.

And now I could see it. It wasn't Hailey that I needed to escape. Because technically, physically, there was nothing to stop us from doing all those things. Hailey didn't really need to escape me in order to walk up the steps of the Louvre. We knew how to walk up a staircase together.

And yes, Bear Pass had been good to us; our teachers and friends and community, taking their lead from our parents, had given us what we needed all these years. But they couldn't give us what we needed next.

I wanted to say all that—to take Hailey's hand and jump out that door with her, however we had to wriggle and squirm to get through it—but the words were stuck inside me. My throat closed up, and I could barely whisper, "I know we have to leave. But I don't know if I can. When we're like this."

I remembered that surgeon on the news clip that my mother had been watching. He'd said the ideal age for separation was nine to twelve months. "It's the best time in terms of their muscular and skeletal development," he'd said, "but also their psychological development, too."

Because after that age—by the time you were, say, one year old—your minds were so intertwined, so dependent on the way they'd grown into each other, was it even fair to say that there was really a place where one person stopped and the other began?

I shifted toward Hailey in bed, my shoulder pressed into hers. "Aren't you worried about how Alek feels about us being attached? Or if not him, if he's not important to you, then just thinking about any other guy you might like for the rest of your life . . ." I let my voice trail off.

"It's not like I don't get what you're saying," she said. "I guess it would take an extraordinary guy to want to be with either of us. But maybe that's the only kind of guy who's worth bothering with anyway."

She shifted around a little, and then she added, "Especially for us, you know? Because I feel like one of the reasons people want that—like, a long-term relationship, or marriage or whatever—is so there's someone to just be together with in life. Someone they can always count on, someone who understands them better than anybody else does and loves them anyway. Just that intimacy and not being all on your own, you know? I mean, I know that's not all of it, but it's part of it, don't you think? And we already have that."

I let that sink in for a while. I thought she was probably right. I just wasn't sure how much better it really made me feel.

Finally I said, "But just walking around in the world—you can't tell me you like having people stare at us and make rude remarks. Aren't you scared at all? How can you never be scared?"

"I don't know," she said. "Maybe it's because I have you to be scared for me."

I half-laughed, half-groaned.

"No, I'm serious," she said. "I've been thinking about it. I think all our lives, you've done the caution and the fear so I don't have to. And I've done the anger so you don't have to."

"Huh," I said, thinking that over. "So it's like each of us hasn't needed to be a full person."

"No, no," she said, "that's not it. We're both full people, but we have our specialties. It's a good thing. You do science and thinking things through. I do art and jumping in. It frees us up, not having to be everything all at once, because we know the other one can handle being whatever we're not."

She went on, "I wouldn't have chosen to have our guts and nervous systems all tangled up with each other, okay? But I also wouldn't choose to die on the operating table, or to end up paralyzed with a colostomy. None of those things would be my absolute first choice. If it was only up to me."

I closed my eyes. Behind my eyelids I could see stars glittering without any pattern at all, close enough to touch.

"And at this point," she said quietly, "I know it's crazy, but I kind of like who we've become together." She got even quieter, so she was half-whispering. "And I can't really imagine us any other way."

What did Hailey feel about me? Not love like you feel for other people, people who matter to you without really being a part of you.

With someone that you love—like, say, maybe your mom—there could be times when you might feel the edges of yourself turning porous and slipping into hers; you might feel in some way that you are not really separate. And then you pull back and you look at this person, you see their whole outline, and you understand that you are not them.

But Hailey and I could never pull back. We could never see all of each other, except in the same ways that we could see ourselves—in a photograph, a mirror image. She wasn't me, but she was part of me, like my hips and knees and heart and thoughts and memories were parts of me. And you don't really love your hips and knees and heart and thoughts and memories, exactly. But what is it that you feel about them? Is it less than love? Is it more?

How could you ever live without them? And who would you be if you tried?

All this time, I'd been trying to tell myself that being

attached to Hailey was incidental to who I was. Or that it should be. But our connectedness had been part of me since long before I was born.

This was who I was. This was who we both were, together.

Hailey raised her head to look toward me, but not into my eyes, and she never would.

"The truth is," she said, "I would rather stay the way we are. But if you want to talk to the surgeon, I will."

In the darkness I shook my head. "No." My voice sounded so firm that I barely recognized it. "We're not going to risk both of our lives for that."

She exhaled, and I exhaled with her, our breath emptying out of us in unison. This fantasy of being solo had been bouncing around in my head for years, but in that moment it slipped out of my grasp—had I only loosened my hold, or had I meant to let it go?—and I watched it drift away like a helium balloon that you know you will never get back.

"Well, then," Hailey said, "what are we going to do?"

I looked around our dimly lit bedroom, with its double dresser, its extra-wide desk, its closet full of specially adjusted clothes, its posters of science fiction films mingling nonsensically with obscure medieval artwork.

We'd moved to this house when we were eighteen months old, and in all that time we had never once slept anywhere else.

Hailey had often told me that the white space between objects is one of the most important parts of any picture, with as much significance as the objects themselves. The shape of the space between the two of us had never changed, and it never would. But the background that filled it in could be different, and surely that would transform the picture too.

I turned as far toward Hailey as I would ever be able to and said, "We're going to get out of here."

36

Hailey

By the time the sun rose, we had created our first-draft college list. When we'd started in the middle of the night, in the yellow-and-blue glow of our lamp lights, it had seemed unreal. I couldn't quite believe that Clara had agreed to this. But as the morning light sifted in through our bedroom window, her enthusiasm only seemed to grow.

It was real. We were going to do this—move away. Take care of ourselves. Face the strangers.

My fingers tingled with excitement. Or at least, I chose to believe that it was pure excitement and not unhinged terror, though I could see how this might be open to interpretation. There was no time to waste either. Some of the colleges had application deadlines as early as November 30, giving us less than three weeks to get them ready.

We were downloading the Common Application for college admissions when Mom burst through the bedroom door.

"Oh good, you're up," she said. "How was the dance?

Did you have a good time?" She looked worried, even though we'd talked to her briefly when we'd gotten home the night before.

Oddly enough, it had been Dad who'd seemed to suspect something last night. When he'd picked us up outside the school, just looking back at us from the driver's seat of the minivan, he'd somehow known that something was up.

"*Someone* had a good time," was all he'd said, but it had been there in his tone, and in his quiet smile. He had known that we'd had more than just an ordinary good time. He had probably known that it had to do with me, and with Alek. And he'd been happy about it. He'd smiled to himself the whole way home.

"Yeah," I said now, to Mom. "It was good. We even danced a little."

"Oh." She brightened. "Well, that's good. I wasn't sure if you would." She hovered in our doorway. "You know, I was thinking, it's good that you're trying new things. And sometime soon we should start to talk about what it's going to be like next year, when you two start at Sutter. There are going to be a lot of new things to prepare for."

My heartbeat quickened, and Clara sucked in her breath. I kind of wanted to not say anything. But we were going to have to tell her soon. It might as well be now.

"Um, Mom," I said, "I think there's something you need to see."

I held up my laptop, its screen facing her, and she came closer to look.

Her face went pale. "The Common Application?" she said. "Sutter doesn't use the Common Application."

I crossed my legs, pulled my spine up straight, and looked right into Mom's eyes. "We're not going to Sutter."

Her eyes widened, and her body pulled back, but Clara jumped in. "We want to see other places and meet new people, people who aren't from around here. We want to give them a chance. Give ourselves a chance. We think we can handle it."

Mom shook her head, looking confused. "It's not like everyone at Sutter is from around here. People come from all over—even from other countries."

"A few people," I admitted. "Not many."

"But also," Clara said, "I never really wanted to study environmental science. And Sutter doesn't have physics or astronomy or anything like that. I want to go where I can study what I really care about. We both do."

Mom kept shaking her head, like she couldn't control it. "Your father is a tenured professor. Do you know how hard it is to get a job like that? We can't just pick up and move wherever you—"

"We're not asking you to do that," I said quickly, glad that I could at least reassure her about this one thing. "You guys can stay right where you are. We promise to visit."

She opened and closed her hands. "You're talking about going without us?"

"Yeah. We are." I forced a smile for her, but before I could say anything more, I felt my fake smile transforming into a real one. "We can take care of ourselves."

Mom came and sat down at the foot of our bed. "I know it feels that way," she said gently. "You two can do an amazing amount for yourselves. You're very independent. But at the same time, you don't necessarily notice all the things that your father and I do for you to smooth the way. Driving you around, tailoring your clothes, cooking your meals, arranging accommodations everywhere you go . . ."

"We can do all of that," Clara said. "We'll learn what we need to. And the stuff that we can't do, like driving, we'll find a way around. Other people manage with bigger disabilities than ours. They manage to live on their own."

"You'd need to get to physical therapy somehow," Mom said. "And learn how to cook, which is going to present some logistical difficulties for you. You'll need to have everything arranged where you can reach it without a step stool and without having to bend down low, because that's so awkward for you. And what happens if you're alone and you get injured? There are so many things that could happen."

"Mom," Clara said, more gently now. "We're grateful for everything that you've done for us, including teaching us to be independent. And you can still help us, okay? You can still fix our clothes and check in with us every day. You can teach us how to cook, and you can visit us and make sure everything's all right. There's a good chance we'll stay in California, so you can visit a lot. We're not trying to disappear."

Mom's head kept shaking. Actually, the rest of her was shaking too. "But where—"

"We're going to apply to a bunch of places," I told her, my voice sounding weirdly calm. "We'll see what happens."

"Hailey. Clara. You're going to need to give your father and me some time to go over all the details of this before we can say yes or no. I can see right now that there are aspects of this that the two of you have not thought through. For instance, with two completely different majors, it will take you twice as long to finish. It's all right at Sutter, because they'll give you free tuition. And you can live at home."

"We'll get financial aid at the other places too," I said. "Mom, I'm sorry, I'm not trying to upset you, but Clara and I have made a decision about this. We're doing this. No matter what you feel about it, we're going to find a way to make this happen."

She drew back. "It's not as simple as you seem to think. Don't you remember your friend Laura Saunders, last year? She got into six schools, and then she couldn't afford to go to any of them."

Something cold trickled down my spine. "Yeah," I said

slowly, "but that's because her parents were assholes who wouldn't cover their share."

"Right," Mom said, nodding thoughtfully. "The financial aid package takes your parents' income into account. It only works if your parents are willing to help. So they have to be behind you."

"Mom," Clara said sharply, "you can't be serious."

"No," said Dad from the doorway. We all looked up quickly. Where had he come from? "She's not serious," he said.

How much of this had he been listening to?

Mom stood up and whirled toward him. "Don't you tell me I'm not serious. Don't you tell me what I mean."

"You're going to control them with money, Liza? I know you can't be serious. Or you're not thinking straight."

Mom turned back toward me, ignoring him. "I'm not saying no. But this is a decision that we're going to make together as a family. And if your father and I decide that we need to put our foot down to protect you, to keep you safe, then that's what we're going to do."

Dad looked skeptical but said nothing. Falling back into place, I supposed, as part of her united front.

"We're just talking about going off to college," I said. Though I thought I felt nothing but anger, my voice came out sounding sad and defeated. "What terrible thing do you think is going to happen to us there?"

"Well, for starters," Mom said swiftly, as if she were glad to be asked, "don't you realize that everyone has a camera in their pocket? You don't notice it around here because it's a protected environment, and we can get that for you at Sutter, too, because it's small and because we've already discussed it with the administration. But out there in the world, there's nothing to stop people from taking pictures and video of you at any time, and doing anything they want with it. You might not even notice they were doing it. By the time you found out, it would be too late."

I looked toward Clara. For the past few weeks people had been sending me videos of the two of us. As far as I could tell, Clara had never noticed that people were taking these videos. Half the time I hadn't noticed it either, even though I'd known about the project and had known that this could have been going on.

"You might think they were just texting their friends," Clara said slowly, "when they're really taking videos of you."

"Exactly!" Mom agreed. "And then anything could happen. They could send it to their friends, or a journalist. They could post it online."

"Liza," Dad said softly, leaning against our doorway. "Honestly."

"It's true, though," Clara said. "They could. And once that happened, it would be too late. You would never be able to unring that bell. The videos would be out there, and then anyone could do anything with them. Keep reposting them in new places. Whatever."

"Exactly," Mom said, triumphant.

"And then when we walked down the street," Clara went on, with just a slight tremor in her voice, "instead of people saying, 'What's that thing?' they would say, 'Oh, there are those girls we saw on YouTube.'"

Mom frowned.

"And then at that point," Clara said, "there would be no reason for us to hide away anymore, because the whole world would already know all about us."

Mom stared at Clara, her face awash with horror and confusion. She must have been trying to figure out the same thing that I was. Was Clara making an argument about how awful it would be to show up on YouTube? Or just the opposite?

And then, from the corner of my eye, I thought I glimpsed Clara's slow, tentative smile.

I looked up toward Dad, where he hovered in the doorway. Mom had her back turned toward him, so she couldn't see his face. She couldn't see what I could. Dad was smiling too.

Slowly, testing all of them, just to make sure that we were really thinking the same thing, I said, "There would be no reason for us not to go away for college."

Clara kept smiling. And Dad did too.

I wouldn't have thought it was possible. But just hours ago, after all, Clara had agreed to leave our cocoon. And if she thought this would help her do it, who was I to argue?

Mom shook her head. "I don't think you're getting my point. We never raised you to be a circus act. We never raised you to be on a vaudeville stage, or on the modern equivalent of it either. That's no way to live your life."

"But neither is this," I said. And then, thinking over the options, I shrugged. "Actually, I guess that *is* one way to live your life, and so is staying here. There are lots of ways. They're all life. But the point is, it's up to us, which one we choose."

Mom's lower lip trembled. Dad looked down at the floor, his expression once again unreadable.

Clara nudged me. "Is that video ready for posting yet?"

"What, mine?" I thought about it. "It's kind of lame right now. And we're not even in it that much."

"I'm sure they sent you a bunch of stuff from last night's dance," she said. "You could add that."

"Yeah, yeah. I guess we could just tack that on. I don't know, though. If we're going to put something out there, I'd rather make it better than just a bunch of random candids. Like maybe more from our own perspective or something."

Mom pressed herself against our bedroom wall. She glanced at Dad, but he wouldn't meet her eye.

"What are you talking about?" she said. "Do I need to confiscate your laptops? Do I need to turn off the Wi-Fi?"

I looked her right in the eye. I could see her fear and confusion—could see all the terrible things whirling through her brain that she felt she absolutely had to protect us from—but I felt detached from those feelings, like they couldn't touch me at all, and it was almost hard for me to care.

Care, I told myself. *Try to care.*

There had been so many times when I had cared. When I had felt for her fear, and for Clara's, too. But this was not the time. This was not that moment.

I took a deep breath and forced my voice to sound as patient as possible. "It won't make any difference. Everything's backed up to the cloud. We can access it from our friends' computers."

"Not if I don't allow you to go to their houses," Mom said, her voice faltering.

"Oh, Mom." I shook my head, losing my grip on my last thread of sympathy. "How are you going to stop us?"

Clara started to giggle nervously, even as tears welled up in her eyes. She elbowed me. "Hailey," she said, "I know what we can post."

37

Clara

By the time the soccer field came into view, as we walked toward it along the cracked sidewalk and then up into the Bear Pass High School parking lot, it was already obvious that the place was packed. Not only was the parking lot full, but the street was lined with parked cars, trucks, and SUVs, many of which I recognized as belonging to my classmates.

Many, but not nearly all. Girls' soccer was big around here, and there would be lots of Los Pinos students and families too.

Los Pinos was about forty minutes from Bear Pass, a bigger town that we never visited, though Mom sometimes went there to shop and do errands.

My nerves jangled, and my mind raced. So many strangers. So many people who had never seen us.

It was noon, and we had spent most of the morning practicing with Bridget, Amber, and Kim, while Juanita had worked on setting up all the details and logistics, and making sure the soccer team and coach were on board. We'd done all of this at Juanita's house, while our mother had presumably sat back at our house, crying or tearing out her hair or making frantic phone calls to family members, or whatever it was that she did when she was alone and worried sick. At least she hadn't tried to prevent us from leaving the house. And although she hadn't said that she would go along with our plan to leave for college, her look of despair as we'd left the house had given me a perverse ray of hope.

We'd been working hard at this, but I wasn't ready at all. I was never going to be ready. As we reached the edge of the field, I realized I was holding my breath. When I let it out, it made a little puff of cold mist, despite the bright sunny sky overhead.

We looked out across the field. Sure enough, our side of the field was packed—the bleachers full and surrounded by foldout chairs, with people huddled into jackets and sweat-shirts and even a few blankets under the cool morning sun. Our classmates and their families, mostly. People we knew.

On the Los Pinos side there were almost as many people, all on foldout chairs. So far, none of those strangers seemed to have noticed us. At least, nobody was staring or pointing, as far as I could tell.

Instead all eyes were on the field, where the Bear Pass girls, in their red uniforms, played Los Pinos, in white and green. I didn't know much about soccer, but I could see that Lindsey was dominating, weaving between defenders as she took the ball down the field with a speed and agility that were frankly beautiful to watch.

"I'll go talk to Amber," Juanita said. "I want to make sure they've got everything they need."

"And Josh," I said as she hurried off. "Make sure he gets the good camera."

Hailey had told me that some of the best videos she'd gotten had been from Josh, and also that he'd seemed eager to help out with her project. I didn't know what to make of that, but I knew that if we were going to do this thing, I wanted it done well. So, fine. Let him help.

As we hovered back behind the bleachers on our side, the ref blew the whistle and the players left the field. All at once all the tensions of the morning, the week, the month, the year, drew themselves into a tight point at the center of my chest, a thing so small and dense that it threatened to suck all my surroundings into its gravitational pull.

Dan and Alek, with a couple of Alek's friends, were setting up a sturdy table and two chairs in the center of the field, while Amber and Kim set up their sound system. In what seemed like just a couple of minutes, though it must have been longer, Juanita ran over to us.

"Come on. It's time!"

I couldn't breathe. Juanita and Hailey stared at me, both

of them smiling. "Come on, come on!" Juanita repeated, beckoning.

Helpless, I followed her onto the field.

All around us now everyone was watching. And that dense ball of tension was still at the center of my chest, but now I was somehow outside it, observing it rather than feeling it, and time felt slow and thick, yet crystal clear as we walked across the field, the center of more attention than I'd ever felt before, its weight heavier, surely, than what we could hold.

When we reached the chairs, Alek and Dan held out their hands; Hailey and I took them, accepting their help as we stepped up onto the chairs, and then from there onto the table.

We turned around and looked at the crowd. On one side, a sea of strangers. On the other, our classmates, our friends, our neighbors. All of them, on both sides, waiting to see what we were going to do.

And in one of the foldout chairs near the front, there was Max, looking up at us with a stillness that I couldn't read, shouldn't even want to try to comprehend.

I should try not to look at him. I should try.

Centered in front of us on the field, Josh held up not a phone but a high-end video camera belonging to Bridget's parents. I tried not to think about what that camera meant.

Just be here. Don't think about it. Don't think. Don't.

And then it came on, through the speakers—Lady Gaga's voice, speaking so loudly and clearly that I thought it could be heard for miles, telling us just what to do.

Following the lady's instructions, our paws went up in the air.

Amber had helped with the choreography and with teaching us how to move. We'd had just a couple of hours to practice, after a lifetime of standing off to the side. Now we were center stage. The moves weren't fancy—not by other people's standards—but they were certainly new to us.

The music revved, picked up, and zipped off into the opening notes of a song that had been on our playlists for just about as long as I could remember: "Born This Way."

Our hands moved first, from left to right above our heads. Our hips came next. The beat pulsed, loud, maddening, demanding.

The crowd was watching. Strangers and friends. Their faces all unreadable. Their thoughts all unknowable. They watched us, and we did our best to dance.

As Lady Gaga's huge voice filled the space around us, spilling out into the parking lot and the street, we moved with painful awkwardness through the steps that Amber and Kim had tried to teach us. We weren't even vaguely in sync with the music, which rumbled and vibrated up through the table.

How many people would end up seeing this video? Would strangers, finding it online, send it to their friends? If we left Bear Pass—*when* we left Bear Pass—would we run into people who had already seen us because of this? And what would that mean, if we did?

I'd always thought that my worst nightmare was to be like the long-ago Hilton twins or Millie-Christine, making a spectacle of ourselves for strangers. But at least those girls had had talent and skills. And no Internet.

So many things were running through my mind that I was only half-conscious of the pulsing music surrounding us. The outdoor speakers boomed, impressively loud, but in contrast to how I'd imagined this moment, the music seemed to have nothing to do with our awkward movements.

This was pointless. We were idiots. What kind of a plan was this? Dance terribly, put it up on YouTube, and expect that to somehow give us freedom? What were we thinking?

Still, I kept dancing, or trying to.

Then Juanita jogged out toward us across the field, and behind her, a dozen of our friends—including, among others, Alek, Bridget, Dan, Amber, and Kim. They gathered around the foot of our table and began to dance along with us, using roughly the same moves that we'd practiced.

I hadn't known they were going to do that.

As Lady Gaga switched to a commanding chant, Hailey

320 • SONYA MUKHERJEE

held out a hand to Alek, who was dancing beside the table. He pulled himself up next to us. The music picked up, and in his own clumsy way, Alek danced with us.

The beat throbbed through the table and up into my feet. It filled the space around us, vibrating out into the air beyond. I felt giddy and ridiculous, like at any moment I might laugh, cry, fall off the table, or all of the above.

I glanced in Max's direction—*stupid, stupid, don't look*—and saw something on his face that might have been a smile. I looked away.

Was it a smile?

Don't look. Don't look. It doesn't matter.

No matter what you do, you'll never know his thoughts.

Another group of Bear Pass kids ran over to dance with us, and then another. A few of their younger siblings joined them, middle school and elementary school kids, kids who had known us all their lives and smiled at us easily now, laughing and jostling one another. The middle school kids were thinking about their own moves, not ours, and the littlest kids weren't thinking about anything at all.

Across the field the soccer teams were stretching, pacing, drinking from their water bottles, paying no attention at all to our dance. Lindsey leaned back in a chair and closed her eyes, as if shutting us out.

But half of our school was dancing with us now—had Juanita planned all of this?—and when I looked over at the

Los Pinos side, a few of those kids were up on their feet, dancing in front of their chairs. They all looked much better than Hailey and Alek and me, as if they could actually sense the beat.

And then the funniest thing happened. I started to sense it too. My hips, along with Hailey's, swung to one side in time with the music, and then they swung to the other side, and we were still in time. I could actually tell.

For the first time in my life, I could feel the rhythm and the music running all the way through me.

Lady Gaga's voice ran through my own silent breath, and where I had been moving out of time to the music, trying to find my alignment, suddenly it was different; the music was inside me, moving me, a part of me. *I'm on the right track, baby, I was born to be brave.*

Somehow I had shifted closer to the edge of the table, toward the Los Pinos side. They weren't that far away, all those strangers from our rival school, and in the front row a couple of guys were nodding along with the music, smiling.

As I looked at them, one of them caught my gaze in his, and just at that moment, maybe by coincidence or maybe because of the eye contact, I registered that he was cute. He kept looking right at me, nodding in time to the music, and his smile grew wider.

Maybe he liked the song or the dance steps. Maybe he thought it was cool that we were brave enough to get up here. Or maybe—most likely, really—he was laughing at us.

But then it struck me. This was the Cynic talking, and she was an absurd little wussy-girl. Always had been.

And Idiot-Girl bounced up to her feet and leapt ecstatically across the ring to knock the Cynic flat on her back, not with a punch but with a ridiculous purple bubble filled with unicorns, which left the Cynic dizzy and down for the count. And Idiot-Girl pinned the Cynic down and whispered softly, teasingly, into her ear, *You've had your turn. Now I'm taking over.*

And I kept dancing in time with the music, and at the same time looking at that cute guy whom I'd never seen before and would probably never see again, and for once I did what I wanted, without waiting to figure out whether I should.

I reached out one hand, pointed at him, and beckoned for him to come over.

His friend laughed, then elbowed him and nodded in my direction, telling him to go over to me.

And he did.

The Cynic, half-conscious on the floor, continued her chant, *He was just doing what he thought he had to do. People were watching, and he didn't want to look like some jerk.*

Idiot-Girl's purple bubbles formed a gorgeous chain, until they spelled out in perfect cursive letters: *So what?*

The cute stranger climbed up onto the table, and he

started dancing next to me. He wasn't great, but he had the beat. Without knowing why, I started laughing, and then he started laughing too.

I looked out toward our side of the field, the Bear Pass side, and almost everyone was on their feet now, dancing with us.

And then I saw them, standing near the bleachers—my parents.

They were looking at us, watching us dance. They had somehow tracked us down.

Neither of them were smiling. Mom looked vaguely shell-shocked, and Dad—well, who ever knew what he was thinking? I liked to think that he was secretly pleased but just covering it up from Mom. Maybe, maybe not. At least neither of them was scowling openly, and they weren't rushing the field to try to interrupt our dance.

I looked away, and I let my body feel the beat.

The night before, sitting out on those bleachers, feeling the shared heat of Hailey's blood stir inside me, I had been bathed in the cool glow of the moon's reflected light, counting lunar craters that I would never be able to explore.

Today, despite the chill, the sun shone brightly between the clouds. Its light fell directly on my face and hands, having hurtled all the way through space to reach me in less than eight and a half minutes. And as I danced among my friends and classmates and this one cute stranger, I felt as if this whole blue-green expanse of planet lay before me, all lit up with mysteries.

And I imagined a hairless, tentacled, teenage girl-creature on another planet somewhere out there in a distant constellation, circling some other star, gazing out across the vast expanse of space toward us here on Earth. I imagined her using her super-high-powered alien telescope to zoom right in on me and Hailey, these rarest of mutations in perhaps the strangest species ever to have evolved on this improbably fertile planet, living and laughing and dancing so awkwardly here among the stars at the edge of the Milky Way.

And I thought, *Well, good. Let her stare. I think we're quite a show.*

Acknowledgments

Thank you for picking up this book. It's had a long journey from its earliest drafts, and I'm deeply grateful to everyone who helped along the way.

Many thanks to Steven Chudney for your wise counsel and guidance, your patience and support, and for making me believe in Santa Claus.

Zareen Jaffery, thank you for giving this novel a wonderful home, and for all your keen insights, which deepened it and brought out the best in it.

Thanks, too, to the entire team at Simon & Schuster Books for Young Readers, especially Justin Chanda, Mekisha Telfer, Krista Vossen, Jenica Nasworthy, Chava Wolin, Katy Hershberger, and Chrissy Noh, for all your hard work in bringing books to life and to readers.

I.W. Gregorio and Abigail Hing Wen, you've been part of this story from the beginning and at every step of the way, nudging it toward its best and truest parts and bolstering me with your encouragement and understanding. I'm forever grateful for your astute reading and generosity.

Evelyn Skye and Jeanne Schriel, thank you for your

thoughtful and immensely helpful reading and advice.

I'm grateful to Askar Kukkady, pediatric surgeon in Waikato Hospital, Hamilton, New Zealand, who generously took the time to answer my hypothetical questions about separation surgery on pygopagus twins; any errors in the novel, however, are very much my own.

Thanks to my fellow debut authors at the Sweet Sixteens for being such a supportive and helpful community. And to the sisterhood of Sixteen to Read: Thanks for your company on this wild and crazy road trip. It would not be the same without you.

To my parents, Rob and Vicky Martinez, thank you for all the books, blank journals, and pens, for always encouraging me to choose my own adventure, and for the kind of love that has made you treat even my failed jokes like frameable art.

Tierra Martinez Crothers and Zak Martinez, you'll always be part of who I am. Thanks for being among the best parts.

Pratap Mukherjee, thank you for supporting me in every possible way as I've pursued this dream, and thank you for making just about all of my other dreams come true. I can't wait to find out what we'll dream up together next.

Finally, Drew and Maya Mukherjee, thank you for bringing a whole new dimension to my universe. Everything in this world means more to me because you're in it.